Soldier Boys

by
Deirdre Savoy
Angela Weaver
Edwina Martin Arnold
J.M. Jeffries

Copyright Page

Parker Publishing LLC

Noire Passion is an imprint of Parker Publishing LLC.

Copyright © 2008 by Deirdre Savoy, Angela Weaver, Edwina Martin Arnold and J.M. Jeffries
Published by Parker Publishing LLC
12523 Limonite Ave., Ste. #440-438
Mira Loma, California 91752
www.parker-publishing.com

ISBN: 978-1-60043-038-1
First Edition

Manufactured in the United States of America

Cover Design by Jaxadora Design

Soldier Boys

Tell It To The Marine

By
Deirdre Savoy

Books by Deirdre Savoy
Spellbound
Always
Once and Again
Midnight Magic
Holding Out for a Hero
Could it Be Magic?
Not the One
Body of Truth
Body of Lies
An Innocent Man
Soldier Boys

Dedication

To the men and women, past and present, who protect our country throughout the world and to the end of the need for their service.
...be the change you want to see in the world.

— Mohandes K. Gandhi

Tell It To The Marine

By
Deirdre Savoy

upbeat, despite the fact fire play could be heard over the band.

Today was different. It was some captain's birthday. She'd been asked to sing him happy birthday and cut a cake that would be served later in the mess. No one had pointed that soldier out to her, but she assumed it was one of the older guys who would prefer to have her rather than the younger woman singing to him.

It didn't matter. She'd do her best to make the soldier feel special on his big day. She wrapped up her next two songs, *The Way You Look Tonight,* which became a tribute to the troops in uniform the way she did it; followed by a bawdy rendition of *I've Got You Under My Skin*, which was all about the places she now had an overabundance of sand.

As the applause died down, she waved for quiet. "I have a special request for a Captain Daniel Reid. Captain Reid are you here?" Vinnie shaded her eyes and looked out into the audience.

The men down in front shifted. One man was more pushed to his feet than rose to them on his own steam. He was dressed, like the others, in camouflage utilities, but even from that distance she could tell he was an officer. Even if she hadn't learned the markings that distinguished an enlisted from the upper ranks, she would have noticed it in his posture and the deference the other men showed him, even as they were pushing him toward the stage.

Well, she knew one thing now—it hadn't been his idea to have his birthday celebrated in this way. Was it his superior's way of embarrassing him or his men's way of honoring him? Neither was her business. For her part, she'd rather get the spectacle over as painlessly as possible. But first she needed to get him on the stage.

"Come on, captain," she urged. "I'm not going to bite you. Not yet, anyway."

The crowd responded with a smattering of laughter. But it didn't speed the birthday boy toward her. He took his time ascending the stairs and walking across the stage. With every step closer he came into sharper focus. She catalogued his attributes: broad shoulders that tapered into trim waist and muscular thighs. His skin was bronzed to a deep brown, accentuating a handsome face with full lips and smoky brown eyes. Vinnie exhaled. "Damn."

He was gorgeous all right, but he wasn't one of the older officers as she'd supposed. He was a baby, at least what she considered to be a baby. He couldn't be older than his mid thirties.

Vinnie tried to get herself together. She was a mature woman who'd been married to a man twenty years her senior. Until Carl's death last year, she'd been a devoted wife helping him battle cancer. She didn't drool over younguns, no matter how biteable they might be.

Biteable. That word sprang into Vinnie's mind, but it was one of her cousin Alberta's sayings. Al wouldn't have a qualm about pouncing on a man she wanted. It wasn't that Al slept around, but once her gonads found someone that excited them she didn't pussyfoot around. If Al were

1

LAVINIA COLE plastered a smile on her face as she looked out at the sea of soldiers awaiting her performance. She was dog tired, having found it impossible to sleep in a place others were bombing. Even under the shade of the canopy covering the stage, the heat was like an overcoat she couldn't take off. If there were any justice in the universe, her intestines would recover from the incredible inedibles that passed for food here, but only time would tell. All in all, she was glad this was the last stop on the tour. She'd done her part and was ready to go home.

For now, she had one more performance to complete. Hers was the opening for someone supposedly more famous but she'd never heard of the woman before they loaded the pair of them into one of those ubiquitous helicopters.

At home in New York, Vinnie played piano and belted out standards for the denizens of the Starlight Room of the New Regis hotel in her hometown, New York City. As much as she could she recreated that act for the troops, given that she wore combat boots and fatigues rather than sequins and heels. Her audience in attendance didn't seem to mind, since applause and catcalls greeted her walk toward center stage where a microphone in a stand awaited.

When the noise died down, Vinnie leaned into the mike. "How are you all doing?"

The applause rose again along with a few shouts and whistles. Vinnie smiled. She knew her reputation probably preceded her. At forty-two she was no spring chicken, but she had a decent body and a sultry way of belting out a torch song most of the soldiers were too young to remember. She didn't mind pouring on the heat for the benefit of them, for in her short stint touring she knew that whatever Iraq had been before the war had turned the country into a hellhole neither side deserved to live in.

A few more innocuous comments, a remark about the weather and then she launched into a rendition of *Fever*. She usually sang the first song alone, but for other numbers she invited soldiers onstage, letting them sing with her or talk about themselves or their experiences here. It was all light and flirty and fun — what they told her they needed. Everything here, she'd say that's what Vinnie's problem was: she'd spent so much of her life caring for someone else that she no longer knew how to care for her own needs. Maybe Al had the right of it, but Vinnie also knew the last thing Vinnie needed was to be having an existential crisis in a war zone.

That thought made Vinnie smile, for real this time. She'd definitely have to wait until she got home to have her breakdown. For now, she had a gorgeous soldier staring at her. "I hear congratulations are in order, Captain. They tell me it's your birthday today."

He nodded, even though she held the microphone in his direction. It wasn't a curt nod or one of irritation, but one that said that if anyone were seeking an afternoon's entertainment they wouldn't be getting it from him. He put up with it because he felt obligated.

Vinnie could appreciate his position. She didn't care to be made a spectacle either. Despite her status as a performer, she only did that on her terms. Early on in her career there had been a promoter who'd tried to convince her to take her music more R&B or more whatever. She knew where her talent and her heart lay. Changing to please someone else would have been a mistake.

So she'd cut poor young Captain Reid some slack and get this over with quickly. But there was one question she couldn't get out of asking him. "And how old are you?"

"Thirty-three."

"Thirty three?" Damn. Even younger than she'd thought, but it figured. Any older and he'd have probably made it higher up the marine food chain already. "I have underwear older than you." The crowd laughed and applauded, but the birthday boy didn't crack a smile.

She motioned two enlisted men in the wings to bring out the cake. "Then there's only one thing left." Once the men had positioned the cake in front of them she burst into her best Marilyn Monroe rendition of *Happy Birthday*, inserting Captain where Mr. President would have been.

He bent and blew out the candles. As expected, she braced a hand on his shoulder, leaned in and kissed his cheek. His hand rose to rest on her back. Before pulling away she whispered, "That wasn't so bad, was it?"

His hand had risen to rest on her back. He said nothing, but his fingers on her back flexed.

She pulled away. Had the gesture been an attempt to flirt with her? Was she reading more into it? Had he noticed the tremor that had shivered through her at his touch? Had he felt it, too? If he felt any attraction toward her, it didn't show on his face, though there was a smile on his lips that hadn't been there before. Maybe he sensed her attraction and was amused by it. The old lady has the hots for you. Big yucks.

No matter. Vinnie took a step back as the enlisted men removed the cake. She turned to the man beside her. "Thanks for being a good sport." To the audience she said, "Let's have a hand for Captain Reid." They clapped as the he left the stage. But rather than retaking his seat, he headed off in the direction of the mess hall. Whatever. Her job was almost done. One more song and she made her exit to be replaced by her younger, perkier counterpart.

She went back to her room, combed her hair into a ponytail and removed most of her make-up. What she wore onstage was way too much for ordinary consumption, and it would be dinnertime soon.

Usually she'd rather skip a meal than indulge in the unpalatable. But tonight she was looking forward to it. She tried to tell herself that anticipation had nothing to do with seeing the captain again. She wasn't quite buying it though. The hunger she wasn't for food but for the sort of carnal pleasure she hadn't known in quite some time.

That was shocking. She'd sleepwalked through the past year grieving for Carl. Without him she felt unanchored. He'd been her rock, even though she'd spent the last few years helping him battle cancer. She couldn't remember the last time the sight of a handsome man had stirred her. If nothing else, her encounter with the marine proved the old Vinnie was still in there somewhere. She wasn't dead inside.

Vinnie walked across the compound with a smile on her face, but when she got to the mess, the captain wasn't there. Just as well. One of the older officers invited her to sit with him. She went along gladly; she didn't need to be reminded of what she couldn't have.

☆☆☆

Vinnie Cole, you done finally lost your mind.

That's what Al had jokingly said when Vinnie'd told her she planned to go to Iraq. But a smile came to Vinnie's lips as she walked into the pick-up area of the terminal at JFK and saw her cousin. Al wore a chauffeur's uniform and carried a sign that read, "My Cousin Vinnie."

"Now look who done lost their mind?" Vinnie asked, coming alongside Al. "What are you supposed to be?"

"Your ride for the afternoon, ma'am."

"If you say so." If Al wanted to play chauffeur, Vinnie would let her. She held out the handle of her rolling suitcase for Al to take.

Al dragged it behind her like a recalcitrant child. "So how was Iraq?"

"Hot, sweaty, enervating."

"That covers the men, what did you think of the country?"

Vinnie shot her cousin a droll look. "Perhaps you've heard. There was a lot of sand."

"No shit. I'll bet you're dying for a hot bath."

"That would be correct. That and a meal that doesn't have all the flavor cooked out of it."

"You're on your own with the bathing, but I've got the food covered."

Unbidden, Vinnie's mouth watered. "Do tell."

Al grinned. "Wait until we get to the car."

Fine. Vinnie could wait. Especially since Al was teasing her rather than fussing. She figured Al would get to that soon enough. Vinnie could wait.

Once they found Al's black *Passat*, the women slid inside. Vinnie pulled off her cap, unleashing a fall of hair that was just as black but not as long as Vinnie's.

Al exhaled. "That's better."

"For you maybe. Where's my food?"

"Hold your horses," Al scolded. "You'll be thanking me in a minute." Al reached into the back seat to retrieve a small red thermal bag. "Some of it might still be warm."

Vinnie took the bag and unzipped it. Immediately she knew, from the aroma wafting up at her, what was in the bag—chicken from the supermarket near Al's apartment. Vinnie had no idea what the store did to make the meat so delicious, but it was soft, moist, well-seasoned, and for the most part short-lived.

Vinnie ignored Al's jibes as she gobbled down a couple of wings then started in on the mac and cheese and *platanos* that completed the meal. In the meantime, Al pulled out of the parking space, paid the parking fee and headed for the highway that would take them into the city.

After a while, Vinnie sat back and sighed. "Thanks."

Al chuckled. "I think I finally know what putting on the feed bag really means."

"I'd get you for that if I didn't want to kiss you. Thanks."

Al's voice turned serious for a moment. "Did you find what you were looking for?"

"I wasn't looking for anything."

"Then did you find the escape you wanted?"

Sometimes Vinnie found it disconcerting how well Al knew her. Al had known she'd needed an escape from focusing on the anniversary of Carl's death. She hadn't mentioned it before Vinnie left, but alluded to it now. For that Vinnie was grateful. "For the most part, yes."

"Good." The smile returned to Al's face. "Now you owe me some serious payback for looking after your place."

"Yes, ma'am," Vinnie said, but she dreaded what sort of payment Al would demand.

☆☆☆

After Al left, Vinnie turned on the shower. She couldn't remember the last time she felt truly clean. She stepped into the stall and shut the door behind her, letting the water sluice over her hair, down her face, over her body. She soaped herself, rinsed and lathered again. Damn the water felt good, cleansing, forgiving.

Vinnie didn't know why that last word popped into her mind. She had no need for absolution, did she? She'd done nothing to be ashamed of. She'd lusted after a man she couldn't have. For some reason his image popped into her mind and the memory of his strong arm around her, the scent of him, and the heat churned in her body. It was all there now, taunting her with what would not be.

Without thinking, she crossed her arms over her breasts, as if doing so would stop the heaviness she felt there. It was no use. Her still soapy hands traveled down her body to meet between her legs. It had been a long time since anyone had touched her to please her, not even herself. It seemed selfish to worry about orgasms when her husband was dying. But now her fingers traveled over her slick flesh, exciting her. It had been so long it didn't take much to push her over the edge.

She gasped and braced one hand against the wall to steady herself on suddenly wobbly legs. Hot tears coursed down on her her cheeks and a sob clogged her throat. It was the most emotion Vinnie had let herself feel in so long that she was overwhelmed by it, cleansed and shaken.

Vinnie pushed her damp hair from her face. She'd found release, but she hadn't found satisfaction. Vinnie Cole wasn't dead, but what was she going to do now?

2

"**REMEMBER THAT** favor you owe me?"

From her perch on the piano bench in her living room, Vinnie slid a sideways glance at her cousin. "Vaguely." She didn't have a clue what Al was talking about, but figured that playing dumb was least likely to insult her cousin or arouse her suspicions as to Vinnie's lack of awareness regarding the subject at hand. For a variety of reasons, Vinnie had been distracted since her return from Baghdad four months ago.

Al frowned in a way that told Vinnie she wasn't fooled. "You know the favor you owe me after picking you up at the airport. You do remember Iraq?"

"Didn't I pay you back by taking you to neuter your cat?"

"No, you did not. And besides, I would have had a more exciting way of claiming my favor and believe me there won't be a cat in sight."

At least not that kind of cat. Vinnie fiddled with the piano keys, tapping out the intro to the O'Jay's *Smiling Faces*. "So, what can I do you for?"

"It's what I can do for you."

Vinnie was afraid of that. Al's well-meaning attempts at getting Vinnie back on track—or on-track in the way Al wanted, were driving Vinnie crazy. Al's idea of coping with loss was to pack up her troubles in her old kit bag and smile, smile, smile. While such tactics might work for Al, it left Vinnie cold. "And what would that be?" Vinnie recounted the ways As had helped her over the years. "What are you going to do for me this time? Run me over with my own bicycle? Fix me up with a man who I threatened to sue for sexual harassment? Super perm all the hair off my head? I can't wait."

Al laughed. "Nothing that exciting. They're having this party tonight by the pier. I need a date."

Vinnie's brows shot up? "*You* need a date?" Vinnie said in a tone that suggested she'd just witnessed one of the final signs of the apocalypse. "Why don't you ask one of your fabulous admirers to take you?"

Al sighed in the dramatic way she had. "Okay, not a date so much as a chaperone. You know what week it is don't you?"

Vinnie shrugged having no idea.

"Fleet Week. You know, gorgeous sailors come here, for R and R. Some fun in the New York sun. You have heard of that, haven't you?"

Every year Al treated the incoming tide of men as if they were her own personal dating tsunami. "Aren't you a bit old to be lusting after teenybopper seamen?"

Al grinned. "I will leave alone that perfectly good intro to a punch line to say, aren't you a bit young to have given up?"

"I haven't given up, I'm just not as," Vinnie gestured, looking for a word. "Outgoing as you are."

"You can say that again. You're the only woman I know who can go to a place where she's surrounded by hot, gorgeous men and not get even a little nookie."

"Aren't hot and gorgeous redundant?" Vinnie said, just to get on Al's nerves, but Al didn't take the bait. "Look, I'm on until midnight tonight, anyway."

Al smiled. "Not a problem. The party won't get jumping until around then anyway."

Vinnie ground her teeth together. It had been this way all their lives — Al the more adventuresome one leading them into the fray while Vinnie, the more circumspect one, tried to keep them out of trouble. It was an arrangement that suited them fine since Al wasn't really all that reckless, neither was Vinnie that much of a stick in the mud.

"Fine," Vinnie said, knowing she was licked and not really objecting much. "Where do you want me to meet you?"

Al slung her pocketbook over her shoulder and stood. "I'll pick you up around midnight."

Vinnie watched Al saunter across the living room toward the front door. For the first time in a long time she dreaded going to work.

☆☆☆

Daniel Reid sat in one corner of the Starlight Bar where Lavina Cole worked, nursing a scotch. Her ignorance of his presence afforded him a few moments to watch her unguarded. Any military man knew the importance of a good recon before jumping into battle. But he'd learned from the best, even before the USMC got their hooks in him. While other kids rode bikes and shot hoops, he and his brother Mike played war games in the woods surrounding their house in Kitterage, New York under the auspices of retired gunnery sergeant 'Granite' Greg Reid, their father.

Most people thought all there was to being a sniper like his father was being able to point and shoot. But that was only part of the equation. There was knowing how to find and stalk a target, how to lay in wait in a way that you forget everything, even your bodily functions, hunger or thirst, anything except taking down the subject. All this with only the occasional "mom" to break up the testosteronefest.

By the time Daniel was twelve, he'd mastered most of those skills, to his father's great pride. Mike hadn't been so lucky. Maybe that's why in their own brand of nature versus nurture experiment Daniel had become a Marine and Mike owned a pottery shop in San Francisco.

But even Daniel hadn't planned to follow so closely in his father's footsteps. However, like God, the Marine Corps acted in mysterious ways. He'd been part of a detail near the Capitol, plagued by an enemy shooter picking off both military and civilians every chance he got.

The kid assigned to the target wasn't having any luck taking him out. So Daniel had taken it upon himself to get the job done. It had taken him a day to nail the bastard.

But as the saying goes, do someone a favor and it becomes your job. He'd brought attention to himself and someone somewhere figured out his familial connection. Then that was that. Despite his rank, he ended up with the gig. Exactly what he'd gone to college to avoid.

He wasn't complaining, though. There were worse things that could happen to a man than to be good at his job and be known for his cool and circumspection. But if he had so damn much self-control, how come he couldn't get Ms. Lavinia Cole out of his mind. He still didn't know whose brilliant idea that birthday cake was, which was the only reason his dignity had gone unavenged. But she'd been gracious enough to wish him well, even if, for a variety of reasons, he was unable to appreciate the sentiment.

He'd been out of sorts, but he hadn't been dead. He'd noticed that electric moment when she'd shivered in his arms. He'd thought he'd imagined it until he'd seen the expression on her face, a mixture of surprise and bemusement. He'd started fantasizing about her and hadn't been able to stop. The middle of the desert wasn't the best place to suffer from unrequited lust unless you were into other men or camels. He'd come here to see if he could get her out of his system.

That's what he told himself. She probably wouldn't even remember him, or if she did, she'd probably brush him off as some young buck in town looking to get laid. Even while she'd sung him happy birthday she'd treated him like a kid. He'd have to teach her otherwise.

His eyes swept around the room once more. It wasn't a large space, though big enough to accommodate the baby grand at which she performed, a small dance floor and a dozen small round tables. She was deep in the middle of Lady Day's *Good Morning Heartache*, emoting in a way that made him wonder who had put the blues in that song for her. The other patrons, most of which appeared to be regulars, seemed riveted to her performance. But he also knew by the clock that she'd take a break in another few minutes. He sipped his scotch and bided his time.

He knew the moment she knew he was there. When her gaze settled on him, something sizzled in her eyes. He inhaled. Damn she looked good, better than he remembered, better than any woman, had a right to. Damn.

Then she turned away, shaking her head as if she didn't believe what she saw. She finished up her song, then leaned forward. "Folks, it's that time again. Smoke 'em if you got 'em, but thanks to *your* mayor you've got to take it outside. Edwin, watch my tip jar. I wouldn't want anyone stealing the, ahem, generosity of others."

She stood and walked toward him. He didn't know if she was aware of how her hands smoothed over her hips as she advanced or the way her tongue grazed over her lower lip, but every inch of him was. He stood to hold out a chair for her, and ignored the gesture when she waved him away.

Once he'd retaken his seat her gaze settled on him. He surmised she was surprised to see him, though not displeased. "Glad to see you're home safe and sound, Captain Reid, but what brings you here? I thought you'd gotten your fill of my voice on the base."

So she did remember him well enough to know his name. Was that a reference to his less than enthusiastic participation in his celebration? He decided to assume that it was. "That had nothing to do with you. Bad day at the office."

She shrugged as if it didn't matter to her. Her gaze traveled over him as if she were assessing something. "You do clean up, nice. I didn't know they let you boys out to mingle with the regular humans."

He chuckled. He'd worn his dress blues to impress her, which thankfully they did. "On occasion."

"Are you in for the week?"

"Something like that." But there was something about the way she asked that made him wonder. "Why?"

She shrugged. "Every year my cousin gets a little man crazy when the ships roll in. She's trying to drag me to some party at one of the piers."

"And that's a bad thing?"

She shrugged. "Al's probably lined up some man to foist on me, too."

He focused on the one word that snagged his interest. "Al?"

"Alberta. She's three months older and thinks she's the boss of me."

"I could run interference for you."

She leaned across the table and squeezed his biceps. "I bet you could. I can handle Al." She picked up the glass and downed another swig. "Enjoy your time in the city, Marine." Calling out toward the waiter, she said, "Edwin, we've got to discuss the rum to cola ratio."

She walked off, dismissing him. He did notice her wave over Eddie and if he read the body language correctly his drinks were to be put on her tab. That was fine. It didn't prevent him from leaving enough money on the table to cover their drinks and a tip. It also didn't prevent him from hanging around until her set was over for the night. Then they'd see who would play interference for whom.

☆☆☆

Clutching her cola, Vinnie leaned her back against the ladies' room door and exhaled a breath. Captain Daniel Reid was the last man she'd expected to see. This man who'd been haunting her fantasies had been such a daydream that she forgot to think of him in real terms at all.

Damn he looked fine, his dark uniform accentuating lean physique.

She'd downed Edwin's godawful drink to quell the heat rising in her body. And when she'd impulsively squeezed his arm, the tempest inside her had grown wilder. Al was right. If all it took to get her this stirred up was touching a man's arm, she really did need a man, bad.

Vinnie exhaled. It was time to get a grip. When was the last time she'd spent time drooling over a man young enough to be trouble. Not that he was dangerous, or at least not to anything but her peace of mind and libido. She was old enough and experienced enough to know when a man wanted her and this one did. She'd seen it in his eyes and the way his body reacted when she'd touched him.

He wanted her, though she wondered why. He could get any woman he wanted. Maybe she reminded him of a once-upon-a-time baby sitter or an older cousin or something. Who knew? And even though she'd decided she wanted to get back into life, it would not be with some young pup she probably needed to school about the finer points of making love. She didn't have the patience for that.

Then again, maybe beggars couldn't be so choosy. There weren't any men she'd consider suitable knocking down her door. All she wanted was a bit of passion. She wasn't ready for anything heavy-duty anyway. Carl's illness had tied her down, tied her to him in ways that never would have transpired if he hadn't been so needy and she hadn't been so scared. She never wanted to tie herself to another man like that again. So what was the problem?

For one thing, she'd basically blown him off before she'd given herself a moment to ponder the situation. For all she knew, he'd left while she was in here pondering her navel. Vinnie pushed off the door. She wasn't going to make herself any promises, but if he were still out there when she went out, she'd consider what to do next.

She took the short way back to the piano. She adjusted the microphone. "I'm back, folks. Did anyone miss me?"

As usual, some of her regulars chimed in with an "I did, Vinnie," or whatever. She looked into the audience, focusing her gaze on Daniel, where she'd left him. Only now he had a companion at his table. Al raised her wineglass in salute before bringing it to her lips.

Vinnie shook her head. How had that happened? Knowing Al she'd strolled in and simply taken up with the most eligible man in sight. Whatever. Mentally Vinnie fastened her seatbelt. It was going to be a bumpy night.

3

THE LAST SET of the night was usually the shortest, since most of her patrons started dragging themselves out about eleven. Aided by her version of last call—*One For My Baby*. It wasn't her job to rout the stragglers, but everyone got the hint it was time to go.

When she finished the song, Vinnie closed the piano and turned to the last two diehards. "I see you two have met."

"Imagine that," Al said, gazing back at her pointedly. The Inquisition would begin post haste. She couldn't blame Al, since she'd never mentioned Daniel and here he was in all the glorious flesh. Damn.

As she stood, Vinnie's eyes went to Daniel. He was already on his feet, standing in a way that reminded her of Burt Lancaster playing a general in some disaster movie or other, except Daniel wasn't acting. Considering that most men stood like they were looking for a place to lie down, she found it refreshing.

"I hope you both enjoyed the show." Her gaze was still on Daniel. With the lights up and his smoky gaze on her, warmth blossomed in her belly. She didn't know what to make of his appearance here tonight. Had he come to hear her sing or was there more he wanted? And if he wanted something else, why didn't he say something?

"If you'll excuse me, I need to make a pit stop."

"I'll come with," Alberta volunteered. She quickly closed the gap between them and took Vinnie's arm, hustling her toward the ladies room.

Vinnie ignored the cheeriness in her cousin's voice. Why shouldn't Al be happy? She was about to get exactly what she wanted—the lowdown on Daniel and any other information she could ferret out. Well, they claimed the best defense was a good offense and she intended to give that theory a try out.

Once they reached the bathroom and closed the door, Al, slapped her clutch purse down on the counter in front of the mirror and turned to her. For the first time that evening, Vinnie really looked at her. Of the two of them, Al was the prettier one, the more slender, the more outgoing. Or at least that's how the family wisdom went. Al wore a sleeveless dress in a subtle leopard-skin print and strappy black stilettos. "I see you're loaded for bear tonight. Any particular quarry in your sights?"

Al blinked in feigned surprise. "Are you referring to Captain Hunky Hunkerson? Funny how I didn't know anything about him until tonight. Why was I not told?"

"There's nothing to tell. At one of the bases I visited I sang happy birthday to him. I wouldn't even remember what his name was if he hadn't shown up here tonight."

The last of that wasn't true, which was probably why Al crossed her arms and cast her a skeptical look. "So you wouldn't mind if I took him to the party instead of you since you're so dead set against going."

Heat flashed in Vinnie's cheeks. "Why didn't you ask him already. You had him at your mercy at the table."

Al laughed. "At my mercy? Oh, please. He didn't say two words to me, 'cause he was so busy gawking at you. And you should have seen your face just now. If looks could kill I'd have a dagger in my forehead right now."

"So what's your point?"

"You like him. He likes you. Grab him and let's go. I mean, seriously, we could both use a night out. I'm not planning on ravishing any too-young bones tonight, but a few laughs, a few drinks, a few dances."

Vinnie sighed, knowing Al was right. "I hate it when you're rational like that. It makes it hard to say no."

"Then don't say no. At least not until you consult with your beau."

"He's not my beau."

"I know, I know. But a little flirting never killed anyone."

No, Vinnie had to admit it hadn't. Not yet.

☆☆☆

A short cab ride later, Vinnie looked down on the party from the top of the staircase leading to the lower level. What she saw below was a crush of bodies gyrating to the driving rhythm of the song, the lyrics of which she could not make out. Not that it mattered. The infectious beat thrummed through her, making her body move. She'd always loved music, from classical to techno and all the stops in between. For a moment she allowed the vibes to claim her as she scanned the room. Seamen in a variety of uniforms mingled with civilians, mostly women dressed in the latest shocking fashions. To be young and on the make.

Al's hand on her shoulder drew Vinnie's attention. She leaned in to hear her cousin.

"I'm off. I see an ensign with my name on him."

"Don't get lost on me," Vinnie warned. "Meet me at the ladies room in an hour."

Al drew an X over her heart. "Have fun." Then she disappeared into the crowd.

Vinnie swallowed. That left her alone with Daniel. It was showtime and she didn't have a thing prepared. But he leaned down and whispered against her ear, "Do you want to dance with me, Vinnie?

She tilted a glance up at him through narrowed eyes. He'd never called her by her given name before, much less her nickname, and there was a hint of arrogance in his smile. Not that she was complaining. The press of the crowd wasn't the only thing making her perspire.

But she couldn't help one of her usual flip responses. She pointed toward the crowd below. "That's not dancing, that's rubbing gonads together."

"Then want to rub your gonads with mine?"

Her body shivered. His smile grew broader and a bit more arrogant as well, prompting her to say, "Maybe."

Shaking his head he took her hand and led her down the stairs and through the throng to a spot where there was a bit of room for movement. "How's this?"

"It'll do." She didn't object as he pulled her closer with his hands at her waist. Given the gyrations of a nearby dancer, it was more of a protective gesture than a passionate one. She still found it rousing to have his hands on her as they moved together to the music. Her fingers traveled upward to settle around his neck. Their gazes locked and there was no mistaking the desire in his eyes or his body's reaction to holding her.

Vinnie lowered her head and inhaled, suddenly needing air. It had been a long time since she was conscious of another person so close to her. She didn't feel like this, so aware of her femininity that she actually ached. She'd never believed herself capable of that. Her relationship with Carl had started as a cerebral attraction more than a sensual one. Carl had been a worldly man for whom sex had been an exercise in technique than an expression of passion. If she'd ever felt any great lust for anyone before, time had erased it from her memory. Feeling it now for a man whose motives she didn't know, was disconcerting.

Feeling his fingers on her cheek, she looked up at him. She saw concern in his eyes. She appreciated that, but she needed some answers before she let her libido completely overrule her brain. She cocked her head to one side. "What exactly are we doing here?"

"I thought we were dancing. I mean, rubbing our gonads together."

Cute, real cute, she'd give him that. "I mean why did you come to see me? You figured you'd try to hit it with the old chick. How hard could it be?"

He lifted one hand from her waist to gesture in a way that encompassed the room. "If you see an old chick in this place, you let me know."

"You know what I mean."

He sighed. "I came to see you because I haven't been able to stop thinking about you since I met you. How's that for an explanation?"

She blinked not knowing how to respond. Weren't marines supposed to be those taciturn one-word grunt of a response type guys? That was a whole two sentences strung together and honestly she couldn't think of an answer she would have preferred. So now what?

The smile was back on his lips. "Any more questions?"

"No, not at the moment." She wasn't sure her nervous system could handle any more of his honesty. But the tenor of the energy between them shifted anyway, intensified. Vinnie dragged air into her oxygen starved lungs. She wasn't sure who moved first, but suddenly his lips were on hers and his tongue invaded her mouth. She gasped and her back arched. Her fingers dug into his shoulders. Way before she was ready to give it up, he ended the kiss.

For a moment she stared up at him. She'd been so consumed with his touch she hadn't noticed anything else, had forgotten where they were. Not that she expected anyone else to be paying any attention to them. Maybe it was something in the Marine code about making a spectacle in public, conduct unbecoming or something.

But she did know one thing: if he kissed like that, she didn't have to worry about schooling him in the art of love. Maybe he'd end up giving her a few pointers.

He took her hand. "I think it's time I got you home."

She cocked her head to one side, studying him. That was a bit much. "Is that so?"

A hint of smile curved his lips. "I mean took you home. You know, catch a cab to your apartment. Make sure you get in the door safely. That sort of thing."

He said that in a tone that implied that any other motives she'd ascribed to him were in her imagination. Yeah, right. But since he seemed to be the one with the restraint, she wasn't too worried. "I need to tell Al."

Surprisingly the other woman wasn't hard to find. She was dancing with two men in Navy whites.

"Look who I ran into," Al said when she reached them.

Vinnie focused on the two young men trailing behind her cousin. Both were tall, dark, handsome and undeniably related. Something in their features was familiar, but she couldn't place it. Vinnie shrugged.

Al shook her head. "You remember the Daly twins?"

Vinnie's mouth dropped open. A lifetime ago they and their parents had lived down the street from her. She embraced each of them. "It's so good to see you."

They exchanged a few more pleasantries before Al pulled her aside, leaving the men standing there.

"So, what are you two up to?" Al asked the moment they were seated.

"Just dancing."

"Yeah, tell that to a woman who doesn't notice your lipstick is missing."

Vinnie huffed. "Well if you already noticed, why are you bugging me about it?"

"I'm teasing you. There is a difference."

If there was one, Vinnie didn't see it. "What are you doing?" she asked, noticing Al rooting around in her purse.

"Open your bag." Curious, Vinnie did as she was told. Al shoved a couple of condoms in her purse.

"Condoms?"

"You may not have dated since the Stone Age, but I believe in being prepared. Isn't that the Marine motto?"

"Boy Scouts."

"Same dif."

Vinnie zipped her bag closed. Unable to let it go just yet, she added, "But Magnums?"

Al nodded in the direction of the men. "Your boy looks up to the challenge."

That he did. Vinnie glanced over her shoulder at him. He was still standing where she'd left him. "Are you going to get home okay?"

Al waved a hand. "I can get a lift with the guys."

Something occurred to Vinnie "What did you say to Daniel while I was talking to the twins?"

Al grinned wickedly. "That I knew his name, rank and serial number and I would hunt him down if he hurt you."

She'd figured as much. Vinnie embraced her cousin. "Take care, sweetie."

"You'd better call me first thing tomorrow." Al pulled back from her. "Don't do anything I wouldn't do."

Vinnie laughed. "If you find out what 'anything' you won't do is, please let me know." Then Vinnie walked to where Daniel waited for her. "Ready?"

He took her hand and led her through the crowd into the dark still night. Compared with the heat inside, the night was cool. Vinnie suppressed a shiver as they walked toward the curb where cabs picked up passengers.

Daniel let go of her hand to shrug out of his jacket and sling it over her shoulders. "Better?"

Much. Not only did the warm, soft jacket cover her down to her knees it smelled of him. She inhaled. "Thank you. How did you know I was cold?"

He glanced from her face to her chest and back again. "Are you sure you want me to answer that question?"

She crossed her arms. "Pervert."

"Maybe."

He opened the cab door for her, then went around the other side to get in. He closed the door, gave the driver her address and sat back.

Impeccable manners. She could get used to this. She had been used to that. Carl was the same way, but she'd never felt so stimulated sitting next to Carl. Anticipation stirred her belly. Maybe it had been too long since she'd held a man's hand in a way that was designed to give comfort. It had been so long since she'd even had the prospect of getting pleasure from a man. Her hormones were rioting.

He slung an arm around her shoulders drawing her closer. "Are you okay?"

"I'm fine." Then she made the mistake of looking up at him. Something about his intense eyes did her in. Even the air she dragged in seemed charged. "Daniel," she started, not really sure what she intended to say. But even to her ears it sounded more like a plea.

He didn't disappoint her. His mouth descended to claim hers and his hand rose to cup her cheek. Moaning into his mouth she gave herself up to the kiss. Her arms wound around his neck pulling him toward her. And when he broke the kiss to bury his face in her throat, she cradled his head in her palms.

His breath warmed her. "I didn't intend to do that."

She knew that. They'd gotten carried away. But he'd promised to be a gentleman and by succumbing to her he considered himself breaking his promise to her. But she had a more pressing question. "Why'd you stop?"

He nodded toward the driver. "I'd rather he not drive into a pole trying to watch the show."

He had a point there. Luckily they were almost to her building anyway. She adjusted her dress and his jacket. Then another thought occurred to her. She lived in a conservative building where most of the tenants were older. That had suited her while Carl had been alive, but now, she could imagine the gossip from having a man arrive home with her at three a.m., particularly since it would be the first man since Carl's death. The fact that everyone would be asleep didn't matter, since Hector the doorman would let everyone knew. The thought brought a smile to her lips.

"What's so funny?"

She shook her head. "Nothing."

Since they had pulled up to her building there wasn't time for him to question her further. Daniel helped her out then paid the driver. By the time she stepped onto the sidewalk, Hector had both the door and his mouth open.

"Good morning, Hector," she said as she sauntered past him. "How are you doing tonight?"

"*Bueno*, I mean, un, fine, Ms. Cole. And you?"

"Very well, thank you."

She waited for Daniel to join her before heading toward the elevators. The car opened immediately when she pressed the button. Once inside the car she leaned her back against the rear wall knowing Daniel watched her.

"Why do I get the feeling there's some sort of joke going on that I don't know anything about?"

"I was just wondering how bad a case of whiplash Hector is getting right now whipping out the phone to dial Mrs. Toucanella to report me."

"Why? We didn't do anything."

"You'd be surprised what passes for gossip in this building."

"Do you want me to talk with him?"

She could imagine big strong Daniel towering over teeny Hector during their "talk." Hector would tell everyone that, too. She shook her head. The elevator was already stopping on her floor. Then they'd get out and he'd kiss her good night at her door. That's the least he would do. Despite the presence of the condoms in her handbag and the fact that she'd been toying with the idea all night, she didn't know what she'd do if he wanted more.

When the doors opened, she stepped out, heading toward her apartment. But before she could get her key in the lock, he took it from her and did it himself.

"When did the military start teaching etiquette?"

"It home training, ma'am." He winked at her.

With her hands behind her, she leaned her back against the doorjamb watching him. "What now, Kemosabe?"

He leaned against the door jam. His eyes gave nothing away. "You tell me. This is your show."

She was afraid he'd say that. She had to make a decision. All she knew was that she'd been lonely too long, and if nothing else she trusted him not to hurt her.

Taking a deep breath for courage, she pushed off the wall, wrapped her arms around his neck and kissed him.

4

DANIEL'S ARMS closed around her, lifting her over the threshold to shut the door behind them. For a moment there he'd been sweating bullets, waiting for her to make a decision. He half expected her to pat him on the head and send him on his way. Despite the combustability of the kisses they'd shared, he suspected a part of her could dismiss any passion she felt as easily as she'd dismissed him earlier.

He knew he had her cousin to thank for changing her mind. He hadn't lied to her when he told her his only interest was in seeing her home, but her sweet lips were on him, making him crazy.

He leaned his back against the door and let her slide down him to stand on her own. He set her away from him, enough at least so that he could see her face. Her hair was tousled and her make-up had smudged a bit, but she was still the most beautiful woman he'd ever met.

He wondered if she'd believe him if he told her that or figure it was some line. She treated the difference in their ages as if it was some big hurdle between them, but it didn't matter to him. Still, the one thing he didn't want to do was rush her into anything she'd regret later. He tilted her chin up. "Tell me what you want."

He'd asked her that already, but he wanted to give her the chance to put the brakes on if she wanted to. Her response was a wicked grin and her fingers went to his waistband to free his T-shirt. He obliged her by pulling it over his head and tossing it aside. He heard her breath suck in as her fingers touched down o nhis bare skin.

Her thumbs strummed against his nipples and he couldn't help himself, he groaned. He wanted to take it slow, but he was losing it already. He crushed her to him, his fingers searching for and finding the zipper to her dress. He rasped it down, but at the same time felt her go completely still.

He turned her so that her back was against the door. For a moment, he rested his forehead against her shoulder, trying to breathe some control back into himself. "What's the matter, baby," he said finally.

Her warm breath fanned his skin. "This is so stupid. I don't think I can do this."

"Why not?"

She buried her face against his neck. "I swear, Daniel. I'm not really like this—wishy-washy not knowing what I want. It's not even that. Do you know how long it's been since I was with someone else?"

He had no idea, but it didn't matter. "I've been in the desert for two years."

"I didn't realize we were playing 'Can You Top This.'"

"We're not." But his control wasn't what it ought to be, either. Neither, it appeared, were his reasoning skills. "Tell me what's going on."

She sighed. "There are things you don't know about me. I was married for fifteen years. By the time my husband died, he didn't remember who I was. Forgive me if I'm a little weirded out showing myself to someone new."

That's what this was about? "Vinnie, what are you talking about? You have a beautiful body."

"That's with clothes on it."

At least she didn't disagree with him. He could understand how she felt, but neither did he intend for her to hide herself from him. "Let me see you." He spoke in a gentle voice, hoping to soothe her.

Slowly she let go of the dress and it sank to the floor. She stepped out of it and kicked it away. But her arms were still crossed in front of her. She didn't resist as he brushed them aside to look at her.

His breath sucked in as his gaze roved over her. This was the body of a self-conscious woman? How was that possible? Her breasts were round and full, her waist slender, her hips curved. He felt himself hardening again just looking at her. "That wasn't so bad, was it?"

She smiled shaking her head.

Encouraged, he traced a finger along the lacey bra cup. She bit her lip. But it wasn't enough. He wanted to see all of her. He unclasped her bra and pushed the fabric from her body. Her hands rose to cover herself, but he pushed them away, figuring it was more of an automatic response than anything else. He had his answer a moment later when he bent to take one of her large, dark nipples into his mouth. A soft sound escaped her lips and her hands cradled his head holding him in place.

Damn she tasted good. He sucked hard, drawing a moan from her. He switched sides than trailed a path upward to her neck. Sweat beaded his skin. He wanted her mouth again and he wanted to feel her bare skin against his. He pulled her to him as their lips met for a wild, wild kiss.

He was burning up, from the warmth of her body, the heat of their kiss. The scent of her was driving him crazy. Her fingers went to his buckle and between the two of them they got him out of his clothes. He retrieved the condom from his wallet, but she took it from him and smoothed it on. He was already erect and throbbing and having her hands on him was too much for him to handle.

Breathing heavily, he pushed her back, holding her hands above her head against the door. She looked up at him, a wicked smile on her face.

She'd known what she was doing to him and was enjoying herself. Was this the same woman who had been afraid to take her clothes off?

He shifted so that he grasped both her wrists in one hand and used the other to lift her hips. Burying his face against her throat he said, "Wrap your legs around me." When she did, he thrust into her, burying himself in her body. Her back arched and she cried out, in pain or with pleasure he couldn't tell.

That sobered him. From the little she'd told him he should have known to be more careful with her. He released her hands and brushed her damp hair from her face. "Are you alright, baby."

She wrapped her arms around his neck. "Who told you to stop?"

Humor rumbled up in him, as well as desire. His fingers tangled in her hair, drawing her head back. He buried his face against her throat as he thrust into her again. She whimpered, but there was no doubt in his mind that it was from pleasure. He thrust into her again, slower this time. She canted her hips and took him deeper, her internal muscles squeezing him in a way that nearly brought to his knees. Her fingers scored his shoulders and what little control he'd mustered snapped. He crushed her to him, pumping into her again and again.

Her breath sucked in and her neck arched and her legs around him trembled. He covered her mouth with his, absorbing her cries as she climaxed around him. Only then did he let his own orgasm overtake him. It rushed up on him with such force that he had to brace his elbows against the door to withstand it.

For a long time he simply leaned against the door, holding her, her legs still wrapped around him, trying to recover. Her lips were at his shoulder, leaving soft, damp kisses wherever they touched down. Her hands wandered over his back in a soothing yet erotic way.

When he thought he might have the wherewithal to move, he lifted his head. "How are you doing?"

She ran her fingers through her hair. "In need of a hot shower," she said.

It wasn't the answer he was looking for, but it would do. He shifted her so that he carried her in his arms. "Where's the bathroom?"

She smacked him on the shoulder. "Show off."

"I'm a Marine. We don't show off. We exhibit our prowess."

"Fine. Then exhibit yourself down that hall," she said pointing.

The bathroom adjoined her bedroom and contained both a sunken tub and a shower stall. He set her down near the door. "How's that?"

She smiled up at him. "It'll do." She walked to the stall and flicked on the water. "I suppose you'll want to be joining me."

She said that in such a put upon voice that he knew he'd disappoint her if he didn't say yes. Not that there was a chance he wouldn't say yes. "If there's room."

She shot him a droll look. "Let's not get carried away with ourselves here."

Chuckling, he disposed of the condom, then joined her in the shower. The warm water felt good. He let it rain down on him for a moment before reaching for her. He wrapped his arms around her waist, bringing her back flush with his front. "Thank you," he whispered against her ear.

"For what?" there was amusement in her voice. "For letting you shower with me?"

He shook his head, but he was sure she knew what he meant. He suspected trusting him had taken more from her than she'd even let on.

"I told you that's not like me. I'm way too old to make a believable tease. It's just that..." She waved her hand dismissively. "Let's not go there again, okay?"

That was fine with him, as long as she wasn't bothered by it. He ran his hands over her scalp and down her hair to settle on her shoulders. "Whatever Vinnie wants."

"How about handing me the shower gel behind you."

He did as she asked, retrieving the bottle, but rather than handing it to her, he poured some of the liquid onto his own hands before returning the bottle to the shelf. He rubbed his hands together then rubbed them over her breasts. Immediately the soap started to lather.

Her back arched and she made that sound in her throat that he liked. "I thought you Marines followed orders?"

He ran his soapy hands over her body, inhaling the flowery scent of the gel, probably getting more turned on than she by his efforts. That's what he thought until he slid one of his hands between her thighs. She gasped and her head jerked back against his shoulder.

"Do you like that?" he asked.

Her throat worked, but no sound came out. He couldn't...

He couldn't' resist smiling as her hips undulated against his hand. He gave her what she wanted, circling his soapy fingers over her clit with one hand and exploring her breasts, hips, and butt with the other. He pushed her legs wider apart and slid two fingers inside her. She jerked again and cried out.

Hearing his name on her lips that way certainly didn't do either his ego or his libido any harm. It just made him more determined to please her. "Come for me, baby," he whispered against her ear.

"I just did."

Her voice was ragged and harsh but he knew she wasn't talking about just now. "Do it again."

And she did. He felt her go still for an instant, then tremors shook her body. He turned her to face him and she clung to him, laying her cheek against his chest. He scrubbed his hands over her still trembling body feeling a sense of satisfaction that had nothing to do with his own appetites. He could get used to having this woman come apart in his arms.

She lifted her head and smiled up at him. "I do believe it's your turn. She reached around him for the gel. "I hope you don't mind smelling like plumeria. I don't have any he-man Marine scents to offer you."

"What is a plumeria, anyway?"

"Damned if I know." Her soapy hands moved over his chest, her thumbs dwelling on his nipples. He sucked his breath, and his hands grasped her hips. His groin tightened and his breathing hitched in anticipation of what she would do. Her hands circled lower, over his belly and lower to grasp his shaft. He jerked and his fingers dug into her hips. He'd known what she was going to do, but the pleasure of it was much more than he'd expected.

She smiled up at him, a wicked expression on her face. "Do you like that?"

The same words he'd asked her, but she hadn't been able to muster a response. His was to lean down and take her mouth. Their tongues met for a slow erotic dance and he groaned as her other hand cupped his balls. He hadn't been far from it when she put her hands on him and now...

She squeezed him with both hands and he nearly lost it. He covered her hands with his. "I want to be inside you."

She cast him an impish look. "I'll be right back." She bolted from the shower and came back a second later with her purse. From it she pulled a short string of condoms and tossed the purse on the bed.

He found himself chuckling as she came back in the shower. He wrapped his arms around her shivering body until the warmth of the water heated her. "Better?"

She nodded. And then her hands were on him, rolling the condom on. He turned her around so that her hands were braced against the wall and entered her from behind. She gasped and when he circled an arm around her waist. It didn't take much to topple him this time. He buried his face against her neck and let his orgasm wash over him.

When he recovered, he pulled her to him and kissed her temple, her cheek and finally her mouth, not with desire, but with something else he didn't have a name for. Her arms wound around him and her hands smoothed over his back.

When he finally pulled back, he looked down at her. Her eyes slowly flickered open and she smiled at him. "The next time we do this has got to be lying down."

"Sounds like a plan." He smacked her butt, then turned her around so that he could rinse the rest of the soap from her. She turned back to do the same to him, but instead of indulging her, he crowded her forward toward the faucets and rinsed off himself. He couldn't trust what he'd do if she put her hands on him again.

"Are you quite done?" she asked with feigned hauteur when he was finished.

He took a step back. "Affirmative."

Shaking her head at him, she turned off the water. "You're really enjoying yourself, aren't you?"

He knew she'd said that to tease him, but he did feel good; better than he'd felt in a long time. Being out of a combat zone had something to do with that, but mostly it was being with her. He grabbed one of her towels, wrapped it around her and carried her from the room.

She shrieked. "Put me down."

He didn't set her down until he reached her bed. He laid her down and came down beside her. She looked up at him with an expression he couldn't quite name, but she cradled his face in her palms. "Do you want to stay or do you have to get back to your ship?"

He probably should have told her that he had no ship to get back to. But he didn't want to worry about the repercussions of her catching him seemingly in a lie. "Are you trying to get rid of me?"

That was the crux of it for him. The expression on her face still gave away nothing. He wasn't ready to shout undying love from the rafters, but what they'd shared meant something to him. Would it really be okay with her if he walked out the door never to be heard from again? Or was he misjudging the reason for the question?

She shook her head. "I don't know how this works. I don't want you to get in trouble because of me."

So, he had been wrong. "I don't have anywhere I need to be." Another half-truth, but that would have to do.

She smiled. "I'll be back." She pushed his shoulder until he let her sit up, taking the towel with her.

"Where are you going?"

"You may not have this problem, but if I don't do something with my hair I'm going to have a rat's nest in twenty minutes."

He knew she was exaggerating, but he didn't tease her. She'd been self-conscious before and he didn't want to bring that back. He swatted her butt as she stood, then watched the sway of her hips as she headed into the bathroom. He got under the covers and lay against the pillows. For the moment he was sated and contented. The sound of a blow dryer, like white noise, was oddly soothing, lulling him into a peaceful, dreamless sleep.

☆☆☆

Vinnie turned off the bathroom light but stood in the doorway between the two rooms watching Daniel slumber. Lord, he was a beautiful man. He'd probably object to that unmanly characterization, but so be it.

She loosened the sash on the lavender robe she'd slipped on, shrugged out of it and got into bed. As soon as she lay down, Daniel stirred, turning to face her and leaning up on one elbow to look down at her with a smile on his face.

She said the only coherent thing that came into her mind. "I thought you were asleep."

"I'm a light sleeper."

"No kidding." She'd barely made a sound.

Chuckling, he stroked his hand down her body to her waist. "Where were we?"

She pushed him onto his back and straddled him. "I'll have to let you know."

5

VINNIE WOKE to the sound of ringing and only became gradually aware that the sound was her phone. Rooting around with her eyes closed, she found it on her nightstand and brought the receiver to her ear. "Hullo."

Even to her own ears her voice sounded raspy and strange. "Vinnie?"

"Who is this?" And why were they calling so early in the morning?

"It's me, Al. The woman you were supposed to call first thing in the a.m. and now it's the p.m."

Vinnie brushed her hair back from her face and glanced at the side of the bed where Daniel had lain. But she knew already that he was gone. She was alone, but her lips were puffy from his kisses and her body still hummed from his lovemaking. The only word she could muster was, "Hi."

"Don't you 'hi' me Lavinia Cole. What happened? Did you sleep with him? Was he any good? Spill!"

Vinnie sat up, resting her elbows on her bent knees. "Give me a minute to think, okay?"

"You mean you're still in bed? Is he still there?"

There was so much hope in Al's voice, but it surprised Vinnie that what she felt most was disappointment. She'd gotten what she wanted, her little fling, her sexual healing. She'd fallen asleep in a man's arms and when they'd both awakened in the middle of the night, they'd gone at it again, but this time without the haste of their first coupling. This time had been slow, erotic and so explosive she would swear every gossip in the building had heard her call his name.

"Well?"

"He left." At least she thought he did. The apartment was silent. Vinnie had no intention of telling her cousin any details of the previous night, but a general impression couldn't hurt. "And let me just say, oh my freaking God. They must put something in the food these guys eat. I think some of his muscles even had muscles."

Al sighed. "I'm happy for you kiddo."

"But what?"

Al sighed again. "Time to get back to real life."

"Guess so. How did you end it last night?"

"The boys saw me home in a taxi. They're just as crazy as they were when they were kids."

"And you didn't…" Vinnie let her voice trail off.

"I told you I wasn't interested in seducing any younguns. That I leave to you. Bye." Al hung up before Vinnie had a chance for a comeback.

It was just as well, since Vinnie had never been as quick with a retort as Al. Besides, the smell of frying bacon reached Vinnie's nose. She glanced at the bedside clock. It was afternoon. Who was cooking breakfast?

She pulled a lavender silk robe on as she headed for the kitchen. She pulled up short finding Daniel bare-chested at her stove. He hadn't made a sound that she was aware of. She hadn't even heard the bacon sizzling. Only the smell had given him away.

"Hungry," he asked.

Her stomach growled its response. "Very."

"Sit down." He motioned toward one of the high stools at her counter. That was a first—being told what to do in her own kitchen. But she sat and reached for the morning paper on the counter. "How long have you been awake?"

"Not long. Enough time to shower."

But he hadn't shaved. Stubble prickled his chin giving him a roguish look. She supposed her lady's razor wouldn't have done him much good. "And to raid the refrigerator."

He winked at her. "I was planning on serving you breakfast in bed until some thoughtless person called and woke you."

He set a mug full of coffee in front of her. She took it black so she didn't fiddle with it. "That was Al," she said before taking a sip.

He shrugged. In fact, Al was about the only person who ever called here, for personal reasons anyway. Her agent called sometimes, or clubs or other venues wanting to book her, but that was business. What few friends she'd cultivated throughout her life she'd let go while she was caring for Carl. As far as family went, she and Al were about it except for the odd cousin or two neither of them spoke to. Vinnie had let her life collapse in on itself while her attention centered elsewhere. No wonder Al worried about her. She should be worrying about herself.

"Can I ask you something?"

His softly spoken words brought her back to the present. "That depends."

"You said you were married. What happened to your husband?"

While that wasn't the farthest subject from hand, she hadn't expected him to care. He set a plate of cooked bacon on the counter. Automatically she took one and bit into it. "He died of cancer last year."

"I'm sorry."

She shrugged. "Don't be. He had a good life."

"You didn't have children?"

"No, but I had two step children who are nearly as old as I am who were ready to fight me tong and hammer for Carl's estate."

"What did you do?"

She lifted one shoulder as she reached for another slice of bacon. "I convinced them there was enough to share. I didn't want much anyway. Just where I lived."

"Nosy neighbors and all?"

"Yeah, them, too. The apartment is paid for. It's convenient. I'm used to it."

"No surprises."

Something about his words aroused a sense of melancholy in her. "Guess not."

He slid another plate in front of her, this one contained toast and an omelet. She hadn't been paying attention to whatever he was doing, so she looked from her plate to him. "Thank you."

"Enjoy."

She forked a bit of the omelet into her mouth. The eggs were well seasoned and she could taste the flavors of peppers and onions. "This is very good."

He took a position opposite her at the counter. "I'm glad you like it."

"Tell me something. How does a man with Miss Manners manners, who knows how to cook, end up a leatherneck?"

He grinned. "I like guns."

She cocked her head to one side studying him. "That's it? You like guns?"

He shrugged. My father was a 'Nam vet. It was a male bonding thing."

Yeah right. She suspected he was being deliberately vague, but she didn't press him. Quite a number of the servicemen she'd talked to had told her about what they'd seen or what they'd done, afraid that people would either judge them or not understand or the experiences were too painful to recount. She couldn't blame him for that.

Probably in response to the skeptical look she cast him, he shifted. "Do you remember that dust-up a couple years back when somebody asked a marine sniper what he felt when he shot someone?"

She remembered the episode. Supposedly the man had answered simply "recoil." "Yes."

"He stole that answer from my father."

Which meant his father had probably been a sniper as well. She didn't know much about who did what in the marines, but she knew snipers were picked for their ability to switch their conscience off as well as their ability to hit a target. Maybe his mother had a softer influence.

"And the manners?"

"That was dad, too." He drank from his mug then set it down. "He was a hard case about everything else, but when it came to women..." he trailed off. "He said you should treat every woman like you're dating Ava Gardner."

"Ava Gardner?"

"Either her or Lena Horne. I grew up listening to Lena, Lady Day and Peggy Lee." He winked at her. "I've always been a sucker for a singer or two myself."

She didn't know what to say. He seemed to be implying there was more between them than one phenomenal night of sex. Was there more? When she thought he'd gone, she'd felt disappointment, but at least it had been a clean break without effort on her part. She'd never been in this position before. How did you tell your one-night-only lover to get his gear and go home? And even if she knew how, did she want to? And why was she finding herself growing attached to a man who within twenty-four hours had managed to point out every deficiency in her life?

She didn't have any answers as she ate her food.

After a few silent moments he asked, "What's the matter, sweetheart?"

Taking a page from his evasion manual, she said, "What makes you think something is the matter?"

"You're too quiet."

No kidding. "So are you."

"That's normal for me."

She paused a moment. "Are you saying I talk too much?"

"No, but there are some things you do with your mouth that I like a lot better."

His word in combination with the heated, hooded look sent desire ricocheting through her with lightning speed. Worse, from the smug turn of his lips she knew he knew exactly what he'd done to her. "My, how verbose of you."

His grin widened. "Are you saying I talk too much?"

"Oh, yeah."

She knew what she was doing—issuing him an invitation for another time with her. Was that wrong? She didn't think so when each of them knew what they were getting into. He'd given her pleasure and showed her concern and he'd listened when she'd told him about her life. That's more than you'd get from most men. Despite the hard exterior, he was a sweet man. And the sex was phenomenal. She shivered just from thinking about it.

He didn't take the bait. He forked the last of his food into his mouth. "I've got to get going." He downed the rest of his coffee then carried his dishes to the sink.

Vinnie blinked. She hadn't expected either the nonchalance or the abruptness of his announcement. Despite any fanciful thinking on her part, she'd known his departure had to come sooner or later. Fine. She'd be a big girl about it. But before she could do much more than swallow, he shrugged into the rest of his clothes.

For someone who claimed to have nowhere to be, he was in a hurry to get there. She slipped from her stool to meet him by the door. He hugged her to him and kissed her temple, which struck her as a particularly tender caress. If she hadn't known that's all there was too this, she'd have melted into that embrace. But she pushed away from him. Not knowing what else to say, she said, "Thank you."

He stared at her with a bemused expression. He cupped her chin and tilted her face up. His kiss was brief but stirred her up and when he pulled away she felt unsettled. He ran a finger down her nose. "I'll call later."

That sealed it. She took a step back. It was just a thing to say, like how do you do. No one ever answered that question, unless facetiously. He wouldn't call and she wouldn't be waiting by the phone and that was that.

She watched him walk out then shut the door behind him and locked it. So now she'd had her little moment, her little fling. Life went on and she had a show to put on in a few hours. She went back to her bedroom to get ready.

☆☆☆

"Somebody's got it bad."

Vinnie looked up from her salad to focus on her cousin. She'd arrived at Al's place a half hour ago and Little Miss Bossy had insisted on feeding her. "What are you talking about?"

"You're like that Purdue commercial—pick, pick, pick. Except you're not eating you're just picking at it."

"I'm not that hungry. I had a late breakfast."

"Wonder why that was? Was a man in your bed?"

Annoyed now, Vinnie snapped, "You know there was. It's not a secret."

Al sat back in her chair and crossed her arms. "Genuine emotion. Most of the time I can't get anything out of you besides flip answers. You surprise me."

Surprised herself, Vinnie said nothing.

"How did you two leave it?"

Vinnie speared a piece of lettuce with her fork. "He said he'd call me. You know what that means." She popped the lettuce into her mouth. "There, are you happy?"

Al snorted. "No, not really. I think you blew it, kid. You broke the rules of having the perfect hook-up."

"There were rules? Shouldn't you have told me *before* you got me into this?"

"I got you into this? You were salivating over him from the moment I saw you last night. All I did was make the suggestion that you act on it."

"How did I screw up?"

"You got too involved—which wouldn't be a bad thing if you actually told him you wanted to see him again, you know, made some plans."

"That would be pointless."

"Remind me why that is again."

Vinnie assessed her cousin. Was Al being obtuse or did she have some other, hidden motivation? "Because he's too young. I don't know anything about him, except he had a crazy sniper father. And he's only here for a few days."

"Interesting. At no point did you say you didn't want to."

That would have been a lie, but she didn't tell Al that. "I'll know better next time."

"Next time? What next time?"

"How should I know?" Vinnie got up and dumped her plate into the trash. "I have to go to work."

"And may I say you look particularly killer tonight."

She could say it as long as she didn't question Vinnie's clothes. She'd dolled herself up on the chance Daniel might show up again, which was kind of ridiculous since if he wanted to see her, all he'd have to do was show up on her doorstep. But then again, she wasn't there.

"You want me to come tonight?"

Vinnie shook her head. Her crowd liked it morose and melancholy. In her present mood, she'd fit right in. "I'll call you when I get off."

"All right. Knock 'em dead."

Vinnie left feeling disheartened and annoyed. Maybe her regulars would cheer her up, but not likely.

6

DANIEL SAT IN roughly the same table he'd occupied the previous night, a glass of scotch in front of him, waiting for Vinnie to arrive. When he'd called her this afternoon she didn't pick up. When he went to her apartment, she wasn't there. Then he'd run into one of Vinnie's neighbors who'd informed him she'd gone to her cousin's apartment. Rather than chase her around Manhattan he'd decided to show up where he knew she'd end up eventually.

At just after five pm, there was no one in the place. No darkness to offer cover like last night. She'd notice him the moment she walked in, which wouldn't be a bad thing, but he wanted to be able to gauge her mood first.

Then she walked in and all he could concentrate on was how beautiful she looked. She'd pinned her hair up, leaving a few wispy curls around her face. The black dress she wore plunged low in the front, leaving little to the imagination. His groin tightened and he downed a gulp from his glass for strength.

As he predicted she noticed him immediately. He stood as she walked toward his table. She'd been frowning when she walked in, but now there was a guarded expression on her face. She stopped at the table. "What are you doing here? You can't be that much of a sucker for a Peggy Lee tune."

"It's not the song, it's the singer." He took her hand. "What happened to you this afternoon?"

"I was at Al's."

"I know. Your neighbor Mrs. Toucanella got a hold of me to warn me of the dangers of preying on vulnerable widows. I think she was hoping I had a friend." He'd made that last part up, but it did its intended job— bringing a smile to her face.

"Then what was with your 'here's your hat, what's your hurry' impression this afternoon?"

He leaned in to whisper to her. "We both know where we were headed before I left." Back to her room. "I had to get while the getting was good."

She cast him a skeptical look. Then he understood. He remembered the surprised expression on her face when she'd found him in the kitchen. He'd thought it was because he was cooking. Now he realized she hadn't expected him to stay. She'd only expected one night. Was that all she wanted?

"What was so urgent you had to take care of?"

He brushed a strand of hair from her face. "A clean pair of skivvies for one thing."

"I guess you can be forgiven. You could have told me that, though."

So it had mattered to her that he'd gone. He brought her hand to his mouth and kissed her palm. "You might not have noticed this, but when I'm around you I lose my head."

She grinned. "I have to get ready. Any requests?"

"Surprise me."

He watched her walk off, then settled down to wait. He wondered what she'd say after she saw what was in her dressing room.

☆☆☆

Vinnie stopped at the door of what could laughingly be called her dressing room. It hadn't actually been a broom closet before she'd appropriated it, but the size felt damn close to one. The only benefit was that, aside from the maintenance guys, she alone had the key. Smiling, she bent to retrieve the florist's package left outside her door.

No doubt the flowers came from Daniel. Even when Carl was well, flowers weren't his style. So this treat was special for her. She pushed through the door, flicked on the light and set the rectangular box on her table. Once she got the box open, she stared down at two-dozen white roses. She pressed her lips together, emotion clogging her throat.

The man was crazy. Then her gaze settled on the card atop the flowers. It read, "What now, Kemosabe?" the same words she'd said to him as they'd stood at her open door. He'd needed that sense of control, even though she still freaked out a bit.

Now, she supposed, the ball was on her turf again, and she didn't intend to relinquish control this time either.

She went to find a vase. Once the flowers were arranged, she broke off one bloom and pinned it in her hair. She broke off another and tucked it in her dress. Hopefully, it would stay there until she needed it.

She heard the band tuning up. They only played on Saturday nights, when she could sing without having to accompany herself. It was the only night couples tended to use of the dance floor, though occasionally someone would get drunk and embarrass themselves to the rest of the crowd's amusement.

In the few minutes she'd been away, a few of her regulars had trickled in. They applauded when she came in, but she waved them to silence. She went to Daniel's table, hoping he only paid attention to the front of her. As usual, he stood when she approached.

"A little birdie left me something in my dressing room." She pointed to the flower in her hair.

"Really? Just the one?"

"Here's another." She retrieved the other bloom and tucked it into the lapel of his jacket. He wore a blue suit rather than his uniform. "No dress blues tonight?"

"I'm a civilian, tonight."

"Thank you." She leaned up and kissed his mouth. Immediately several oooohs could be heard from the patrons. Vinnie waved a hand. "Pipe down, folks. I'm going to get the real show going in a moment."

To Daniel she said, "I'll see you later. Order anything you want, Edwin will put it on my tab."

She walked to the stage and took her place in front of the microphone. The band struck up her first song, *The Way You Look Tonight*. For the first time ever, she felt nervous singing. It had always been her escape. Like some people turned to acting to take on different personas, her performance was her mask. Even while going through the worst of it with Carl, she'd been able to come here and forget temporarily, that her life was off kilter. But the presence of one man had changed all that.

When the first set was over, the band put on some canned music and she went to join Daniel.

But before she could sit, he took her hand. "Come dance with me."

"Now?" A few intrepid couples had been on the floor while the band played, but they'd disappeared once the live music ended.

"Now."

She didn't argue. She followed him to the dance floor and let him pull her into his arms in a traditional hold. Vinnie couldn't suppress a grin. Dancing like they had last night was definitely out in this environment.

He tilted her chin up with his fingertip. "What's so funny?"

She shook her head. She was definitely not bringing that up now. A few other couples joined the fray, offering them some cover. She laid her cheek against his chest and inched closer to him. His arms tightened around her and she sighed. She could definitely get used to being with this man, who, for all his youth, offered her more warmth and security than any other man she'd known. She might not have him forever, but for the short while he was available to her she wanted as much of him as she could get.

When she looked up at him, he was already watching her with that intense gaze of his. No matter. She took a deep breath and let it out. "Stay with me."

"I'm not going anywhere."

"Not now. Stay with me until you have to ship out."

"Vinnie—"

She placed a finger over his lips. "You don't have to answer me now, just think about it. Okay? I have to get ready for the next set." She pulled away and left him standing there while she hurried back to her dressing room.

☆☆☆

Daniel went back to his seat. If she'd waited, he would finally have had a chance to tell her that he wasn't going anywhere anytime soon. But it also occurred to him that part of the appeal of being with him was that she assumed the temporary part was built in. Not in his mind it wasn't.

He sighed. What would it take to convince her to at least give them a decent try? He didn't know, because he wasn't sure what she was afraid of. He knew she'd had to watch her husband die. He didn't know how much she'd loved the other man, but he doubted it was ever easy to watch someone you cared for deteriorate to the point of death.

Was it the difference in their ages? It shouldn't. She'd married a man almost twice her age and it hadn't fazed her. Or was it the fact that she was the older one this time? He couldn't fathom it either way. But as soon as he could get her alone, he'd explain things to her.

In the meantime, he'd enjoy her performance. She really did have a beautiful, sultry voice designed for the type of material she sang. Now if she'd hurry up and finish they could get the hell out of there.

☆☆☆

Once the lights came up and the last patron had straggled out the door, Vinnie came to him. "You have to stay home next time."

Daniel's eyebrows lifted. "Why is that?"

"You keep staring at me. You give me the willies."

"Aren't people supposed to look at the performer?"

"Not like they're imagining what I look like naked."

He laughed. "Was I that transparent? Well don't keep me in suspense, woman." Since no one was around, he hooked a finger in the front of her dress and peeked down to see the lacy cups of a black bra. "Not bad."

Playfully, she smacked his hand away. "Barbarian."

"Yup." He considered slinging her over his shoulder, but she worked here so he'd behave. "Are you ready to go?"

"I want to bring my flowers home if you don't mind."

He retrieved them for her. When they got to her apartment she placed them on the living room coffee table. She straightened and turned to face him. "Thank you again, Daniel. They're beautiful."

He cradled her face in his palm and stroked his thumb over her cheek. "No more so than their owner."

"Daniel," she protested.

She stepped away from his hand and he let it fall to his side. Didn't that husband of hers ever pay her a compliment? Whether he did or didn't was none of Daniel's business, but he found it telling that she'd be so overwhelmed by a simple gift of flowers.

She started to walk past him and he caught her around the waist. He lowered his head to explore the column of her throat. She moaned and her neck arched. His groin tightened in response. Damn. She could heat him up faster than any woman he'd ever known. All she had to do was make that sound and he was a goner.

He turned her and hoisted her onto his shoulder. She shrieked and hit him, but only because he'd startled her, he was sure. He carried her to her bedroom and set her down. Her cheeks were reddened and her hairdo was ruined.

"What is your problem?" she asked, but there was humor in her voice.

"Just living up to my name."

"Daniel?"

Clearly she'd forgotten and there was no point reminding her. He pulled her to him and claimed her mouth. At the same time, his fingers went to her hair, pulling out the pins. In a moment, the full mass spilled into his hands. His fingers tangled in her hair, pulling her head back so that he could look at her. Her eyes were wide and luminous. Her lips were moist and already kiss-swollen. God, he wanted her, but he inhaled trying to muster a bit of control. After last night, she probably needed tenderness from him more than anything else. If he allowed himself to rush, that's not what she'd get from him.

But her fingers were at his lapels, pushing at his jacket. He shrugged out of it and tossed it onto a chair. His tie followed. Then her fingers were at the buttons on his shirt, quickly unfastening them. She had it open and out of his waistband before he had the time to stop her. Her mouth touched his chest, warm, moist, teasing. His breath sucked in and then he groaned from the pleasure of her mouth anywhere on his body.

But he broke the kiss and stepped backward so that he could sit on the foot of her bed. He pulled her to stand between his legs. "I thought we needed to talk."

"Is that what you really want to do right now?"

No, he wanted to bury himself inside her, but he wanted to make sure things were okay between them first. He probably should have thought of that before bringing her in here, but that was another story.

She pushed him away from her and he obliged by leaning back on the bed, watching her as she pushed the straps of her gown from her shoulders. It slithered to the floor leaving her bare except for her bra and panties. He'd been wrong, the bra wasn't black but a deep purple that seemed more erotic. He shut his eyes. "Have mercy."

She laughed and knelt between his legs. Her hands braced on either side of him. "Who's Mercy?"

It was the sort of non-sequitur that ordinarily would have made him laugh, but all he could concentrate on at the moment were her breasts, pushed by her little half bra. He reached up and covered them with his palms. She gasped and her back arched. He undid the front clasp of the bra and her breasts sprung into his hands. The sight, the feel of her caused him to groan. He leaned up and took one nipple into his mouth and then the other, sucking hard until she moaned and her body became restless. Then he took both nipples at once and she jerked, crying out.

"Easy, baby," he said, his hands going to her hips to keep her still. His fingers gripped her buttocks and she jerked again, pulling back. For a moment, she leaned back, looking down at him. Her eyes were half closed and her breathing was heavy. It seemed to him she was on the verge of saying something, but she didn't. She leaned down and pressed her mouth to his. His arms closed around her, but she shrugged them off.

She broke their kiss then moved down his body, leaving moist, heated kisses along his skin. His stomach contracted as her tongue delved into his navel. He undid his cuffs and managed to slip out of his shirt as she reached for his belt buckle. He toed off his shoes and she divested him of the rest of his clothing. She stood for a moment and shrugged out of her bra then tossed it aside.

He reached for her, but instead she knelt between her legs and took him into her mouth. It was too much. His fingers gripped the sheets and he nearly came off the bed. She had the nerve to laugh. She enjoyed having him at her mercy, which bothered him not at all. Then her hands were on him, rolling a condom onto his shaft.

He leaned forward, grasped her by the arms and hauled her on top of him. Then he pushed her back on the bed and came over her. Her arms closed around his neck, but he held them over her head so he could look his fill at her.

Lacing the fingers of one hand with both of hers, he used his free hand to roam her body, over her breasts and belly and lower to cup her over her panties. He felt the moist heat through the thin fabric that covered her, inhaled the aroma of her arousal. She squirmed against his hand and he didn't disappoint her. He pushed aside the fabric to slide two fingers inside her. She was ready for him. He brought his fingers to his mouth to taste her juices, then kissed her letting her taste herself on him.

She moaned, her body restless. He pushed her panties off, spread her legs further apart and plunged into her. It felt so damn good, his whole body shivered. He let her hands go and pulled her on top of him. With his hands on her hips he set a slow, erotic rhythm that drove them both mad. His hands wandered over her breasts, her belly and between her thighs. He stroked her clit with his thumb, watching her orgasm play out on her face. Her legs tightened around him and an instant later her body spasmed.

He couldn't hold back anymore. He pulled her down to him and pumped into her until his own explosive release overtook him. He held her to him until the last waves of pleasure receded and they could breathe with some normalcy. He tilted to the side so that she could lie next to him, even though their bodies were still joined.

He brushed her hair away. "How are you feeling?"

She grinned. "Want to have that talk now?"

He hugged her to him. "Give me a minute, okay?"

She nuzzled her nose against his neck. "Fine by me."

He inhaled, willing his heartbeat to settle. After a moment he arranged them under the covers with her lying against his chest. "Now I'm ready."

"Have at it."

He took a deep breath, since what he intended to say was serious. "I want you to understand something about me. The only reason I was in the audience to be ambushed with the cake was that I couldn't get out of it. Some asshole up the line declared all the men should enjoy themselves."

"Thanks a lot."

"The day I met you I'd just gotten news that one of my buddies' convoy had hit an IED. That's a—"

She cut him off. "I know what that is."

He supposed anyone who'd been in Iraq any amount of time had already had their fill of talks of bombs and other explosive devices. "I wasn't in a partying mood."

"I guess not."

"You know the only thing I remember about that day is you kissing me. Right here." He touched the spot on his cheek. "You trembled when I touched you. It was the only good moment in an otherwise hellish day. So I didn't lie to you when I told you I wanted to thank you. Or that I couldn't get you out of my mind since then."

"I never accused you of lying to me."

"Maybe not, but you seemed to believe I had some ulterior motive I wasn't sharing."

"I thought you just wanted to get laid."

He couldn't repress a grin. "There was that. But that's not all I wanted." He paused waiting to see if she showed some inkling of knowing what he was talking about. When there was none. "I wanted a shot with you, Vinnie, a chance to see if there was anything real between us."

"Why do you think I asked you to stay here?"

"For a few days before you think I have to leave."

"Don't you?"

"I probably should have made this plainer before, but no. I asked for and have been assigned to a special counterterrorist training team to the NYPD."

He let his words sit there for a moment. If he was right that she was only interested in the short tern, he'd know if a few minutes. "You mean you're stationed here?"

"Yes."

She sat up. "Why didn't you tell me that?"

"I had trouble getting a word in. Does it matter?"

"I don't like being misled."

"It wasn't intentional."

She slid from the bed, found her purple robe and put it on. "Maybe you should go."

He shook his head. "I don't understand you, Vinnie. First you treat me like a kid when you married a man twice your age. Is that how he treated you? Then you tell me let's just have some fun since I won't be around long enough for anything to happen. Then I tell you I'm not leaving and you're upset. Tell me that makes sense."

"I'm not trying to tell you anything. Is it so hard to believe that maybe I just wanted to get laid. You don't know what it's like to have to nurse someone else, someone who promised to be strong for you, see their life wither away and you are left with nothing. Is that what you're looking forward to?"

Daniel ground his teeth together. "Oh, please, Vinnie. The difference in our ages is negligible. And someone you love can get sick at any time. I'm not asking for the moon. Just a chance. Tell me what's really going on with you." He waited for her to respond. But when she said nothing, he added in a quieter voice. "If you want me to go, I'll go, but that's on you."

He rose from the bed and dressed. When they were in decent enough order to step out into the street he walked out, but he had no idea where he was heading.

7

AFTER DANIEL left Vinnie wrapped her arms around herself and sank down on the bed. He was gone. In her heart she knew she'd done the right thing—gotten rid of him before things went any further. He'd known she wasn't leveling with him, but that didn't matter. What she withheld she'd kept to herself. Even Al didn't know and would be furious with Vinnie for not sharing such information. But it didn't matter now, did it?

That was enough self-pity for one day. Losing a man must make her thirsty because she was parched. Or at least that's what she intended to focus on—physical needs that had nothing to do with sex. She'd get a water from the fridge and get some sleep if that were possible.

Once she got to the kitchen she noticed something she hadn't before— a green post-it note on her refrigerator. *In case you need me—.* Scrawled below was a cell number to a New York exchange. At the bottom was a big D.

The only time he could have left that note was this morning. So this afternoon, instead of obsessing about his whereabouts, all she'd had to do was look at her own refrigerator? If she'd eaten at home instead of at Al's she might have noticed that. Damn. It didn't really change anything, but at least she'd realized how thoughtful he was before he'd walked out her door. Amend that—before she'd driven him out. What was for the best and what she really wanted often proved to be two different things.

Tears formed in her eyes, threatening to spill. It was juvenile, but she wanted what she always wanted when she was down. Al was going to kill her, but then she'd kill her anyway once she heard what Vinnie had to say.

Al lived in about the only building in Soho that hadn't been gentrified in any way. The walk up three flights of stairs was preferable to waiting for the elevator, which might not actually show up.

Vinnie trudged up to the landing then across the hall to Al's door. It had to be around four in the morning, and the way Al slept the only thing that might wake her at this hour was a neutron bomb. So it surprised Vinnie that Al answered the door almost immediately.

Al had her hair down and one of her fancier robes on. Definitely not an

I-don't-have-a-man-here attire. "Did I come at a bad time?"

"Is it ever a good time to show up on someone's doorstep at four in the morning?"

"I suppose not. I meant do you have a guy here?"

"Not exactly."

Vinnie focused on the not part and stepped over the threshold. "I'm sorry to be a pain in the ass, 'cuz, but I need to talk to you."

Al closed the door behind her. "No, by the look of you, you need grandma's cocoa."

"How did I know you'd understand?"

"Been there, done that, ran the marathon wearing the T shirt."

Vinnie laughed, but there was no humor in it. "We've been through a lot together, haven't we?"

Al led the way toward the kitchen. "And it appears we are about to go through some more."

"Not us, just me." Vinnie took a seat at the kitchen table. "I know I did the right thing…"

Al poured milk into a saucepan. "Then how come you look like crap?"

Vinnie stretched her arms across the table and laid her face straight down in defeat.

"I take it this has to do with Daniel. I thought we settled that this afternoon."

Vinnie sat up. "That was phase one. Phase two is that he's not leaving. He told me tonight that he's staying here in New York."

"That's great, 'cuz."

"That is not great." She sighed. "I ended it before either of us became too attached."

Al glanced at her over her shoulder. "What do you mean before either of you became too attached? You're not still hung up on this age thing are you?"

She shook her head. "I kind of told him I was, but it's not that."

"I'm glad because it seems a bit hypocritical to me to be able to marry a guy so much older and not even date a guy who's not even half as much younger."

Vinnie's brow furrowed, as she tried to make sense of Al's math. "It's not hypocritical, it's practical."

Al brought two mugs of steaming cocoa to the table. "What does that mean?"

"An older man, one who was married before, who already has all the children he wants isn't looking for a new wife to give him any more."

For a moment, Al said nothing. Vinnie recognized the look on Al's face, one of complete puzzlement. "Huh?"

"A younger man wants kids. I can't give him any."

Al's only response was the same puzzled look. "You haven't had so much as a hot flash yet, which I am jealous about by the way."

And she never would. Vinnie sighed out her frustration. "Do you remember right after college I was in that car accident?"

"Of course. You broke your leg."

That's what she'd told everyone. "I broke my pelvis, which perforated my uterus and it had to be removed." Bobby Lincoln, her fiancée at the time had deserted her the moment he found out the extent of her real injury.

"I'm so sorry, Vinnie. Why didn't you tell me?"

"I don't know. I guess I was smarting from having the man who supposedly loved me bolting on me. At least he kept his mouth shut like I asked him to, the weasel."

"You settled for Carl because you thought no one else wanted you."

"Something like that. It was just easier, I guess."

"And you broke up with Daniel because of that? How do you even know this thing between you will go anywhere? How do you even know if he wants kids?"

Because being with him felt like coming home, that's how. Everything she knew about him made her want to know more. "Why should I put him in that position of having to choose? Everyone talks about adoption or surrogacy or in vitro like it's nothing, but it's a pain in the ass and expensive. There's a reason people do it the old fashioned way, and it's not just because it's fun."

Al patted her hand. "I'm glad you told me this. I was beginning to think you were a bit teched in the head for letting a great guy like Daniel go." Al inhaled and huffed out a breath. "I kinda have a confession, too."

Vinnie scanned her cousin's face, definitely not in the mood for any fun and games. "What?"

"I'm very fond of Daniel. I slipped him my number to call me if you gave him any trouble. I'd tell him how to handle you."

"How to *handle* me?"

"Something like that. You really hurt him."

Vinnie surveyed her cousin. "How would you know?"

"He's kinda here, and he probably heard every word."

Vinnie rose to her feet so fast that the chair fell out behind her. She turned to look at the entry to the kitchen behind her. Daniel stood there with his shoulder braced against the doorframe.

"Make that definitely," Al said.

Vinnie watched as Daniel walked toward her, righted her chair so that it was out of the way and pulled her into his arms. "I'm sorry, baby."

"You didn't do anything."

"For pushing too hard. For making you dredge up unpleasant memories."

"It's okay. I didn't realize until now how much I was letting the past rule my thinking, making me afraid."

He kissed her temple. "In a funny way, I didn't realize how much the past was prodding me to change things in the present. I guess neither one of us is guilt-free."

"What happens if you want children?"

"How about we go on a date that doesn't involve you singing before we decide that."

"Sounds like a plan."

"Here's another." He lowered his mouth to hers.

8

"HE'S LATE, as usual."

Vinnie closed the oven door and looked over at her almost husband. They'd planned a small ceremony to take place in three days. Daniel's brother was to serve as his best man and their dinner companion that particular evening, but he had not yet arrived. She knew Daniel wanted his brother's approval of her and their life together, but, aside from the night he'd proposed, she didn't think she'd ever seen him nervous before.

"Relax, he's coming. Al's late, too."

Daniel cast her a look that said what else was new.

She'd taken the last of the hors d'ourves from the oven. She put a few on a plate and offered them to him.

He sat on one of the counter stools and pulled her close to stand between his legs. He took the plate from her and set it on the counter. "I've got a taste for something else." He leaned forward and pressed his lips to the valley between her breasts.

"Daniel," she protested. "He'll be here any minute."

"I'll be quick."

He pushed her straps from her shoulders, baring her breasts. She moaned as he took one nipple into his mouth and his hand delved between her thighs. He hadn't lied. In a few short minutes he had her moaning his name as she climaxed. He head lolled forward as she tried to normalize her breathing. Then the doorbell rang and they both froze.

Her head snapped up. "God, I hope that's Al."

Daniel had the nerve to laugh, but she would get him later. She fixed her hair and her clothes and went to the door. She glanced through the peephole, squinted, looked again, then opened the door.

For a moment, she and the man on the other side of the door surveyed each other. She knew that face and the arrogant amusement of his expression. There was no doubt in her mind that he knew exactly what they'd been doing before she came to the door. So be it. He extended his hand toward her. "You must be Vinnie."

"Hello, Michael, nice to meet you." She glanced over her shoulder at Daniel then back to the man in front of her. "Daniel didn't tell me you were twins." Identical twins, in fact, save for the fact that Michael sported a goatee, wore his hair a bit longer and lacked the military posture she favored in Daniel.

"Didn't I?"

She ushered Daniel inside, only noticing then the liquor store shopping bag he carried. He extended it to her. "I hope you like it."

Well, he had the family manners as well. As she moved to close the front door, Al appeared.

"Sorry I'm late." She was fiddling with her own shopping bag. Finally Al looked up straight into Michael's eyes. For a moment neither of them looked away. Neither of them spoke.

Vinnie pressed her lips together to keep from laughing. Worse things could happen to a woman than to fall in love with the last man she expects to. She managed to close the door behind her cousin. She grinned at Daniel. She'd have to remind him of that later.

Author Bio

Native New Yorker Deirdre Savoy spent her summers on the shores of Martha's Vineyard, soaking up the sun and scribbling in one of her many notebooks. It was here that she first started writing romance as a teenager. The island proved to be the perfect setting for her first novel, SPELLBOUND, published by BET in 1999.

Since then Deirdre has published more than a dozen books and two novellas, all of which have garnered critical acclaim and honors. Deirdre has won two prestigious Emma awards. Her work has been featured in a variety of publications, including Black Issues Book Review, Romantic Times, Affaire de Coeur and Blackboard Bestsellers List.

Deirdre lives in Bronx, New York with her husband and their two children. She enjoys reading, dancing, calligraphy and "wicked" crossword puzzles.

Love Freefall

By
Angela Weaver

Books by Angela Weaver
By Design
By Intent
Taking Chances
A Love To Remember
No Ordinary Love
The Very Thought Of You
Bound By Moonlight

Dedication

This story is dedicated to my cousin, Mary Helen, a gorgeous lady who lives life to the fullest, loves with all her heart, and keeps a smile on everybody's face. You are an inspiration.

Love Freefall
By
Angela Weaver

1

MARISSA BARROW felt as if her heart would beat her chest to death while her knees shook like a washer in spin cycle.

Why did she have to stop and lean up against the side of the aluminum building that served as ground zero for the skydive school? Not because she was afraid of heights. Not because she was afraid of dying. She'd be jumping out of a plane with a virtual stranger tied to her back.

No, she closed her eyes and inhaled the crisp morning air. Her heart continued to hammer the mess out of her because of the tall, handsome, broad-shouldered man getting out of the airplane and walking across the tarmac. It was the fear that she might spend the rest of her life, no matter how short it might be without seeing the stranger up closer and real personal.

Her tongue darted across her dry lips. She'd heard of women's sex drives increasing after thirty, but she'd just celebrated her birthday forty-eight hours ago. It was too soon for her libido to skyrocket. She continued to study the stranger's very nice stride. Not too confident, not too slow, but just right. And she'd bet her retirement account that he would carry the same perfect rhythm into the bedroom.

"Earth to Marissa. Girl, you can't freak out on me yet."

"What?" She tore her eyes away from the chocolate Adonis.

"You're not getting sick on me are you?"

Marissa smiled as she met Robin's concerned stare. They may have shared the same schools, grandparents, and maternal genes, but on everything else, they could have been virtual strangers. Robin was a free-spirit; she'd been born that way. Her independent nature had given both her parents grey hair. Only after a stint in the Peace Corp did her cousin return home and take up a career in graphic design.

Unlike Robin, who hated scheduling even visits to the dentist, Marissa had a plan for everything. And when things didn't go the way she wanted, she would just switch to plan B. Her decision to become a physical therapist came after she'd unsuccessfully interned with a general surgeon at the local hospital. She enjoyed helping people; it was just the blood part that didn't sit well with her. "I'm alright." Even to her own ears, Marissa's reply sounded weak.

"Good. Cause I paid for both of us and these people have a no money back policy."

"Along with a no liability should you have a heart attack on the ground, on the plane, or die because of a parachute malfunction?" she quipped.

Robin nodded. "All that too."

"This idea of yours is getting better and better, cuz."

"Wait a minute here! This was your idea."

"Right...right." Marissa frowned. She remembered proposing the idea between her third margarita and her second tequila shot. She'd had misgivings this morning when she'd woken to the possibility that she would be risking her life. But the video highlighting the parachute, equipment, and live footage of what would happen as soon as they reached fifteen thousand feet had reassured her of her alcohol induced craziness.

"You're not having second thoughts are you?" Robin asked.

Marissa nodded. "I've lost count of the times I wanted to chicken out after seeing that video."

"This is perfectly safe, girl. Come on? Have you seen the statistics? We're safer jumping out of a plane than we are driving on the expressway in rush hour."

"It only takes one time." *I will not panic, I will not retreat. I survived finding out Roy was cheating on me, I will get through this.* Just remembering the night when her fiancé called her up and told her their engagement was off because he planned on marrying his Korean girlfriend, still set her teeth on edge.

After spending an evening searching for the bottom of a Sangria pitcher, she'd spent the next morning lying on the bathroom floor, praying to the porcelain Goddess. It was at that divine moment, she'd looked over to the pile of books she'd kept in the bathroom and found hope bound in a white cover. *Getting Over The Ex: Getting Great Sex And A Better Life.*

"Girl," her cousin's amusement laden voice intruded. "We're not sleeping with anybody. Although I wouldn't mind seeing the inside of the owner's jeans. The man is gorgeous."

Marissa shook her head and laughed. "Same old Robin. Only you would want to go after a skydiving instructor."

"Don't knock it. Aren't you supposed to be cutting loose?"

Marissa angled her chin upward. "You're right." She looked toward the sky and crossed her fingers.

2

AIR FORCE Captain Grant Edwards stepped into the Freefall Adventures office and walked toward his step-brother sitting behind a grey desk. "Jay, did you…"

"Wait a minute; just let me check my teeth first." His brother's booming voice interrupted his question.

Grant folded his arms across his chest and waited. Jason Waters was not only the co-owner of Freefall Adventures and an Air Force flight instructor, but also his best friend.

He waited until after Jason looked up from the small mirror to complete his earlier question. "Did you see the two ladies out front?"

"You mean the 'sweet-Jesus-beautiful-take-home-to-mother, sexy chocolate ice cream sundaes' in the waiting area?"

Grant chuckled. "Yes, them."

"I sat with them through the video and coaxed them through signing the release forms."

"Are we taking up their husbands?" Grant asked the question, but didn't want to hear the answer. He flashed back to the glimpse of the woman he caught earlier. A sistah that good-looking couldn't be crazy and no man in his right mind would let her risk her life without being by her side.

"Through some smooth intelligence moves, I know that Ms. Sexy and Ms. Gorgeous are single, with no kids."

"Intelligence moves?" Grant's smile widened.

Jason almost crowed in his own triumph. "I checked the fingers. No engagement rings, no wedding band, no tan lines. I took a look in their cars, while they were watching the video. Didn't see toys, no car seat, or snacks."

"They could have clean kids." Grant believed that both of the women were most likely single without children.

"Trust me, these ladies don't have any crumb snatchers or baby fathers around. Both of them were two-door cars. No parent in their right mind would own two-door cars with kids."

Grant's eyebrows rose. "I'm impressed, big brother."

Jason shrugged. "I'm on a mission."

Grant was taken aback, but decided to let the comment go. "So they are clients. Tandem or Free-fall?"

"Tandem."

Grant nodded. Most of their clients wanted tandem jumps. Every now and again, they got college kids looking for a rush, or mid-life crisis men needing a crash course in gravity reality.

"So is this a repeat or for certification?"

"They're just like everyone else. First time."

Grant respected that. Not too many people willing to jump out of a plane.

"How's this going to run? I fly and you and Donald dive?"

"Nope. Eddie's flying. He needs more flight hours."

"I get the day off?" The time he spent at the jump zone was outside of his work hours and free of charge. He got a couple of cases of beer and flight time.

"Not today, little brother," Jason stood up and grinned. "You're gonna be my wingman."

Grant turned and walked out of the skydive trailer like a man with marching orders. In his hand he held a scrap of paper with the name of the woman he would be taking in a tandem skydive. Although he was well on his way to have over five hundred jumps under his belt, he always felt uncomfortable when jumping with another person.

In his job as a cargo pilot for the Air Force, he ferried equipment, materials, and troops from base to base. In the pilots' seat with a closed door to the rest of the aircraft, he had anonymity. For the next few hours, he would be working with a stranger.

Risking his life with a civilian who just wanted to experience a thrill made him nervous. He looked down at the sheet. Correction, not just a civilian but Ms. Marissa Barrow.

Grant raked his hand over his head. Jay was on a mission and the single-mindedness of his impending pursuit had him feeling sorry for Robin Webb. Whether she liked it or not, her world was about to be invaded by an army of one.

The only thing he could hope for was that the woman his brother intended on pursuing wasn't the lady in blue. He didn't believe in love at first sight. More like lust. He'd gone through that phase many a time.

He started walking toward the training area and his eyes widened as he caught sight of two women. If there was a God in Heaven looking favorably down on him, then the woman he'd glimpsed as he walked across the barracks would match the name in his hands. He wasn't one to poach on another man's girls and technically Jay had seen both women first. But, his older brother still owed him favors and Grant was prepared to call in every one of them if he had to.

"Good afternoon, ladies. Which one of you would happen to be

Marissa Barrow?"

The woman with her back to him turned and Grant wasn't certain if his breath caught in his lungs because his allergies had taken that moment to flair up again or because his eyes had landed on the sexiest combination of cheeks and lips.

"That would be me." She held out her hand.

A scent of sandalwood washed over Grant as he grasped her outstretched hand.

"And you are?"

"Grant Edwards. I am going to be your tandem instructor today. If you will follow me over here, we can start practicing your freefall form."

"What about Robin?"

Grant barely managed to pull his attention from the beautiful woman's face much less concentrate on anything other than her rich alto voice. Stealing a quick glance back at the staging area he watched his step brother turn on the charm. "She's in good hands. My brother will make sure of it."

Marissa blinked. "Jason is your brother?"

He noticed the way she scrutinized his features. He was used to the surprised stares. He and Jay looked nothing alike. "He's my step-brother."

"I have an older brother."

Her answer caught his attention as his thoughts shifted away from the sight of her kissable lips. For more than the second time he thanked God he'd had a brother instead of a sister. If he'd had a sister as pretty as Marissa, he would have spent his entire life fighting with her suitors.

He chuckled. "I'm surprised he isn't here dragging you away."

She gave him a startled look. "I don't understand."

His grin widened. "Because that's exactly what I would do if I had a pretty sister. Does he live here?"

"No, in Connecticut. My parents and I go up and visit at least once a year, preferably before winter."

"Ahh, the good old family vacation."

She smiled. "It's the longest car ride of the year. Do your parents live here?"

"For about nine months out of the year, then they rent a mobile home and tour the country for three months."

"That's exciting."

"It's my father's latest version of retirement. He's spent the last three decades as an industrial machinery mechanic. When he official retired, he opened up a tool repair shop. It's has pretty heavy volume, so much so, that my mother has to constantly remind him that he's retired."

She looked away from him, a blush rising underneath her brown skin. "Oh. I didn't mean to be nosy."

"Ask me anything."

"Am I going to live through this?"

"I haven't lost a student yet."

"And you've been doing this for how long?"

"Ten years."

She let out a breath. "That should make me feel better."

"But..."

"It's not."

"Well, why don't we have you practice your freefall form? Maybe that will loosen you up a little." He led her over to a mat. "Now I need you to lie on your stomach and then lift your body so that only your stomach is touching the pad."

"This isn't so bad," she said.

"I couldn't agree with you more," he muttered as he watched the way her hips rose up in the air as she arched her back. His body hardened at the thought of her arching underneath him. Shaking his head, he took two steps back and gestured towed the equipment shed. "I need to finish up some paperwork before we jump, why don't you do three more and then head over to the changing area and get into your jumpsuit."

After retrieving his flight book, Grant should have been logging the time he spent in the plane that morning, but he found he couldn't tear his eyes away from her, though. He'd taken hundreds of tandem jumps and had always found everything leading up to the jump, tedious. Except now with Marissa, everything she did suddenly became fascinating.

Little things...like her hair sweeping gently over her shoulder as she leaned forward, listening to his instructions. The way her eyes, like soft brown velvet, widened a little when she suddenly understood exactly how they would be falling.

He was in big trouble.

☆☆☆

Marissa leaned up against a tree and stared at the twin engine airplane fifty yards away. She stroked the large altimeter on her wrist, terrified that she was actually going through with her wild plan to skydive. She took a deep breath and hoped she didn't look as nervous as she felt.

What if the plane went down? What if the parachute didn't open? What if they landed in a tree?

Grant and Jason had spent a half an hour showing them a parachute and all the equipment that goes with it. Then, both he and his brother went though a brief description on what everything was, how it all worked, and emergency procedures.

During their presentation, her thoughts drifted. The only thing she could recall with any clarity was the part about what to expect should the main parachute fail to open. Normally, Marissa could focus like a laser on important things like pulling a cord that would save her life, but the sight of her cousin ogling the instructor and damn near drooling on the man had her mesmerized. She wanted to blame Robin for her inability to concentrate, but Marissa knew the main reason had another name and a face: Grant.

"Not thinking about backing out on me, are you?"

The words spoken so close to her ear were in one of the sexiest voices she'd ever heard. He had a deep bass tingled with a nice southern twang. The icy fear in her veins transformed to steam. She turned her head and stared at him, as she examined the wonderful curve of his eyelashes.

Although they had just spent the past half an hour practicing for the tandem jump, she hadn't been this close while facing the new object of her lust. Damn, if the man didn't have flecks of gold in his eyes. Her gaze took in the small veins of grey in his hair, then cruised south to take in the strong nose, clear semi-sweet chocolate complexion and sexy mouth.

His features far away were nice. Up close, he was striking and she could just imagine the wonderful feel of that slight five o'clock shadow on her skin. After having her back pressed up against his while practicing a simulated freefall, Marissa couldn't help but notice that the man wasn't adverse to the gym. Unlike her, nothing on his body jiggled, not the muscled thighs, hard biceps nor the solid abs. Try as she might, Marissa couldn't help believing that his naked body would be so much more enjoyable in her body and in her arms.

Mentally she shook herself. She just met the man and here she was imagining making love to him. Yes, she knew his first name, his occupation, but for all intents and purposes he was a stranger. After schooling her features to hide her inner thoughts, she faced him. "I'm sorry what did you say?"

"I was wondering if you're thinking about backing out."

She took a deep breath and took in the scent of his spicy cologne. *Lord save her from a man who looked good and smelled good enough to eat.* Grant fit both her and the book's ideal of post-breakup male requirements. "If I said yes, would you hold it against me?"

"Everybody's afraid their first jump. I'm impressed that you would admit it."

"One of my professors said that there was nothing to fear but fear itself."

"And you believed him?"

"Her," she gently corrected. "I'm really trying to because if jumping out of a perfectly good plane doesn't kill me, the thought of hitting the ground will."

The intense warmth of his gaze launched a swarm of butterflies in her stomach. "I promise that nothing will harm you as long as I'm around."

"I'm going to hold you to that." She managed a small smile.

"Good. We're going to be going up in ten minutes. Want to practice your freefall form one more time?"

"Is this where I lay on the mat with my back arched and my hands crossed like I'm lying in a casket?"

A low chuckle curved those kissable lips of his. "I've never heard of it described that way."

She shrugged her shoulder lightly and broke eye contact. "What can I say; I have a way with words when I'm nervous."

"Are you nervous about jumping or are you nervous being so close to me, Marissa?"

His grin bloomed wide. In that instance Marissa took in his deep dimple, killer smile, and gorgeous brown eyes. Damn, Grant was good-looking. Her mother had always warned her that looks could be deceptive. But none of that seemed to matter as her pulse rocketed upwards. She bit the inside of her lip.

She wanted to lie almost as much as she wanted to stand on her tiptoes and kiss him, but common sense beat back the embers of desire. Yes, he made her nervous. Yes, he made her nipples tingle, and her secret garden bloom. Until she knew more about the man, she was leaving her cards on the table.

"Both," she softly replied.

Several heartbeats passed silence until Jason's shout. "Planes fueled. Ready to get going?"

"Showtime, beautiful." Grant looped his arm with hers and turned them both toward the plane. He lowered his head. "And I can't wait to freefall with you in my arms."

The shock of his statement left half of Marissa's brain paralyzed. That the sinfully good-looking man was flirting with her. But before she could come to her senses, Grant managed to hustle her towards the plane. She stepped into the passenger cabin and took a moment to look at the small seats, rust colored rug and aluminum colored side panels. Robin walked over to the back of the plane and sat next to her.

Marissa started to stand back up, but an arm crossed her lap and buckled her in. She turned her head, still trying to process the warmth of the hand lingering on her thigh and the steady gaze of Grant's brown eyes. Before she could speak, Jason closed the door and the plane's engines roared to life.

"Just relax," Grant shouted in her ear.

"Right," Marissa barked sarcastically. Relax? She was sitting next to the sexiest man she'd met in years and about to jump out of a plane. How could she relax?

For a few moments she forgot the purpose of her flight and enjoyed the scenery, until she jumped, when she felt a tap on her shoulder.

"Time to hook up." Grant's voice rose over the sound of the engines.

With trembling hands, Marissa unbuckled her seatbelt and stood on wobbly legs. It was now or never.

☆☆☆

"You can do this." Grant smiled as he placed a helmet on her head. As she closed her eyes, a sweep of lashes brushed her cheeks. Grant stared at the rapidly beating pulse in her throat. He wanted to kiss her.

She raised her face and her eyes locked with his. "What do I do?"

"Just keep breathing for me, little bird." His finger automatically tightened the chin strap as he continued to hold her stare. Those dark brown of her eyes had darkened to black with fear. He'd seen more than his fair share of new recruits punk out on their first jump. It was human nature to be afraid of heights, and damn smart to be afraid of hitting the ground at a high rate of speed.

Feeling the plane start to circle around to return to the drop zone, Grant re-checked the equipment. When he finished, he gave the thumbs up to both the pilot. He placed his hands on her shoulders. "I need to get you attached to my harness."

He turned her body around and for a moment he hesitated, feeling the tremors along her muscles. Carefully securing the gear, Grant pulled down his goggles, then motioned for Marissa to do the same. Moving out of the way so Jason and Robin could get in front; he took a deep breath and inhaled her scent.

"Open'er up, Eddie," Jason called out.

The rush of wind that accompanied the opening of the aircraft door flooded the cabin. Instinctively Grant put his arms around Marissa as the temperature dropped another ten degrees. Five minutes later, Jason and Robin jumped. Moving forward, Grant grasped a strap inside the open cabin door and placed them squarely at the doorstep.

"Is it too late to change my mind?" Marissa shouted over the sound of the wind.

"Remember what I taught you about exit positions?"

"Yes!" She hooked her thumbs under the harness shoulder straps.

"Good. Now, one, two arch," he shouted and pushed them out the door and into the clear, cool, bright blue Carolina sky.

Grant didn't remember anything about the jump except for being close to Marissa. It seemed like only seconds until they hit the ground. He felt her shaking body next to him and he quickly got them unhooked and out of their harnesses. "How was your—"

Marissa grabbed his cheeks in both of her hands and kissed him. It was fast and hard. She pushed herself away from him and took off running toward her car.

What a woman.

☆☆☆

Marissa walked through the garage door of her townhouse and took off her shoes. What a day! Not only had she jumped out of a plane, she'd kissed a stranger. Then Robin dropped her bomb; Grant was in the Air Force. That ruined everything.

Why did he have to be in the military? Her problem wasn't that he was divorced, had kids, an ex-felon, or a skydiving junkie. No, it was far worse. He was committed to the military. Just like her ex-fiancé. And the last thing Marissa needed was to put herself in the middle of that possible train wreck again. Nope, she affirmed. Not again.

3

IT WAS BARELY past five in the morning when Grant brought his truck to a stop in front of the air base gates and presented his badge to the security personnel on duty. Even at this time of the morning, he watched the headlights of trucks, jeeps, and planes moving through the darkness. With the overseas reduction initiative starting up, base activity would only increase.

Instead of driving to his office, Grant headed toward the hanger bays. Within minutes he was making his way across the concert to the hangar facility. One of the biggest on the airbase, Grant knew exactly what to expect as he used his badge to unlock the door. However the sight that greeted his eyes always gave him a thrill. The U.S. military gray painted C-17 aircraft sat empty with its large aft door lowered. The huge machine with its four turbine engines could carry paratroopers, equipment, or supplies.

Grant walked toward the rear of the plane and entered via the lowered ramp. Once on deck, he looked upward and whistled. It didn't matter that mentally he could understand how the aircraft flew, his spirit was still amazed at the cargo compartment's twenty foot ceilings. On more than one occasion, he's seen the space packed with large wheeled transports and tracked vehicles, tanks, helicopters, and missiles.

Taking a deep breath, he made his way to the cockpit, but just as his fingers touched the handle, he heard the hanger door open and shut. Turning back, he walked toward the rear exit. Technically, Grant was on leave and the last thing he needed was to get on the service chief's bad side.

Grant came to a full stop and straightened as he glimpsed someone in a blue dress uniform. Upon recognizing Lieutenant Colonel Baker, his senior officer, he saluted.

"At ease, Captain."

"Good morning sir." He lowered his hand. He'd served under Baker from the start of his commission.

"Didn't expect to see me this morning?" The man's silver eyebrows crooked upward.

"I didn't expect to see anyone this morning, sir."

"You do know that today is your first day of leave?"

Grant grinned. "I have some reports I need to file and I'm taking off."

"Will you be back before we start the hops to the West Coast?"

"Yes, sir."

"You can still log some hours on the paratrooper jumps."

"Making sure I'll come back?"

"Civilian life can be tempting especially to man who hasn't had a vacation in over three years."

"No worries, sir."

"Good. I'll see you when I'm back from the Pentagon."

Grant saluted. "You do the same in Washington, sir." Grant's mouth twisted warily as he watched the Lieutenant Colonel walk away. He leaned against the bulkhead and took a deep breath.

Three days ago he wouldn't have thought there was anything better than flying. But that was before a certain dark-haired daredevil had inserted herself into his thoughts. Marissa's perfect curves had caught his interest the second he'd seen her standing next to the skydive office. Her lush lips had snared his attention. But it was her attitude that had earned his respect and admiration. The lady didn't back down. And that kiss she laid on him rearranged his universe. He would never forget the feel of her mouth on his.

He chuckled silently recalling how she'd screamed through the freefall and laughed as they floated down. He'd jumped plenty of times before but he'd take the memories of that jump to his grave. The combination of Marissa's joy and the sheer beauty of the mountains on the horizon had taken him off-guard. But, what happened when they both had their feet on the ground would forever keep a grin on his face. After a perfect seated landing, after he'd unhooked the harness, Marissa just turned around and grabbed him and pressed her mouth to his in a mouthwatering kiss, and without a word, she'd walked away leaving him brain dead with surprise.

Grant straightened and exited the cargo plane. Four weeks to do whatever he wanted, whenever he wanted. And at that moment, he knew exactly what he planned to do with his time. Sticking his hands in his pockets, he strolled toward the exit of the hander bay to being his next assignment.

The seduction of Ms. Marissa Barrow.

☆☆☆

The first thing Marissa noticed when she drove into the parking lot of the physical therapy facility was that almost all of the spaces were filled. With a sigh she realized that not only was it a Monday, but that it was the Monday after the high school football championships.

Inside her office she picked up her first patient file and she buzzed the reception area. "Morning, Louisa."

"You've got a nice one waiting for you," the receptionist answered.

Interesting, she thought. "Please send them back." Normally, she would have sat down and reviewed the patient referral information and medical history, but having arrived late, she didn't have the time.

After passing into the workout area, she took a seat in her treatment room and waited. After taking a deep breath, she blinked as she watched her client strolled through the doorway.

Grant Edwards.

Although the shock of recognition should have left her paralyzed, she opened the file, picked up her pen and tried to pretend they'd never met, never dropped out of a plane, and never kissed. Tensing, Marissa turned her eyes away from the doorway, but her ears couldn't miss the sound of a person's heavy footfalls on the floor.

"Mr. Edwards, please have a seat." She didn't look up as he took a seat.

"Marissa."

She cleared her throat and hoped her smile was professional. "So what happened, Mr. Edwards?"

"Call me, Grant. And I tripped."

"Really? How did you trip?"

"I was trying to catch up with this beautiful lady before she ran away. *Focus, girl, focus.* "Did you fall on the concrete or on the ground?"

He raised his eyebrows. "Ground."

"Are you in pain?

He moved forward and she moved back. "Yes, Ma'am."

"Where?"

He pointed to his head.

Marissa compressed her lips into a thin line. "Do you have a concussion?" She swiped her sweaty palms on her pants.

"Just my pride. It's pretty banged up."

Marissa raised an arched brow. "I'm a physical therapist, you need a psycho therapist."

"No, I need you to have dinner with me tonight."

Marissa blushed. He had looked up and caught her staring at him.

He cocked one of those perfect eyebrows and smiled.

Marissa pulled her gaze from his, and then she noticed how tightly her fingers gripped the pen in her hand. She shook her head. "Look, Grant. Saturday was..."

"The beginning."

"Of what?" she echoed confused.

"Introduction, first meeting, first chapter, first lesson."

"Saturday was a mistake. I wasn't thinking straight. I was full of endorphins and raging hormones when I kissed you."

"Enjoyed it, didn't you?"

Marissa's heart pounded. She then wondered if she were losing her mind because he was telling the truth. She barely knew the man but the thought of kissing him again kicked her sexual appetite into a frenzy. "Grant..."

"Marissa, no need to lie, I'm irresistible."

Her brows drew together. "What?"

"Yep." His lips hitched upward. "Girls, women, and grandmas love me. It's a curse."

"Curse?" What was wrong with her? When did she develop this inability to articulate a complete sentence?

"Yes. But you broke it."

"I did?"

He put both of his elbows in her desk. "With that kiss and the sexy exit the other day."

"You're no longer irresistible?"

"I'm not sure," Grant replied. His hand whipped out with lightning fast swiftness and grasped her wrist, stopping her thoughts in her tracks as he pulled her hand toward him.

She fought to regain her composure. It was harder than it should have been. Marissa usually maintained a calm, collected demeanor but she was truly taken aback and for a few seconds she'd felt as if she were losing herself in his penetrating gaze. "You are not irresistible."

"Irresistible or not, something is happening between us and you know it." His voice gave him a dangerous quality. He hadn't let go of her hand yet, and she found her heart beating a little faster at the way his fingers traced over the smooth contours of her palm. "I don't have to acknowledge it."

"Your pupils are dilated, heart rates up, cheeks flushed, breathing slightly heavy. You want me."

"I'm glad your ego has recovered from its injury." Marissa tried to free her hand. "But you're mistaken."

He laughed then lifted her hand to his mouth.

Marissa's breath escaped in a trembling hiss as she felt his lips brushing the inside of her wrist.

"I don't think so," Grant murmured, his breath a seductive murmur against her skin. "What are we going to do about it?"

She opened her mouth and closed it again.

"Marissa, I just heard…"

The door opened and the sound of someone's voice shattered the moment. Marissa pulled her hand from Grant's and stood abruptly. She rubbed her hands against her pant legs, forcing herself back in focus.

Emily, her co-worker was standing in the doorway, an amused grin on her face.

Marissa's face heated as she watched her friend's eyes dart back and forth between her and Grant.

"Captain Grant Edwards, this is Emily Wright, she specializes in sports injuries."

"Hello, Emily. Please call me Grant."

"Grant?" Her eyes seemed to twinkle. "If all military men were as handsome as you, I might have joined the service."

His good-natured chuckle echoed in her office. "Thank you."

Marissa swallowed a groan. "Did you need me, Emily?"

"Yes," she flashed a smile toward the man seated in her office. "I need to ask her a question about another patient."

Marissa was giving a new meaning to dazed and confused as she moved into the hallway and closed the door.

"Is that's the skydiving instructor?"

"How did you guess?"

"Guess? Shoot, the man should have a 'SS' on his chest for Super Sexy."

"I think it should be more like "Super Stubborn.""

"Let me guess. He's faking an injury to get an appointment and ask you out."

Marissa eyes almost popped out of her head and her mouth opened in disbelief. How the heck did she know unless...

"No, I'm not a physic and I didn't arrange this. I just know men and that Air Force captain sitting in there isn't going to leave here without your address and a phone number."

She'd be buried in quicksand before she'd admit it, but her heart did the electric slide at Emily's words. "He wants take me out to dinner."

Emily rolled her eyes. "What's the problem?"

"You know how I feel about military men."

Emily ran her manicured fingernails through her short curly hair. "You're kidding me. Marissa, you don't have to love him. Just break bread and sip some wine. He saved your life."

"No, he didn't."

"That's right I forgot. You were committing suicide."

"Skydiving," Marissa corrected.

"Same thing. Go to dinner. You have nothing to lose."

"Did you need me or did you want to get a good peek at my fake patient."

She snickered. "I just wanted to drool over Super Sexy before I started my class. The ladies up front couldn't stop talking about him."

"This is so not good."

"You are the only woman on earth that's not happy about having a gorgeous, employed, intelligent, sexy man sitting in your office just waiting to wine, dine and seduce you."

"Please. He's not that into me. We just met."

"Marissa. I wear contact lenses not blinders and the man was looking at your backside as if it were a T-bone steak."

"Enough." Marissa held up her hand. "I'm going to get him out of my office and I don't want to hear another word."

"Nope."

☆☆☆

Grant's eyes fastened on the woman returning to her office. The whole time between meeting her at the jump site and sitting in her small office, she had been a constant thought in his mind. With her hair pulled back into a bun and a doctor's white coat covering her lushness, his body hardened at the memory of the body underneath.

No matter what he was doing he recalled the delicate bow of her mouth, the elegantly arched eyebrows, her kiss, the smell of her skin, the press of her backside against him as they entered freefall. Somehow even his last night flight reminded him of Marissa's hair. How the cloudy night was as dark and lush as her soft, thick, raven colored tresses. "So is it because you're afraid of me or this chemistry we have going on?"

"I am not afraid of you."

"Then why won't you have dinner with me tonight?"

"Because I don't want you to take me to dinner tonight."

"Chicken."

"Conceited jerk."

"She hits below the belt. Did I strike a nerve?"

"No, you are getting on my last nerve. What is it with you military people? The world doesn't revolve on your every whim and women don't have to drop at your feet because you're protecting the country."

He chuckled. "Now I see."

"See what?"

"You're a pacifist."

Marissa huffed. The man would try the patience of a saint. "Hardly."

"You just hate the military."

"I respect the military. My father was a Marine and was injured in the Beirut barracks bombing."

He paused. "If it's not the principle than it's personally?"

This guy just didn't quit. "Can we drop this?" She put her hands on her hips.

"Will you let pick you up at seven tonight?"

"No."

"Then consider the subject still open. Let me guess. Your fiancé died in the Gulf War?"

"I wish." At least she could have mourned him instead of spending weeks feeling sorry for herself then feeling like fool. At least now she realized what kind of man she'd almost ended up marrying. Roy had done her a favor. If he hadn't cheated on her, she never would have taken back her life.

She raised her hands in a sign of defect. "All right. We were engaged. He shipped out to Korea, met a Korean girl, and dumped me. End of story."

"So you naturally assume that because I'm in the Air Force that I'll spend all this time getting to know you, ask you to marry me, and then run off with some random foreign woman. Or are you really afraid you will fall head over heels in love with me and I'll end up breaking your heart?"

"My heart is off the market," she replied firmly.

"Good, because I don't want your heart yet."

Marissa's brows furrowed. "What do you want?"

"You want the truth?" His hot dark eyes looked down at her as he stood up and took a step toward her. When he stood close enough to see the warm liquid brown of her eyes, the smooth skin of her neck, his hard won self-control started slipping away. His gaze moved to her mouth. Lord, he was tempted to kiss her again. Some small voice in the back of his mind which had been dwelling on the sweet taste of her lips knew that he'd probably never get enough of her lips. "Can you handle it, little bird?"

The central air conditioner clicked on cooling the office.

"Bring it on," Marissa declared, refusing to give into the urge to look away, she rose to stand in front of him. Her office, which wasn't large to begin with, seemed to get smaller.

She knew the kiss was coming, but she didn't anticipate strong arms circling her, drawing her close against his chest, and that her brain would shut down.

His mouth took hers; his tongue took hers, drew it into his mouth and took her breath as she felt a wave of desire sweep across her body. His hands wrapped around her waist, and she sagged in his arms, unable to do anything else as his ravaging kisses left her every muscle weak.

"No." she whispered against his lips. He caught her bottom lip between his teeth and sucked, and she found her hands pushing against his chest. "This is wrong...it's too fast..."

Panting as he lifted her head, Marissa leaned against him and trying to breathe. "I can't believe you did that."

He grinned and responded. "I can't believe I waited that long." He let her go. "Nothing to say?"

She leaned back against her desk. "I'm speechless."

Grant took her hand, lifted it to his mouth and placed a kiss on the top. "Then that makes us even because you had me speechless when you gave me that kiss."

Marissa eyes widen. Everything about him was new, exciting, and wonderful. The way he looked at her made her feel as if she were a treasure.

"I'll pick you up tonight at seven." He smiled again.

"Look, Grant." Marissa rubbed her hand against her cheek in an effort to bring a semblance of order to her chaotic thoughts. "I've risked my life with you and kissed you in the heat of the moment, but I still don't know anything about you except your occupation and bad habits."

"I'm thirty-six years old. My biological father died in Vietnam a few months after I was born. I grew up in Virginia, met a lot of people, and studied hard. I didn't always know what I wanted to be, but my parents taught me to be better and my step-brother taught me to go after my dreams."

"After graduating high school I entered the Air Force Academy, I received a Bachelors of Science. After graduating, I started pilot training, and a year later earned my wings."

"Impressive. So what?"

His hands came from his sides and he reached up to brush his fingertips against her cheeks. "I'm telling you all of this, so you will know I'm not a man who takes things lightly or I don't give up. Your doorbell will ring at seven."

Her heart began to race. "I didn't give you my address."

The corners of his lips hitched higher. "I've memorized your skydiving agreement form, little bird. I know exactly where you live."

"Then why did you ask?"

"A gentleman always asks."

"Are you a gentleman?"

"I was until a couple of days ago."

"And what are you now?"

He leaned down and kissed her hand. "A man on a mission."

4

AT FIVE O'CLOCK, Marissa ran through the door of her two story townhouse and headed upstairs to her bedroom.

At six o'clock, she stood in the middle of her walk in closet wearing nothing but a towel and a fierce frown. What did a girl wear on a date she supposedly didn't want, with a man she wasn't supposed to be insanely attracted to?

It took her ten minutes to pull on a pair of slacks and a top, and five minutes to comb her hair and apply her makeup. After she placed on her earrings, Marissa stared at herself in the mirror. She inhaled a deep breath. It had been long time since she'd felt so feminine. Her mind flashed back to the hours she'd wasted preparing for a date with Roy. Before the negative thoughts could intrude, the doorbell rang. Marissa's heart skipped a beat. She glanced at her watch; it was seven on the dot. Military men were punctual.

Taking a quick second to dab perfume on her wrists and behind her ears, she left the bathroom and headed downstairs. Marissa opened the front door and the sight of the man standing on her doorstep made her wish they were having breakfast in bed instead of dinner in public.

When she'd had her arms around his neck and he'd had his tongue doing nice things in her mouth, Marissa had discovered that he was in shape. As her eyes scanned him from head to toe, she had clear view Grant's well-defined muscles. "Hello. Come inside. I just have to grab my shoes." She turned and moved back into the townhouse.

"Nice place," Grant commented.

Marissa paused from looking through the hallway closet, turned around, and flashed in a quick smile. "Thanks."

"And you look very nice, but..."

Her hands stopped searching and she turned around to give Grant her complete attention. "But?"

"You might want to change into jeans," he suggested.

"Why jeans?" she asked.

"What you're wearing isn't exactly motorcycle gear."

Her eyes widened. "We're taking a motorcycle?"

He pointed toward the window and her eyes landed on the Harley Davidson sitting in the middle her driveway.

"Nice evening for it." He raised an eyebrow. "Any objections?"

"N-no...it's just..." She paused. "I've never been on a moving motorcycle before."

Glad he could surprise her, he grinned. "Well, there's a first time for everything."

In less than ten minutes, Marissa had exited the townhouse wearing a tight white blouse and blue jeans, and over it she wore a black leather jacket. Grant's eyes followed her, unable to keep his eyes off her legs in those tight jeans as she stopped next to his motorcycle. "You ready?"

Marissa bit her bottom lip. "I think so."

His heartbeat sped up as she moved closer to him, the spicy scent of flowers and sandalwood surrounding her. "Let's ride."

"Are you sure about this?"

"Why? You want to back out?" He jiggled his eyebrows. "We can always stay in, order pizza, and play truth or dare."

She lifted her chin. "I'm ready now."

"Here." He tossed her his spare helmet.

She caught it deftly and placed it on her head, tightening the neck strap with a grin. "I shouldn't be surprised that you ride a motorcycle."

"Don't worry I'll pick you up in my truck next time."

Marissa looked over the motorcycle, then guided her eyes t his as she formulated a response. "You are awfully confident there's going to be a next time."

"Remember what I said this morning?"

"How could I forget? You are irresistible to women."

He swung a leg over the seat, settling his hands on the handlebars. "Exactly."

She laughed. "What do I need to do?"

"Get on the seat behind me, and hold on."

She laid a delicate hand on his shoulder and swung her leg over the seat. When she settled in, Grant could feel her trembling as she pressed herself against his back and slid her slender arms around him. "Are you nervous?"

She laughed, her voice shaking. "I'm terrified."

Then she'd hold on tighter. "I haven't crashed yet."

"Didn't you say there was a first time for everything?"

"Don't you trust me?" Before she could answer he kick-started the bike and eased it into first gear. It roared to life, and he felt her arms tighten around him even more.

He drove the motorcycle through the empty streets and out onto the highway, the wind whipping past them. They drove in silence, conversation impossible over the roar of the engine, but Grant was content to drive, enjoying the feel of Marissa's warm body pressed against him. He stole a quick glance down at her brown hands, clasped across his stomach, and a shiver of excitement ran through him.

He leaned into a curve and she leaned with him, and they cruised toward the ocean with only the light traffic surrounding them and the wind howling in their ears.

5

SMOKEY BONES was a favorite haunt for Air Force personnel to get together and blow off steam. The interior decor was simple and spare: concrete flooring and tables covered with paper tablecloths, as well as big-screen TVs at each end of the open dining room.

It wasn't just the atmosphere that drew the men and their families to the restaurant, it was the food. The owner was a second-generation barbeque pitman. Everybody know that retired airman, Mitch Ronnal learned his craft from his dad, Harry, who'd been the captain on the competition barbecue team that had won numerous awards and championships around the country.

The jeans clad waiter escorted them to their tables and handed out menus. They took their seats, ordered their drinks. "The décor might not be too fancy, but I can promise you that Mitch has the best baby back ribs east of Memphis."

"I've heard a lot about this place, but I've never been here. It's pretty exclusive."

"Yeah. Over half the men in here are military."

"And the other half would be the small group of civilians allowed in your illustrious presence." Even with the edge of sarcasm, the woman had an amazing voice, rich like espresso.

Grant sat back. "I don't think I've ever met someone so dead set against the military."

"I am not against the old military. Remember my father was in the Marines. I'm just so impressed with the new military."

"We're all human, Marissa," he answered after the waiter deposited their drinks.

She shrugged. "Maybe."

Grant heard the doubt in her voice and planned to argue when he looked up and spotted a buddy entering the restaurant.

"How about we put your preconceived notions to the test?"

Her brow wrinkled. "And how do you propose doing that?"

"A buddy of mine just came in. Would you mind if I invited K.C. to eat with us?"

Mind? Marissa had felt like she'd been given a chance to breathe. After the most exhilarating ride of her life, she was having trouble just keeping her scattered thoughts together. Grant's intense eyes weren't helping her nerves either. Nodding, she managed a small smile. "Not at all. Why would I?"

"Because we're on our first date."

As she turned away to look down at her white napkin in mild annoyance, she caught his eyes moving over her.

"Who said we were on a date?" Marissa asked, surprising him. "This could be called dinner between two people getting to know each other."

"Did I invite you to dinner?"

"Yes."

"Pick you up at your door?"

She reluctantly nodded.

"That's called a date," Grant stated simply, grinning at her.

"Must you always do that?' she asked with the barest edge of irritation

"Do what?"

"Contradict me." Marissa's chin came up and her eyes narrowed. She wasn't blind or dumb and Grant's humor at the situation lit up the table.

"Only when I'm right," he answered and took a swig of his beer. "And I am right."

"What is your colleague's name again?"

"K.C."

"Nice name." She glanced toward the bar. "Is he single?"

A chill swept over her skin as Grant's dark eyes seemed to glitter. "Married two decades with a half dozen kids."

"Funny, he's not wearing a ring," she replied. "And he looks too young to have that many kids."

Grant shrugged his shoulders and leaned back in his chair. "I guess he must have left it at home."

"Well I guess we'll find out over dinner."

"I'll go invite him over."

Marissa shook her head. "Let me." Ignoring his frown, Marissa lifted her hand, aimed the biggest smile she could conjure at the man sitting at the bar, and waved him over. Much to her delight K.C. left his seat and began to walk over to their table. When he'd less than three yards from the table, Grant stood and turned around. The two men greeted each other with a handshake.

"Grant, man. I didn't see you over here. How's it going?"

"Great. K.C. I'd like you to meet, Marissa Barrows. Marissa, this is my ace, K.C."

"Nice to meet you, Ma'am."

Marissa shook his much larger hand. "Please call me Marissa."

K.C. looked back and forth between the two. "Well, I don't want to interrupt your dinner."

"Actually we haven't even ordered. Why don't you join us?" Grant took a seat.

K.C.'s brow wrinkled. "I don't want to intrude."

"I insist," Marissa gestured toward the empty seat. "Besides I need someone to back up all the wild tales that Grant's been regaling me with all evening."

K.C. pulled out the chair and sat down. "You know I can't turn down a pretty lady. Not to mention who could pass up the opportunity to get the scoop on Crash's girl."

"Oh, he and I—"

She never finished her statement because Grant reached over, placed his hand atop her own, and squeezed.

"K.C., why don't you tell Marissa here how I got my nickname since she doesn't believe a word I say."

She reached for a glass of iced tea. "Oh, I have no problem believing that you've crashed."

"No...No," K.C. laughed. "It wasn't like that at all. Grant here was hauling up a group of new recruits for their first jumps. Well, none of them wanted to go and he was already behind schedule so he faked an engine problem and told them all they were going to crash. Needless to say, they couldn't wait to jump out of the plane fast enough."

Grant laughed. "I was reprimanded, but the sight of all those recruits leaping out of the plane was worth it."

"You think that was funny," K.C. added. "You should have seen how fast that Major pushed those greenies out of the way to get out of the plane."

"How long have you and Grant known each other?" Marissa asked as she turned her attention to K.C.

"Since the Gulf War—we were stationed at the same base."

"Air Force buddies?"

"Yep."

Marissa took a sip of sweet tea and let the warm and friendly mood at the table seep into her bones. K.C. had finished ordering another round of beers before she asked another question. "Are you a pilot as well?" she asked.

"Me?" K. C. grimaced. "I don't like flying. The only thing I like is seeing the take off and the touch down."

Marissa's brow creased with confusion and seeing it K.C. explained. "I'm a loadmaster. In most cases, I just make sure that the cargo is on the plane."

"Don't be so modest K.C." Grant added. "He not only gets the plane loaded. He always get's it loaded the right way. Trust me, his job is just as important as mine. Improper weight or balance can bring down a plane."

☆☆☆

Much later after a great meal, Marissa removed the tablecloth from her laps and stood. "Excuse me, gentlemen I need to go to the ladies."

They both stood and Grant was unable to keep his eyes off her legs in their tight jeans she weaved between the tables.

"Four kids, Grant?" K.C.'s rumbling voice snapped him from his reverie. "Are you crazy?"

"You have two kids and two dogs." He pointed out.

"Did you forget to put in the soon to be ex-wife?"

"No need."

K.C. sat back and took a swig of beer. "Well I'm feeling the need to let her know I've been without a steady woman in my life for the past year and could use a little TLC."

"Do that and I will have you sitting on piggyback flights from Germany to Japan for the next two months," Grant threatened.

K.C. visibly shuddered with the thought. "All right then. So does Marissa have any sisters?"

"An older brother. Not your type. If I were you I would ask about her friends."

"Are they cute?"

Grant tipped his bottle in his friend's direction. The Loadmaster had a bad habit of chasing nice looking brain-deficient women. "Better than that. They're intelligent."

"So, Crash. You getting' serious?"

Grant shrugged. "Not sure. But what I do know is that she's too good to be true. It's like I won the lottery."

K.C.'s normally flippant expression sobered as he took a swig of beer. "All I can say is don't mess up like I did."

Grant nodded his head and sat back in his seat. Although K.C. didn't have to ship out, he still spent a lot of hours away from home. After five years of patience, his wife just called it quits, packed up the kids, and moved back to New Jersey. By the time he'd calmed down enough to go get her, she'd already served him with divorce papers.

Grant took a deep swig of his beer and put the bottle down. "Advice duly noted, my friend."

☆☆☆

A few hours later during the ride back to her house, Marissa took in Grant's scent, which was subtle, a faint hint of tobacco, amber and musk. Strangely appealing, like the man himself. She rested her chin on his shoulder, and reflected that his motorcycle, unlike her older brother Mark's crotch rocket, this bike seemed as if it were definitely built for two.

After dinner, he'd challenged her to a game of pool. As they'd spent the next couple of hours playing pool at a billiard's place across the street from the barbeque restaurant, Marissa wished she'd worn glasses instead of contacts. Actually, she wished she could have worn sunglasses because it would have allowed her the freedom to slide her eyes over his incredible physique without a single soul being the wiser.

Grant...the heat from his back as she had clung to him on the motorcycle. The smooth tautness of his stomach muscles beneath her clasped hands...the thought of him made her knees weak and sent a delicious shiver through her body.

Grant brought the bike to a stop in her driveway killed the engine and put down the kickstand. He got off the bike first and Marissa paused a moment more, then smiled and took his hand as he helped her to a standing position.

She took off the helmet and shook her head while taking a deep breath of the sweet night air. A tingle of desire ran through her as took off his helmet and gloves, placed them on the bike then reached over to clasp her hand.

Flustered, she tugged at her hand and was surprised when he didn't let go.

Grant found he liked the feel of her hand in his, the touch of her fingers soft and warm against his rough ones. "So when can I see that pretty smile of yours again?" he asked.

"In your dreams," she teasingly replied.

"I've got a better idea. How about in the morning?"

Her eyes narrowed in annoyance but his smile widened.

"My...my, Marissa Burrows. You've got a dirty mind. I was going to meet you for breakfast."

She sighed. "Look Grant. I enjoyed tonight."

"Then we can do it tomorrow."

She shook her head. "I can't allow this to go anywhere."

"Are you saying you can't go to the movies, dinner, or a sleep over at my place?"

"No, I'm saying that our relationship can't be serious."

"What gave you the impression that I don't want the same?"

Speechless, her lips drooped and then after a moment she recovered. "I just got the feeling that you don't take things lightly. I mean look at your profession."

"You're right I don't. But there's always a first time, if someone's willing to take that chance."

He took the helmet from her hand and hung it on the handlebars and before she could draw another breath, he leaned down. "Are you willing to take a chance on me, Marissa?" Grant dipped his head close to hers, closing his eyes and kissing her forehead, her eyes, her lips...her breath sweet from her parted mouth as she kissed him back hungrily. Her hands slid over the muscles of his shoulders, the leather cool beneath her fingers. Only the sound of a dog barking broke the spell. Marissa broke their kiss but all she had to do was inhale deeply and her lips would lock again with his.

"You make it hard to say no." Her voice sounded sultry to her own ears.

He ran a fingertip along the curve of her jaw. "Then don't. What do you have to lose?"

The question echoed in her mind. "I don't know."

"Nothing. I won't take anything that you're not willing to give. And if you ask, I'll give it back."

Pulling further away, Marissa sighed. "I've had too much food and too much fun to make rational decisions about you, Captain Edwards."

"Love it when you call me that, little bird." His voice deepened and she blushed with the heat of his stare. Bedroom eyes, she thought.

"What was it you said to me when I asked why you would jump out of a plane?"

Sensing a trap she replied slowly. "I wanted to try new things and live life to the fullest. Take chances."

"Take a chance on me, Marissa and I promise new adventures on a daily basis."

Her brow rose at the confident boast. Having grown up with a military family, she had first hand knowledge of how plans could change at an instant. "And how are you going to promise that when you're in a plane over the ocean?"

"I'm on leave from active duty."

"As in you're on spring break."

"A much needed session of R&R."

She lifted an eyebrow. "So would you call this a spring fling?"

"Is that what you want to call it?"

"I don't know."

"I don't think you've ever had a Spring Fling, Marissa Burrows," he commented.

"And you would be right."

"I don't think you've even done too many impulsive things in your life," he added.

"You would be right."

"I'm more than willing to give you ample opportunity to prove me wrong, beautiful."

6

MARISSA STARED at a man standing on her doorstep with his face hidden behind a bouquet of lavender roses and purple lilies. Over the past couple of days she'd gotten flowers, candy, and stuffed toys delivered to her office and to her home. She was the envy of many of her female colleagues and the topic of the week around the break room water cooler. It seemed as if the man had launched some kind of campaign to win her over.

"Flowers for the pretty lady."

She shook her head and reached out to take the flowers and stopped when he lowered the bouquet blocking his face. "Grant Edwards. What are you doing?"

"I'm bribing you with flowers."

Marissa smiled. He was too cute. Standing there with a baseball cap partially covering his face and that killer dimple aimed right at her she couldn't help but feel happy. "They are lovely, just as beautiful as the roses and daisies. You've made a florist very happy this week."

"The plan is to make you happy. Did I succeed?"

She took the flowers and buried her nose in the petals to hide her face. Marissa didn't need a mirror to know she had a big ultra cheesy grin on her face. Her pulse started playing hop-scotch. Inhaling deeply, she lowered the flowers and looked him in the eyes. The intensity of his gaze and the honest warmth of his expression

"I thought you were going to be in the air today," she called out over her shoulder as she placed the vase of flowers on a small foyer table.

"Something's wrong with the plane. No jumps today."

As a neighbor drove by and waved, Marissa remembered her manners. "Please, come in. Can I get you something to drink?"

"No thanks. I've had more than my quota of fresh sweet tea while taking care of my neighbor's lawn this morning. I'm hoping that you've got some free time today.

"I do. What do you have in mind? A movie?"

"No. Close your eyes and open your hand."

She did as he directed and something heavy and metal was placed in her palms. Balancing it's with in her left hand; she used her right to run her fingertips over the metal and along the rubber grip. Without opening her eyes, she knew exactly what it was. "A Glock nine-millimeter semiautomatic," she announced before opening her eyes. The expression on Grant's face was absolutely priceless. She took the gun and handed it back to him handle first. "Do all Air Force officers have concealed carry licenses?"

"Most," he answered. "How did you know about that?"

"Surprised that I know about firearms?"

"Impressed. Something you want to tell me about? Maybe a hidden gun room?"

"My father was in the military. We had weapons in the house, he taught my brother and I to have a healthy respect for guns."

"Did he teach you how to shoot?"

Marissa shook her head. "Barely. I was more interested in fashion than ammunition."

"So you can't shoot?"

"Just because I'm not in the running to be a sniper, doesn't mean I can't shoot rings around you, Captain."

He took a step closer. "That sounds like a challenge?"

She shrugged. "What are you putting on the table?"

"Dinner."

She raised a lovely eyebrow. "Too easy."

"A home cooked dinner."

"I'm always ready for a home cooked meal," she replied, her near-perfect imitation of his slow drawl making him chuckle.

He took a step forward and before she could anticipate his next move, Grant leaned close, catching her face between his palms as he bent his head and pressed a slow, lingering kiss against her lips. Marissa closed her eyes, and with both hands resting on his broad shoulders, she leaned into the kiss. Their mouths parted, tongues darting in and tasting each other.

He eased away and looked at her with heated tenderness in his eyes. His fingers traced her lips and smoothed her check, and tipped her chin upward. "I wanted say that I'd like you to put your money where your mouth is, little bird. But I couldn't resist stealing a kiss first."

"I wouldn't have known you were a thief."

"I wouldn't have guessed you were a Temptress. Now would you like to go to the gun range because if I keep looking at you for much longer I don't think I'm going to be able to make it out the door."

Blushing, she waved him toward the informal living room. "Make yourself at home. I need to run upstairs and change clothes." She turned and had gone up a few stairs when something compelled her to look back. Her gaze settled on the tall man standing at the edge of the foyer landing. A slow smile spread across his face, looking both handsome and charmingly boyish. Fighting both a flirtatious wink and a giddy happiness she turned around and resumed her steps, only this time she had a little more sway in her movements.

☆☆☆

The shooting range on base was in a windowless concrete building on the northeast corner. As Grant opened the door and stood aside to let Marissa enter, he chuckled internally at the sight of curious excitement in her eyes. It had only taken a few dates for him to figure out that Marissa Burrows liked surprises. He stepped inside the air-conditioned outer room and inhaled. The smell of gunpowder, metal and oil perfumed the air.

Grant purchased a couple of boxes of bullets, headsets, and safety glasses from a rather large gentleman behind the counter, while Marissa eyed the numerous glass cases. Firearms of every shape and size imaginable lay settled in the glass display case. Grant felt his blood pressure and his pulse increase just looking at her. Feminine and playful. Sexy and sassy.

His mind snapped back to reality when the man behind the counter handed back his military identification. "You're all set, Captain Edwards. I've got you in lane nine at the end."

"Thank you."

He turned to find Marissa standing by his side. "I'm assuming you've been to an indoor range before," he said.

"As a matter of fact, this is my first visit to an indoor range. My father brought us to the old outdoor base by the river before the EPA shut it down."

"Looks like I'm in for one surprise after another with you Marissa Grant." Grant stated with a warm, crooked grin. He placed his hand on her back and led her to a set of metal doors. The closer they progressed to the shooting gallery, the louder the gunshots became. They walked down a long hallway until they came to the end of the room and then stepped into a booth. He took a moment to hang up the circular target and activate the electrical pulley. Once the target reached the fifteen-yard line, he returned his attention to Marissa.

Grant pulled the gun out of his holster, clicked the latch and the clip dropped out of the gun's grip. He then proceeded to slip back the release, revealing an empty chamber. "Remember to always check the chamber. One of the frequent causes of accidental shooting is that someone thinks just because the clips empty, the gun is harmless."

Marissa nodded.

He proceeded to quickly load the bullets into to the clip. "Rule number one, never point a gun unless you plan on firing it. If you point it at a person, it should be to kill, if you point it at a target it should be to score."

"I didn't think the Air Force would be so into weapons."

"As a rule, we are not. But my step-father was a competition shooter." Grant grinned.

She leaned toward him, her cupid bow lips looking perfectly kissable, her hand outstretched palm upward. "I like fish."

"What did you say?"

"I would like fish for my home-cooked meal."

His grin widened even further at the boldness of her challenge. He reached over to the small shelf, picked up a set of set ear protection and placed it over her ears, then handed her the safely goggles. He handed over the gun and stood back, watched her move into the gun lane, place her feet at least shoulder-width apart, lean forward, and raise her arms.

Leaning back against the concrete wall he watched as she emptied the gun clip in to the black section of the target.

If he hadn't been sure before then he certainly knew now. Grant had finally met his match.

7

IT WAS WITHOUT choice and without protest that Marissa ended up taking Grant up on his promise to show her new things. And true to his profession and his word, Grant more than delivered. For the next several days, her workdays were filled with smiles, laughter and excitement.

He took her to the airfield and she learned how to identify the different planes and jets. One night they had dinner on the beach complete with a fire and toasted marshmallows. They spent an entire Saturday on the motorcycle cruising down the highway. When they'd returned to her house, they'd given each other back massages and she'd fallen asleep in his arms only to wake up the next morning to an empty house but a smile on her face.

Now as she stood in front of the mirror preparing for dinner at Grant's house, Marissa inhaled and shivered. The man was going to drive her crazy. Who would have thought the scent of gunpowder and aftershave could harden her nipples and send a heat wave south of her stomach. When they'd been at the gun range, he'd stood close to her and wrapped his arms around hers to show her how better aim his semi-auto. Lord, and when he spoke, the warmth of his breath on her neck had sent a tingle down her spine. It was a miracle that she'd actually hit the paper target instead of the ceiling. How in the world could a woman concentrate with a man that handsome behind her?

☆☆☆

An hour later after taking a tour through Grant's home and then excusing herself to use the restroom, Marissa followed her nose to the kitchen. Pushing through the swinging door, she stepped into what could have doubled for a Williams Sonoma print ad. Dark grey commercial sized anodized pots and pans hung from strategically placed hooks over the stove and shiny gourmet appliances sat neatly on the countertops.

As her nose took in tantalizing cooking aromas, a smile crinkled the skin around her eyes as they landed on Grant standing next to a gas range with a metal spatula in his hand. Marissa leaned against the island countertop and let out an appreciative whistle. "This is a pretty serious kitchen, Mr. Edwards. I'm impressed."

Grant turned and smiled, "Believe it or not, I'm a pretty serious cook."

"You cook, fly planes, shoot guns, and go to church regularly. You have the making of the perfect man. Better watch out or you'll have every man in America trying to take you down," she teased.

"Why would they do that?" He turned over the salmon.

"Let me clue you in on something, my very naïve Captain. Right now it's only the single woman that chase after you while the married women dream about being single and dating you. If the press got wind of your culinary skills, married women everywhere will have something else to nag their husbands about."

Grant laughed before turning around and peeking into one of the double ovens. "You should have been a comedian instead of a physical therapist. You're talents are being wasted."

"I get to do both. Laughter helps my patients make it through the pain. And, I don't have the patience for show business. I'll leave that to you. So what's cooking and how can I help?"

"We're having salmon with sautéed garlic spinach and baked red potatoes. For dessert, I've got spiced apple tarts."

Marissa's eyes widened and her stomach growled. "Please don't tell me you bake, too."

"I could lie," he answered. "But I'm not a baking kind of guy. These tarts came with simple directions. Remove from box and place in oven."

She walked towards Grant. "How can I help?"

"See that dining room over there?"

Her head turned to follow his fingers and her eyes landed a romantically decorated table complete with place settings and lit candles. "Yes."

"I would like you to take a seat facing me, so I can look at your gorgeous smile while I serve you dinner."

Marissa had known from the minute Grant had opened the door that she was in trouble. Just how much she didn't know. Taking in a deep, calming breath, she turned and walked into the dining room.

After the meal she went into the cathedral ceiling living room and stood next to a chocolate leather sofa. The house decorated with a masculine hand had sleek and modern furniture, accent pieces and an aura of warmth. And he'd worked overtime on the den. A large screen television was against one wall, cockpit leather chairs and a loveseat. She barely glimpsed the corner speakers. They'd shared an incredible dinner and now she'd been sent in here to pick a nice movie.

"So you're just like every other boy," she called out over her shoulders.

"What makes you say that?" Grant answered. Marissa eyed the way he walked. No, he swaggered down the hallway.

She pointed to the video game console. "Your toys?"

"That's work actually," Grant replied ushering her into the center of the room.

"Really?"

He took a step closer to her enjoying the twinkle in her eyes, but he loved it that he could put it there. "I see I have a skeptic in the house tonight," he observed while turning to pick up the remote control with one hand and hitting the on button for the game console with the other.

"Really, Grant," she said with an indulgent tone. "It's okay to have toys."

"I'm testing a flight simulator prototype. This is the home version. We had a full scale version with a virtual cockpit on base."

"Is it difficult?"

"Very."

"How hard can it be?" She shrugged.

"How about you test it out? There's a beginner's level."

"Here," he handed her the game controller. "What's the worst that could happen?"

Her brow rose. "I could crash."

"Not a problem; there's a reset button for a reason. Why don't you fly solo while I get us something hot to drink?"

Ten minutes later, Grant paused in the doorway watching Marissa as she chewed on her bottom lip in frustration. Somehow sensing his arrival her eyes darted from the screen and collided with his.

"This is impossible. I haven't been able to get on the runway much less get in the air."

He placed the two mugs of tea on the coffee table. "Difficult, but not impossible." Then he moved to stand beside her.

"Stand up for me."

He chuckled as she did so without her eyes leaving the television screen. He sat on the sofa, put his hands on her hips, and then guided her to sit down between his legs. The second his manhood came into contact with her jean clad bottom, he couldn't help but stiffen and bite back a curse.

Damn. There was a fine line between torture and pleasure.

Smothering a groan as she relaxed against his chest, Grant inhaled. The soft feminine scent of her enveloped his already overheated senses. Using an extra portion of willpower he didn't even know he possessed, he reached around Marissa's sides and placed his hands over hers on the controls.

"This is as real as the Air Force could make it. So it might look like a game, but you have to following real-life protocol, like releasing the brakes and checking in with the air control tower."

"Oh," she said. "Where are they?"

"Bottom right, little bird. Now pay attention to the instrument panel," he said slowly in her ear. "Turn. Good. Easy on the control. You wouldn't want to get a speeding ticket."

Forcing his eyes to stay on the screen, he tracked the progress of fuel trucks realistically dashing across the tarmac.

"Do they actually give out speeding tickets?"

His chest rumbled with laughter. "I was teasing."

"You're doing a lot of that tonight, Captain."

"Would you like me to stop?" His voice deepened.

Her tongue flicked out to wet dry lips. "No. Now that I'm moving what do I do?"

Grant reached around her and turned on the sound volume. Immediately the sound of a simulated voice with a Boston accent filled the room.

"Now you the follow ATC's instructions and taxi to the required runway, and hold until released to take off."

"ATC?"

"Air Traffic Controller," he explained.

As she turned the plane, Grant relaxed into his sofa until she reached the next stage.

"All right. Congratulations, looks like you are ready for take-off. Now I need you to pay attention to the control panel and watch for the speed. Given the weight of the plane, thrust, and runway length, we need to get to 225 to 275 km/h before you can take off."

"Do you fly often?" she asked as the plane began to gain speed.

"Not this type of plane, but yes I do."

"Grant?"

"Yes?" He stroked the back of her hand with this thumb.

"I can't do this," she said quietly.

"Why not?"

"Because I can't concentrate."

He stilled. "Would you like me to move?"

"Stay."

"Pull up, Marissa. Slowly."

"I did it!" she exclaimed turning her head around to face him. Her expression of childlike joy heated him faster and hotter than drinking straight moonshine.

"Yes, little bird you did. You are a natural." He smiled. "Now bring up your landing gear. Good. Go east."

"All right."

And while the compass rotated and the plane turned eastward, Grant's hands moved north. He started at her curve of her neck, running his fingertips along her skin, feeling the soft warmth. He heard her breath hitch and his nostril flared at the intoxicating scent of female arousal.

Wanting to have all of her attention, he plucked the game controller from her hands.

"Hey, this is my game," she said in a sultry protest.

"So are these," he whispered back, leaning down to cover her lips with his. She made a tiny noise as she returned his kiss slowly, tasting the delicious salt of her sweat. He broke the kiss gently, his dark eyes locking with hers. "All mine."

"Are you making a claim on me?" She palmed his cheek, stroked his lips with her thumb.

He caught her hand with his, and a long beat of silence passed between them before he spoke again. "Maybe I am," he said softly. A sudden seriousness came over his face. He was reluctant to meet her eyes, and instead looked at her hand, tracing the smooth contours of her palm with his fingers. "So shall we work out some rules of engagement?"

"What—" Marissa murmured. "I'm not sure what you mean." Her body melded even more closely into his own.

"I think it's time to begin negotiations," he replied.

"I think I'm at a disadvantage."

"If you can feel me, I am too. I want you, little bird."

He leaned forward and let his lips replace his fingertips and he lightly kissed her neck. "I want to strip every stitch of clothing off your body and look at you naked. Then I want to touch and kiss you from your lips to those lovely hips and then lower. I want to take your tongue in my mouth as I move inside of you. I want to fall asleep with you in my arms, and I want to wake up still inside you."

For a moment he thought he might have scared her.

A faint breath escaped her, a sigh so small it barely existed. "How long are you on leave?"

"Three more weeks."

Marissa reached up and framed his face with her fingertips. Grant locked his gaze with her.

"I can't get involved in a serious relationship with you."

"Is that one of your terms?"

"It's the only one," Marissa whispered.

He lifted his brow. "You want a no strings relationship?"

She began to undo the buttons of her blouse. "Two adults with emotional and physical needs sharing each other."

The emotional part of Grant that had already decided to claim Marissa as his own protested, but his body overruled as his eyes remained glued to her fingertips. The urge to taste Marissa again beat at him. He leaned over and ran his lips along the hallow of her breast, lightly nipping her skin with his teeth. The feel of her body shuddering against his was all he needed to seal his agreement.

Feeling as if he'd wasted enough time, he placed his hands underneath of bottom, stood up and carried her to his bedroom.

He took his time, slowly undressing Marissa. With each piece of clothing he removed, his eyes admired her body, while his fingertips caressed her bare flesh. Seeing her standing in the soft glow of the lamplight clad in red lace panties and a satin bra, a ragged sigh escaped him.

"Do you know what you do to me?" He was nearly undone as he looked into her face, her lips and eyelashes fluttering a millimeter from closed.

"No...tell me," she said softly.

"How about I show you instead?" He moved his hand behind her back and unsnapped her bra. Her firm breasts and dusky erect nipples made his heart thunder in his chest. Mesmerized, his hand cupped her breast and he lowered his head and slowly guided the cocoa-tinted nipple into his mouth.

Grant sucked her nipple gently, his eyes still holding hers, then he gripped it lightly between his teeth, teasing the tip with a series of butterfly-light flutters of his tongue. When the sound of her moan reached his ear, he hooked his thumb underneath her panties and slid them down over the soft curve of her hips.

With her naked, Grant lowered Marissa into the bed, atop the satin sheets. She made no attempt to cover herself, content to lie still against the pillows, her breasts rising and falling with her rapid breathing as she watched him standing over her. His gaze never strayed from her face as he reached into his back pocket and pulled out his wallet.

Within seconds, he'd withdrawn a condom and placed it on the nightstand. Although the thought of her having his child warmed his heart, he wanted his daughter's conception after happy months of trying. The thought of a holding miniature Marissa made him all the more hungry and possessive.

After kicking off his shoes, he pulled his shirt over his head, unbuckled his belt and then pushed his slacks and boxers off. When he joined her in the bed, he took his time, kissing her, stroking her, loving her.

Grant was fascinated by the softness of her skin, mesmerized by the sound purr of her throat as his fingers journeyed between her naked thighs and found her warm and moist. Her legs parted and what little control he'd had vanished at finding out how ready she was for him. His mouth fastened on her neck and something akin to a growl escaped his throat. He didn't know how long he could take it. Yet his one overriding thought was that he wanted to make damn sure he pleased the woman in his arms.

"Grant," she whispered.

"Baby?" His eyes locked with hers.

"I can't take much more."

Pausing, Grant reached over, took the foil-lined condom from the bedside table, and donned protection. He leaned down and greedily took her mouth in his at the same time he entered her. She murmured and he slowly began to move inside her, rocking his hips gently against hers. Her breasts pressed against his chest, teasing him with their softness, and he bent his head down kissing her deeply, catching her tongue between his teeth and sucking it as he concentrated on the feel of her body around his like a tight glove.

Every nerve in her body thrummed with pleasure as she felt him move inside her. Marissa ran her fingernails along the hard muscles of his back as he buried his face in her neck, his breath hot and moist against her skin. She closed her eyes as a wave began to build somewhere inside her.

"Grant..." she moaned, gripping his shoulders. His name on her lips seemed to inflame him. His breathing became a harsh pant in her ear as he slipped his hands up and over hers, interlocking their fingers as he lifted her arms and held them down on either side of her head. He was kissing her hard, and she arched her back, returning his kiss with a passion she didn't know she had, the pleasure increasing with his every thrust until she thought she would pass out from it if there wasn't some relief.

And when the wave crested, Marissa flung her head back and cried out as something exploded inside her. She pressed against him, her legs locked around his hips as Grant poured himself into her.

A long silence passed between them with the room quiet except for the sound of soft, ragged breathing.

"Did I hurt you?" he asked softly.

"No," she murmured.

Grant rolled off her gently and onto his side, wrapping his strong arms around her and pulling her into his embrace. As the aftershocks of their lovemaking eased, her gut told her something her mind had known all along. This wasn't an affair; it wasn't a fling. Making love with him had touched something deep in her soul. In the place of a couple weeks, he'd gotten into her blood.

☆☆☆

Marissa lay soft and relaxed in Grant's protective embrace. Nothing she'd ever experience could compare to the sensation of his fingers caressing her skin. She stirred beneath the gentleness of his touch, taking his hand in hers. As her heart rate descended her brain began to wake up from its passion drunk stupor.

"With you as my pillow, little one, I don't think I'll ever want to sleep again," his voice rasped close to her ear, his warm breath stirring the hair at her neck.

His statement implied permanence, caught her off guard. "I'm not spending the night, you'll get plenty of sleep."

Before she could move, Grant turned her around and wrapped his muscular arms around her torso. The lips that had been burning her skin moments before were pressed together in a frown. "Explain."

Doing her best to hide her growing nervousness, Marissa swallowed. "We met two weeks ago when I was jumping out of a plane. We've been friends for less than that and now we're lovers. But we both agreed that this isn't long term and I don't think it's a good idea for us to be sharing breakfast."

Anger glittered in his gaze. "So I can make love to you, but I can't hold you in my arms as you fall asleep?"

Sitting up, Marissa pulled the comforter over her naked breasts. Annoyed, she clutched the fabric tight in her hands. "Don't twist my words."

"Then tell me the truth."

"Fine," she snapped. "I snore," she lied in order to stave off telling him her real reason. The truth was making love with him had been unlike anything she'd ever experienced. He'd showered attention on every part of her body and brought her to an earth-shattering climax. And as much as she wanted to run from his bed and hide from the reality of the situation, she wanted more. Just like her grandmother's chocolate chip cookies straight out of the oven, she couldn't just have one. A lump settled into her throat, making it difficult for her to swallow as she thought of what her life would be life after Grant returned to active duty.

His anger seemingly evaporated and a grin lit his handsome features. "Darling, if I can sleep with aircraft landing on my bedroom roof, then I can sleep through a little snoring."

A panicked frown furrowed her forehead. "That's not just it. I like sleeping alone."

"You'll like sleeping with me better."

"I *need* to sleep alone, Grant."

"No, little bird, you *need* to let the past go and give us a chance."

She shook her head. "There is no us."

"There is for the next two weeks, unless you want to go back on your word…"

Closing her eyes, she sighed. "I'm not backing out."

"Is what I'm asking from you so difficult to give?"

"No, it's just that I've been badly burned."

"Once bitten, twice shy," he surmised.

Her eyes clouded for a moment. "Exactly."

"He really did a number on you didn't he?"

"It wasn't entirely his fault. I let myself believe in love and happy endings."

"There's nothing wrong with that."

"Fairy tales are for kids not adults, Grant."

He chuckled softly. "Does that mean I don't have to rent a horse and dress up in shining armor?"

Marissa smiled and relaxed enough to slide down deeper into the bed. "I like you better without the armor. Actually…" She aimed a smoldering look at his broad smooth chest and muscled stomach. "I like you better nude."

Grant moved closer and wrapped his arm around waist and lowered his face into hallow of her throat. Marissa whimpered as his teeth grazed her neck. He opened his mouth and bit her soft skin, just hard enough to elicit a gasp from her, then he closed his lips around the skin. "Then it's a very good thing that we princes like to please a woman."

8

MARISSA BARELY managed to get in the door to her townhouse before the phone began to ring. Tempted to let it go to voicemail, she checked out the caller id box and decided against it. Knowing her best friend, she had programmed the phone to automatically redial until someone picked up.

"Good morning, girl."

"Good morning, my behind. It's one o'clock."

"Oh."

"I called your cell phone last night and it went straight to voicemail."

"Battery must have died," she off-handedly replied while cradling the phone between her ear and shoulder. Marissa slipped off her shoes and began moving toward the stairs.

"Really? Let me see. You have a date with a gorgeous pilot, don't answer the phone and you sound like you were up all night doing the horizontal tango. So how was he?"

"You know a lady never kisses and tells," Marissa replied primly with the hope that it would put Robin off.

Several moment of silence passed. Determined to wait it out, she walked into her bedroom and flopped on the bed.

"Marissa?" Robin questioned.

"Yes?"

"You know your mother called me looking for you're behind last night. She wanted to know if we wanted stuffed pork chops or Cornish hen for Sunday dinner."

She closed her eyes and then opened them to look at the ceiling. "All right...all right." A smile drew her lips upward. "Let me just say that man doesn't need a plane to take a girl to the clouds."

"It was that good?"

"He put it on me," she said smugly.

"Wow. Must run in the family. Jason had this girl singing notes I didn't know I could reach. Thank goodness he lives in an older subdivision. If we'd been in one of those new cluster homes, we would have kept up the neighbors."

Marissa clutched the phone. "T.M.I. cousin."

"Don't go all bookish. So what's up between you two?"

"Does there need to be anything else? I think what I just told you was pretty big."

"Nah. That was the tip of the iceberg. Come on spill it."

Marissa eyed the phone and not for the first time that her cousin was spying on her. "He manipulated me into going away to the mountains with him for the weekend."

"Oh, yeah. That's what I'm feeling. Girl, I can't wait to let my mom know she can start brainstorming on an Spring double wedding."

"Your sister's getting married too?"

"You know as well as I do Vanessa's man won't pop the question until she dumps his commitment phobic behind."

"Then who's getting married?"

"You and me. Grant and Jay are the marrying kind, girl. I have no doubt those two will be ring shopping before the season is over."

Marissa shook her head. "Not happening. I made sure Grant is well aware our relationship ends as soon as his leave is up."

"Have you lost your mind?" Robin screeched.

Marissa pulled the phone away from her ear.

"This time I'm keeping my heart and my common sense."

"Just because you had a bad relationship with Mr. Navy, doesn't mean all military men are bad."

"Maybe, maybe not. I'm not up to taking that risk."

"I was there for you when everything went south. Honey, I know what that bastard put you through. Grant is a good man."

"I never said he was bad. I'm just not looking at this one for the long run."

"Whatever. Mark my words, yee of no faith. You're not messing with a boy this time. Grant is a real man. No matter what you've got planned, he's going to be calling the shots."

☆☆☆

Grant rose into the air, catching the overstuffed punching bag, hanging from one gym ceiling, with his knee. Not stopping with that, shifting his weight he executed a tight back flip mid-air stretching out his left leg in an attempt to connect with the bag a second time, only to miss his intended target and fall flat on his back.

Rising onto his elbows, he looked up at the black bag and swore. "Dammit if that thing isn't laughing at me," he muttered. "I've been working that flying one-two for the last year and I still can't get it right. Hell, I used to be able to pull that off blindfolded. What the hell am I doing wrong now?"

"Not concentrating." Jay's humor filled voice answered.

Disgruntled and still mumbling, Grant stood up adjusting the belt of his martial arts uniform.

He should have been feeling like a man on top of the world when he walked into the base recreational facility, that morning. Instead, he'd had to convince a woman to spend the night in his bed. Not to mention, he'd had to practically blackmail Marissa into agreeing to take a trip to the mountains.

Yeah, they'd both enjoyed the days hiking and the nights in each others arms. Hell, he couldn't remember having a better weekend. Now after having knowing her two weeks, he still couldn't break through her personal barriers and get her to realize that what they had could stand the test of time and distance. She was still determined to end their relationship in less than twenty-four hours.

"Got something you want to talk about, little brother."

"More like someone."

"Let me guess: Marissa."

Grant nodded, turned to the left, and began mimicking his brother's punching technique. "She's driving me crazy. Bro, she's like a drug. The more I'm around her, the more I need."

"Women will either turn your life around or turn it upside down." Jay gave Grant a searching look. "From the looks of things I would say that you've got a little of both."

Grant gave a loud grunt and stopped in mid motion. The urge to pummel the body bag had disappeared with his step-brother's assessment of his current mental state. The question was, how did he solve the problem? There was no doubt in his mind that after Sunday night, Marissa would hightail it out of his life on the first thing smoking.

"Jay, karma is no joke."

"Why you say that, man?"

"Marissa is playing the love me and leave me card." Grant began to unwrap the tape around his hands and wrists. "Now I know how the women we skipped out on felt."

"Ouch! Keep that to yourself. Robin thinks I'm a hero."

"Lucky you."

Jay shook his head. "It's not luck. As Momma tells me: it's a blessing. Now all I have to do is put a ring on her finger and get her to say the vows before the truth comes out and she leaves me."

Grant stopped what he was doing and stared at Jay in disbelief. "Are you serious?"

"I'm serious enough to figure out how much I'm going to have to spend on an engagement rung."

"Damn."

"You're surprised? You're thinking the same thing."

Jay put his arm around Grant's shoulders. "I was thinking it; not saying it out loud."

"Please it's the only step. You know you like following your big brother's foot steps. Not to mention you can't leave me hanging. I'm not doing this without you."

"You know I'll be your best man."

Jay laughed and his Grant on the back. "I'd rather you be a better man. Just don't take no for an answer."

"I'll see what I can do."

9

"SO SWEETHEART, do you want to tell me about the nice young man you've been seeing?" Marissa's mother said sweetly.

Marissa's loosened her fingers and let the knife in her hand drop to the side of the cutting board. After wiping her fingers on her apron, she turned to her mother and smiled. It didn't surprise her that her mother knew about Grant, but what did catch her off-guard was the amount of time she'd taken to bring him up. She and her mother had always had an open dialogue with one another.

Patient and understanding, her mother would wait until Marissa was ready to talk. The only exception had been with her ex-fiancé. When that relationship had crashed, her mother had questioned Marissa relentlessly until and she had been forthcoming with his infidelity.

"His name is Grant; he's a pilot in the Air Force."

"Your father and I know about all that. I just wanted to know when you plan on bringing him by the house for supper. Your father would definitely like to meet the young gentlemen."

"That might not be a good idea."

"Baby, you know that whole rivalry between the Air Force and the Marines is a bunch of nonsense."

"It's not that, Mom."

"Then what is it, sweetheart?"

Marissa bit the inside of her lip as her mind struggled to come up with an appropriate answer to her mother's questions. It was the third week of their relationship and soon Grant would be returning to active duty. They had seen each other almost every other day. When Grant wasn't working in his step-father's shop or flying an airplane, she was in his arms. Persistent and loving, Grant had erased most of her misgivings and charmed his way into her heart.

She released a quiet sigh. "I don't think the relationship is going to last." Actually she knew it wouldn't last; Marissa had already begun making plans for their last evening together.

"I don't want to be nosey here, but why" her mother said while reaching into the refrigerator.

Marissa shook her head from side to side. "Yes you do."

"I'm your mother so I get that privilege. Are you sure that you're not feeling this was because of what happened with Roy."

"No, I'm not sure. I refuse to set myself up for heartache, Mom. Once was enough. When Grant goes back to active duty, I go back to my life."

"You mean you go back to work and try to hide yourself from the world?"

"No, I'm going to keep dating. I'm going to make sure I get a nice civilian man."

"Sweetheart, you can't dictate what kind of man you're going to fall in love with."

"Maybe."

"Oh, Lord. I believe I hear Zachariah Burrows in this kitchen. You sound just like your father; thinking he can control everything. Well, you keep thinking that and when the truth hits you in the eyes. Call me." Her mother walked out of the kitchen leaving Marissa speechless.

10

IN THE WEE hours of Monday morning when Sunday was still fresh in the memory, Marissa woke and slipped out of bed. She went to the window and looked out into the starlit night of Grant's backyard. How could she describe how wonderful last night had been? How could she walk away from that kind of love? She closed her eyes and felt herself yearning back toward the bed as if by some inexplicable pull. It would be so easy to slip back into the sheets and fall asleep with Grant's scent on her skin.

Her body still ached sweetly in remembrance. All it had taken was a hot bath. She remembered leaning forward and running her soapy hands over his wet muscles. She remembered bending tenderly to him, feeling how he trembled in desire and anticipation. His hands, so strong yet gentle, had found her breasts, and his mouth had hungrily suckled her neck.

She remembered letting her hand sink underneath the water to cup him and how he had thrown his head back when she touched him, how his body had moved, how the sound low in his throat seemed to shiver through her bones.

She remembered how he had carefully peeled away her robe, and how she'd nearly come just from the warmth of his hand cupping her mound. And how he'd guided her into the Jacuzzi tub, spread her open, lifted himself to meet her, parting her slowly but firmly, and she'd eased down, almost unable to breathe, until they were fully locked together, her inner thighs against his hips, and she'd opened her eyes then to look at him and their eyes met, joined in every sense of the word.

Love, she'd thought.

And she had laid on his chest, feeling him shift within her, to rest her head below his chin. And he had wrapped his arms around her, enfolding her, whispering her name and kissing her hair. She remembered how he had started to move, a slow rocking, and she had moved with him, pressure waxing and waning. And she came not in a singular explosion but in a series of waves rolling in and cresting, each higher than the one before, washing over the beach that was her body.

And she remembered feeling his every muscle tense, his jaw locked against a shout, his eyes blazing, hands holding her to him, nearly withdrawing and then burying himself deep. She'd felt the contraction of his release and heard the shuddering groan that escaped his gritted teeth.

And most of all she remember her words. The words from her heart. She'd told him that she loved him.

"What am I doing?" She murmured aloud to the glass window. As much as she would have loved to deny it, she'd somehow managed to fall in love the type of man she'd sworn she'd avoid like the plague. Not to mention that this situation was far worse than the last one because she'd willfully ignored all the book's recommendations and her own common sense.

"I don't know. You tell me."

Startled, she looked away from the window to notice that Grant sat on the bed watching her. "What do you mean?"

He ran a hand over his head. "Come on, Marissa. I saw the way you reacted at dinner the other night when K.C. mentioned a possible assignment in the Middle East."

"I don't know what you are talking about," she replied through clinched teeth.

"Sure?"

"I'm telling you the truth." Or a portion of the truth, her conscience whispered. Even Marissa had yet to accept the possibility that she could be in love with a man she'd known less than a month.

"Then why do I get the feeling that you're lying?"

"I don't know," she replied. Intent on beating a hasty retreat, she picked up a fleece throw from the bottom of the bed and wrapped it around her like a towel. "You tell me?"

Grant stood up and grabbed her arm. "Do you always run away from your problems?"

She tried to pull free, but he only tightened his grip. "I'm not running."

"Then sit down and talk to me," he patiently ordered. "Tell me what's going through that head of yours." He insisted as he pulled her down beside him. "Are you afraid for me?"

She nodded her head in confirmation. Actually it was more terror than fear. "When I was in high school, my father volunteered to go to Africa to help train U.N. Peace Keeping Forces. While he was there a land mine left over from World War II exploded. Their guide was killed in the blast and my father was injured." Marissa's voice trailed off as she remembered the moment her mother had received the international phone call. The days afterward with her father in a third world hospital would forever be etched in her memory. The gray pallor of her mother's face, the oppressive silence of the house, and the waiting had left her nauseous.

"But your father came home," he stated. All along he'd pictured some faceless Naval officer as the source of Marissa's refusal to commit. He should have figured out that it was much deeper than a failed engagement.

Marissa covered her face with her hands. "He had to go into another hospital for a round of surgery to remove the shrapnel.

"You were afraid he was going to die."

She shook her head. "Even then, I didn't comprehend the possibility of my father's death. All I knew was the fear that my father wouldn't come home."

Grant wrapped his arms around Marissa, looked down into her tear filled eyes, and his heart turned over. Never in a million years would he want to be the cause of her pain. Yet, he had a duty to his country and a love of flying. It was selfish, but he wanted both. He wanted to fly and have her close for the rest of his life.

"I love you, little bird."

"Grant…" She started but he put a hand on her mouth silencing her.

"I'm not asking for any promises, Marissa. I'm just asking that you give us a try."

She laughed. "Well, I'm asking you for a promise."

Grant pulled back in surprise. "I'm confused."

"That's makes two of us. I don't know when or how it happened. But I love you. And if you're sure you're willing to be stuck with me, then you've got me. A twenty-four hour, seven days a week friend, lover, mate."

Grant leaned in and kissed her hard on the lips. "I don't think that I've ever wanted anything more in my life."

Epilogue

One Year Later
Daddy's coming home.

MARISSA PLACED her hand over her eyes and watched the cargo plane coming in over the horizon. The beauty and power of the enormous aircrafts he piloted never ceased to amaze her. After becoming Grant's wife in a private ceremony three months earlier, she didn't think she could be happier. However a trip to the doctor this morning revealed how much more joy she could actually feel. In her pocket was the official confirmation that a new Edwards would be arriving in less than eight months.

With a smile on her face, she turned toward the man standing at her side. Grant's best friend along with his older brother had taken her under their wings and constantly checked in on her when her husband went out of town.

"K.C., do you remember when we first met and I asked you if you were a pilot?"

"Yep," he chuckled.

"How did you respond?"

"That I only like to see 'em go up and come down."

"Me too, my friend." She waved her hand at the approaching plane.

☆☆☆

Author Bio

A Southern Girl by way of Tennessee, Angela Weaver grew up with jazz, country and the blues. An avid reader and occasional romantic optimist, she began writing her first novel on a dare and hasn't stopped since.

After spending a few years living in the north and abroad, Angela now calls Atlanta, Georgia, home. On weekends, she can be found horseback riding in the mountains, reading a book under a tree, or working away in front of her computer.

She loves to hear from readers and can be reached via email at neri22@yahoo.com

Recruiting Dora

By
Edwina Martin Arnold

Books by Edwina Martin Arnold
House Guest
Chocolate Friday
Jolie's Surrender
Eve's Prescription

Dedication

I would like to thank my husband, John Arnold. Writing love stories is a whole lot easier when I've been involved in one for twenty years. Next, I would like to thank Jen, Gil, and Connie who have provided constant love since they were born. Last, I would like to thank the women of my writer's group who have listened to my ideas ad nauseum.

Also, if you would like to get in touch with me, I can be reached at www.edwinamartin-arnold.com.

Recruiting Dora

By

Edwina Martin Arnold

1

FROM HIS WINDOW, Captain Joe Bolin watched the angry woman stomp across the parking area. It was a clear sunny day and very few people were in the lot, so when he looked up from his paperwork his eyes were drawn to her. Her beauty made him continue to stare although she wasn't attractive in the clone-like way that was for sale with any plastic surgeon. Her mouth was too full, her nose was too prominent, and her high eyebrows were clearly unplucked. She wore her long black hair in a loose knot, the effect was a cross between school teacher and seductress. The woman had his attention and as she made a beeline for his storefront, he knew she was coming to see him because the boy he suspected was her son had warned him.

"Damn," he muttered because he realized it wouldn't be a pleasant exchange. He wanted to meet in a nightclub where he could send her a drink, or a café where he could send her latte, or even while running where he could offer to wipe her sweat. Anywhere but in this stark Army office in the small recruitment facility located on Grady Way in Tacoma, Washington.

Whispering to the empty space, he said, "I knew I shouldn't have let that kid enlist." But the boy had been so eager, came into the office asking his clerk where he had to sign to become a soldier. After the boy had put his signature on the dotted line, he'd warned Joe that his mom might show up. Joe should have ripped up the contract until he met with the boy and his mother. He'd learned a long time ago that recruitment was always better if the parent was on board. The kid wouldn't hear of it, though. In fact he had a good argument that he was nineteen, a senior, and knew what he wanted.

"My mother's just overprotective," the kid claimed. When he'd asked about the boy's father, the kid made it clear the man wasn't involved in his life. So against his better judgment, he'd let the kid enlist.

How could he not when the boy reminded him so much of himself at that age. Joe had to admit that he had been a little surprised at the kid's enthusiasm, yet he wasn't shocked that he was there. In the last week, many of the high schools in Washington had hosted career days, and his unit knew how to put on a show. Nobody had toys like the United States military. Rolling up to schools all around the Fort Lewis area in Humvees painted with orange flames, blasting the latest hip hop songs did it every time. It drew the kids to them like a sponge in water. Then, they opened the doors to the customized vehicles, and the youths fell over themselves trying to get to the game controllers for America's Army, a video game that was developed to show what military life was like.

The woman had reached the outer office now. The boom of the door slamming let him know she had arrived. Sighing, he stood up and opened the door quickly because he wanted to intercede before security was called.   Private Adams stood red faced unsure of how to address the woman screaming at him. Yes, this had to be the boy's mother. Although much bigger, her son had the same broad nose, high arching eyebrows, golden skin. Joe stood and watched for just a second, acknowledging the fact that even though her face was contorted with rage, the woman was striking.

Raising his voice, Joe said, "Ma'am, if you come this way, I will assist you."

Her mouth closed and dark eyes full of fire turned on him. The woman needed to explode at someone and since he was the man in charge, he knew it had to be him. Joe stepped aside as she marched into his office. He had barely closed the door when she whirled on him. "Are you the one responsible?" she threw papers which landed at his feet.

Picking them up, he glanced at the name and confirmed his suspicions, "Yes, I spoke with Deshawn Lamont. Are you his…"

"How could you do such a thing and wear a uniform that implies honor?" As if to physically challenge him, the woman moved closer while taking off her long wool coat to reveal a white polo shirt over jeans. She wore an apron, and Joe assumed she was a waitress because pinned to her impressive chest was a nametag that he couldn't quite read. A lock of hair had escaped the bun at her neck and fell over her eye. She hurriedly placed it behind an ear and tossed her coat on a chair while Joe peered at the tag. It read, *Dora*.

When Joe didn't respond fast enough, she continued. "Are you a parent," she paused to stare at the stripes on his chest, "Captain?" So she was familiar with the military. "Have you ever held a tiny child that is innocent, and you know it's your job to sacrifice everything to shield that precious life?" As she spoke, she continued advancing, eyes narrowed, while she pointed a finger up at his face.

Joe held his ground even when her fingertip pressed into his tie. A slight citrus scent teased his nose, making him pause. It came from her hair or perfume; he wasn't sure. Whatever the source it was pleasant, no that wasn't the right word, alluring, yes that described the scent much better. The finger pressed harder and her head tilted, clear clues that she thought his silence strange. So he said, "I don't have children."

"How sinister is it to come into our schools and lure children away to war with hot cars and video games? Only a monster would lead children into a battle zone!"

Joe was astounded that so much fierceness could come from such a petite package. She couldn't be a hair over five three, standing before him, quivering with rage. She was a miniature missile, very nice and curvy with large breasts, like an old-fashioned soda bottle about to blast off. He'd learned through a conflict resolution course that it was best to let angry relatives have their say before trying to have a conversation. If he'd adhered to his normal routine and insisted that he and the young man talk to a responsible adult before enlistment, he wouldn't be standing with his back against the door being berated by a beautiful waitress. He listened and nodded when appropriate, wondering what her age was. He knew her son was nineteen, so she had to at least be in her thirties. Her bronze skin gave no clue; it was smooth enough for her to be a teenager.

"The bullets are real. When people are shot, they don't get to start the game over. Did you tell my son that before you dangled all your gadgets in his face?"

She paused, glaring at Joe, and he responded by holding up his right hand that was missing the last two digits. "Ma'am, I showed him this." Extending his hand towards her, he said, "My name is Captain Joe Bolin, and I was on the receiving end of one of those real weapons. It's a pleasure to meet you."

She took his hand and squeezed hard. Again Joe was impressed by her strength. If only the circumstances were different. He admired women with vigor.

☆☆☆

Dora Lamont was hotter than fish grease. Catfish, to be exact, a favorite at Soul Kitchen the restaurant she managed. However, some part of her was a little ashamed that she intentionally gripped the soldier's hand as hard as she could. When he didn't flinch, guilt washed over her. Surprising herself, she flipped the hand over, palm down, and looked at it. The scar tissue had keloid and was a shade darker than his oak brown skin. Subconsciously, she rubbed a thumb over the scar before releasing him. Then she asked, "Knowing the dangers how could you?" Her voice was barely above a whisper.

Nodding slightly, the man side-stepped her, and she realized how close she was to him. She'd had him pinned against the door.

"Won't you have a seat?" He pulled back a chair that was positioned in front of an ugly, green metal desk. She remained standing and crossed her arms, trying to be imposing. The struggle came compliments of the fact that she was short, a reality she hated at times like this, and she was well aware that sitting would do nothing to help her cause. She glared at the man who had to be at least six-three, the height of her son, and just as fit. On some level, she acknowledged that Captain Bolin was gorgeous in a rough, military, crew cut kind of way. He looked fabulous in uniform. The light tan of his shirt was a seductive contrast to his dark skin and his olive green slacks hugged his hips. But she wasn't here to drool. She was here to protect her son.

"Ma'am, I do feel as if I owe you an apology. Usually, I don't sign young adults without speaking to a parent first. However, Deshawn was so persistent."

Dora interrupted, "Listen to yourself. One second you call him an adult, and the next you admit he's less than. If DS was grown, you wouldn't need to speak to a parent."

"Ms. Lamont, Deshawn is old enough to enlist on his own. However, he's still in high school, so he's at an awkward stage. I realize how vital it is to have the support system on board when big decisions are being made. That's why I like to speak with those important to the enlistee even when I'm not obligated to."

Dora shook her head before glaring. Through clenched teeth, she said, "How hypocritical it is to say a child can kill or be killed at eighteen, but can't drink until twenty-one? If they are grown enough to die, they should be grown enough to drink."

"On a personal level, I happen to agree with you, Ma'am. On a professional le..."

Not giving him a chance to say more, her voice became louder, "Your rules, regulations, personal practices are all bull when faced with the reality that you're dragging kids out of their mother's arms to face bullets."

"With all due respect, Ma'am, nineteen is far from a baby."

She didn't respond at first, painfully admitting there was truth in what he said, and she was getting far too emotional. She refused to cry in front of this man. Looking directly into the Captain's eyes, she crossed her arms. "Well, don't add my son to your quota requirements yet because this is one boy that you're going to have to fight for!"

Knowing the tears were near, she turned and grabbed her coat, then snatched the door-knob open. She didn't look back as she slammed the door.

☆☆☆

Joe walked to the window in the outer office to watch Ms. Lamont stomp to her car. She still held her coat over an arm, and his eyes were drawn to the natural sway of her hips. He really couldn't blame the woman. War was an ugly business. But someone had to stand up and grab the gun, or America would quickly disappear. Flexing his three fingers, he knew that he couldn't grab the gun anymore, but he was still a soldier and doing his part to protect the life-blood of the military by recruiting new members.

Joe was drawn out of his musings when Adams exclaimed, "What a firecracker!"

The tone of voice struck Joe wrong. It had too much male appreciation in it. "Private," he said.

"Oh, excuse me, sir," Adam's face was beet red again.

"We both have work that won't get done by itself. Let's return to it."

"Yes, sir," Adams saluted as Joe made his way back to his office.

2

DORA REACHED her car, slammed the door after she got in, and took a deep breath. "Dammit." She slapped the steering wheel, then gripped it tightly as water flowed down her face. After the tears stopped, she counted to ten slowly and started the car, yet she still pulled out of the parking lot much faster than she intended. "Calm down," she told herself. Four o'clock traffic was just beginning and there were too many cars for her to be zipping around because she was mad.

Dora focused on her driving, and as she drove along Interstate 5, she tried not to be irritated with a black BMW that had just cut her off for the second time. The man at the wheel was talking feverishly on his phone and gesturing wildly, sometimes taking both hands off the wheel. Dora tried to relax into the cloth seats of her older model Nissan Maxima, but it was hard, especially after her confrontation with the perfect soldier.

Captain Joe Bolin. Tall, chocolate, and handsome, too damn handsome. When she'd had him pinned against the wall, she couldn't help but notice how broad his shoulders were, how narrow his hips were, how good he smelled. He wore a rich cologne that mixed well with his natural scent. All were things she wasn't supposed to acknowledge when she was angry. But she'd have to be dead not to appreciate that strong jaw, the high cheekbones, and the gorgeously full mouth. "Probably helps him recruit lots of babies," she muttered before cursing loudly when the BMW clipped the left, front fender of her car. Dora barely avoided swerving into the other lane. The BMW pulled to the side of road with Dora right behind. She ripped off her seat belt and threw open her door in a rage ready to call the man every name in the book. Looking at her car, she noticed the damage was minimal, but she was still furious. If she hadn't controlled the Maxima, she could have ended up in a major accident.

She stomped towards the man who was getting out of his car. When he met her half way with the cell still attached to his ear, Dora shouted a few choice words before the man grabbed her arm. She socked him in the chest and backed up, her anger becoming tinged with fear.

The man's hand went to his front, pants' pocket and Dora was turning to run back to her car when she saw he pulled out a wad of money. He shoved it at her, saying, "Look, lady, I'm sorry I hit your car. My wife's in labor and there's complications." Dora noticed tears in his eyes. "I'm just trying to get there. Here take this," he waved the money, "I'm sure it's enough. I need to leave."

"Just go," Dora told him, feeling horrible. "My car's so old and dinged up, another dent won't matter."

Dora backed up when the man rushed her. He put the money in her apron and ran back to his car. She was still standing there when he took off.

When Dora got back in the Maxima, her head slumped on the steering wheel. She'd hit a man trying to get to his ailing wife and unborn child. "Dear Lord, I'm sorry." Usually, she was calm and reasonable, but ever since DS had came into the restaurant at lunch and announced he'd joined the Army a couple of days ago she'd been crazy.

Sighing deeply, she admitted that her confrontation with the Captain was a bit misguided on her part. As much as she wanted to blame it all on the military, she knew her son was mostly at fault. The boy had always been a daredevil. The more she preached caution, the more risks he took, from making suicide ramps to launch his bike from when he was kid, to the hang gliding he'd done just last week!

"It's his father jumping out in him," her daddy would say, referring to Deshawn Sr., the man she'd loved who'd left before his son was born. The last time she'd seen him he told her she'd always have his heart, but he wasn't meant to be tied down, there was too much out there to explore and see. Then he'd kissed her and told her to take good care of their child. In a blink of an eye, he was roaring off on his motorcycle. She'd named his son after him, believing that someday he really would come back. After several years, she'd given up hope.

Dora still remembered being hysterical that day he'd left. Crying, yelling, and chasing after his bike when she was six months pregnant. Thinking of it now, she felt embarrassed and since then, she swore she'd never make a fool of herself over a man again. When her son asked about his daddy, she explained that his father loved him, he just loved adventure, too. Thank God for her father, Jasper Williams, who had stepped up and spent a lot of time with his grandson, providing that all important male support.

Dora hit the dash board. "I've worked so hard to give DS choices!" She'd scrimped and saved to have enough for him to go to college, and she was so proud of her son's grades, a 3.7 to be exact. Why did the boy want to join the military when she'd struggled so mightily to give him what she'd never had? She'd wanted to go to college, but she had a baby to support at eighteen. When Deshawn had showed her the enlistment papers earlier, it was like waving a red flag in front of a bull. Her anger convinced her that if she couldn't get DS to listen, then she'd yell at the person who had allowed him to sign-up. She felt guilty, especially about the Captain. Although she didn't care for the President, she appreciated what the men and women of the Armed Forces did for the United States. She groaned, remembering how she'd squeezed the Captain's hand with all her might. She'd behaved poorly, and she knew she'd have to apologize.

"I wouldn't mind if he just waited," she whispered. "If DS would go to college, get his education, then enlist I wouldn't mind at all." Sighing, she knew that wasn't completely true. No matter when her son joined she'd be worried about his safety. She'd just be more comfortable with his decision if he were years out of high school. Why couldn't DS listen to reason?

When she walked into the restaurant where she worked a little before five, she was still pondering the question. Mr. Hillard Cook, who owned Soul Kitchen, walked towards her with his cane. "How you doin' today, gurl?" He was the only man Dora let get away with calling her anything less than a woman. She allowed it because when she'd started working for him before the pregnancy, she'd been a girl, and she knew it was harmless. In fact, her boss treated her like a daughter.

"I'm good, Mr. Cook. How are you?"

"Hey, your voice don't sound right. Somethin' wrong? Do you need to tell me about this personal business that you flew outta here to take care of today?" He put a hand on her shoulder and his cane dangled from the other while he looked in her eyes.

Dora preferred not to tell him about DS. In Mr. Cook's opinion, she babied the boy too much. So instead she said, "I just hit a man whose wife is in labor."

Mr. Cook frowned at her. "Come again?"

Dora told him about her ugly response to an unfortunate situation. "Going off at the handle doesn't sound like you, gurl. What's really wrong?"

"Nothing, Mr. Cook. I better go check on things." Dora glanced around to see the restaurant was half full. "You know we'll be packed in about fifteen more minutes."

Mr. Cook blocked her path. "Listen, both of us know you really run this place. I couldn't have done it without you for years now. If somethin's eatin' at you, you better let me know 'cause I can't do it without you."

"Okay, sir," she said with a smile. "Have a seat and let me get to work."

3

JOE WAS TIRED when he reached his house just off base in Lakewood around 5:30. The place wasn't a mansion, just a three bedroom tri-level with a lawn he could mow in fifteen minutes, but it was his. After growing up in apartments, then living in barracks most of his nineteen year army career, it felt good to come home to something he owned. Taking off his pea green overcoat, he hung it over the couch and loosened his tie. Chuckling he remembered Ms. Lamont's finger pressing where he was now touching. "Probably wanted to strangle me."

Looking in the refrigerator, he decided to eat just an apple. He was meeting some buddies in about thirty minutes to lift weights and shoot some hoop. Opening the refrigerator again, he decided to grab a beer as well. Hell, it was Friday, and he deserved it after having his butt chewed out by the cute waitress.

Three hours later, the aroma of fried fish and collard greens made Joe's stomach grumble as he stepped out of his car at the restaurant. A dozen pick-up games of basketball did that to a brother. Although he was hungry and tired, he felt much more relaxed. The restaurant looked like a converted Denny's, but the neon signed blinked out Soul Kitchen in bright red. Joe sure hoped the food was as good as it smelled, and according to his friends, it was. "Just like momma's," his boy, Jared had claimed. A bachelor, Joe ate out a lot, and he wondered how he'd missed this place so close to base.

Jared left his car, joining him, and the two men walked in together. The delicious aroma was stronger as they opened the front door. Joe's stomach grumbled loudly in appreciation. "I heard that," Jared said. "The way your jumper was on today, I guess you deserve to eat, but you need to work on that defense."

"Man, what are you talking about?" Joe's head tilted. "I believe I was knocking your sorry shot all over the gym."

Jared started limping beside him. "Only because I have this bad ankle."

"Bad ankle, bad wrist, bad eyes. It was all bad today."

"Yeah, but wait 'til tomorrow. My game will be unstoppable then."

"Uh, huh," Joe said as he followed his friend.

Jared looked around the crowded restaurant. Red booths lined the wall and wood tables sat in the space in between. "Hey, there's a spot in the back. It's seat yourself," Jared said over his shoulder as he rushed to the table.

After they were seated, Jared said, "Guess what? My neighbor flashed her breasts and booty at me."

"What?" Joe said, clearly surprised.

"Yep, no lie. Ms. Jones lives in the duplex next to me. Sunday afternoon, she knocks on my door and asks me to help wash her car. I feel obligated because she's always baking me cookies, and when I'm out of town, she checks my mail and takes care of my cat. So I go out there and she's in daisy dukes, meat hanging all out, and she has on a white tank top!"

"Really? I know the sun was out last weekend, but it didn't hit sixty degrees."

Jared nodded. "Next thing I know, she's managed to wet her whole front. I could see everything. Problem is she has to be at least sixty years old."

Joe burst out laughing.

"You know for an old chick, she wasn't bad. Her booty still had some bounce, and she had big nipples with only a little sag..."

"Why am I not shocked by the subject of this conversation?" a female voice asked.

Both men looked up remorsefully, but Joe did a double take when he saw who the owner of the voice was. Dora Lamont, the enraged mother he'd faced earlier in the day. She wasn't angry now. In fact, she appeared to be holding back a chuckle. He felt even more shameful when he couldn't stop his eyes from straying to her lush breasts. Joe shifted in his seat as his lower half acknowledged the beautiful woman standing before him. Lord knows what she'd think if she became aware of his aroused state.

"Here are your menus." She handed him one and a small smile appeared adding to the twinkle in her thickly lashed, brown eyes. Joe couldn't decide which version he liked better: fiery or teasing.

She turned to his friend. "I bet you were a mess in high school, Jared. Half the time your conversation is worse than my son's."

Jared jumped up. "I apologize, Dora. I was just telling my friend about my neighbor. Let me introduce you to Joe. It's his first time at your fine establishment."

Joe stood as well, although he didn't want to. His daddy and the military had trained him to be a gentleman, and if Jared was standing, he should, too. He hoped his baggy shorts didn't reveal any of his secrets, though. Extending his hand to Dora, he said, "Nice to see you again." A crooked smile appeared on his face. "Hopefully, it's safe for me to eat here. You were less than happy with me earlier." He was close enough to inhale her warm, spicy fragrance. It went well with the slightly rough texture of her hand. He didn't like his women too soft.

She laughed, a full robust sound, which was music to Joe's ears. "I promise there will be nothing but top quality ingredients in your food."

Joe sat down, feeling himself stiffen more. Damn, he hadn't had a rise-up like this since he was a teenager. Glancing at Jared, his friend looked as if he was about to ask him a question. Joe shook his head, and Jared seemed to get the point.

A bus boy came up with a towel and Dora said, "Thanks, Jim, I'll do it." She took the rag and began wiping their table. Joe was hypnotized by the gentle sway of her breasts as her arm moved back and forth. Erotic fantasies filled his head, the most prominent being his face buried in what he was ogling. He was close to slapping himself. When he looked at his buddy, Jared seemed transfixed on Dora, also, and it wasn't himself that he wanted to hit now.

Jared looked at him and mouthed, "What?" so he knew he must have been frowning pretty severely.

Straightening, Dora said, "I'll give you two a chance to look at your menus. Can I take your drink order before I leave?" They both asked for beers.

When she'd gone, Jared said, "Now you know the second reason I come here, Dora, the most gorgeous waitress in Washington. How do you know her?"

Joe explained what happened earlier in the day.

Jared smirked. "She doesn't seem mad at you now."

"I know. It's weird. If she'd had a weapon, other than her mouth, I'd be dead."

Jared nodded. "DS is a good kid. He'll make a fine soldier."

"That's if he joins. I need to speak with both of them. I want him to be sure of his decision."

"Shoot, I wish the guy who recruited me had been more like you. I tried to back out and he threatened to sue me."

"Those types of tactics don't work in the long run. I think the military is learning that now."

Jared shrugged. "It took a little while, but I'm pretty happy I joined now. I've seen the world, met all kinds of people, and I'll have twenty years when I'm thirty-eight next year. I can retire and start a whole new career."

Joe listened with half an ear. His eyes had found Dora, and he watched as she moved through the room checking on customers. "How well do you know Dora?"

Jared smiled. "Do you have a thing for her? People yelling at you gets your fire up?"

"Could be," Joe responded. "Maybe, I'm just curious since I'll undoubtedly have to talk with her later."

"Uh, huh." His friend didn't sound convinced. "She always has a smile on her face and something nice to say. She's no pushover, though. She's got a sharp tongue if someone gets out of line. She's not the owner, but she really runs this place. Did you notice the reader board outside when you drove up?"

"Nope," Joe answered.

"Well, check it out when you leave. It was Dora's idea to keep count of the total number of soldiers lost in Iraq, as well as the ones from the bases around here. Also listed, are the names of local soldiers who have died in combat during the last week."

"Wow, how did I miss that?"

"I don't know. As many shots as you made we know you're not blind. You're just slippin'."

"Thanks buddy."

After his friend finished laughing, he pointed. "See the old guy sitting near the cash register?"

Joe looked around, spotting a thin gray haired man dressed in a brown suit with a cane across his lap.

"He's the owner. Looks like he's on his last breath, doesn't it?" Jared didn't wait for an answer. "Rumor is Dora's trying to buy the place, and he's waiting on her to get the financing. I hope she does and keeps it going just like it is. Look at the pictures of the military soldiers in planes, ships, and tanks on the walls. Those were given by customers, and see how many service folks are in here. It's a place where we feel welcome. Check out the menu."

Joe opened his and looked. He smiled as he read the military inspired names. Meatloaf and mash potatoes were the Marine Special while chicken fried steak and macaroni were the Airman's Deluxe. "I think I'll have the Navy SEAL catfish with a side of collard greens."

A voice he knew he'd never fail to recognize again said, "I've got it." The woman sure liked to sneak up on people. He admired the muscles in her arm as she reached near him to place the beers on their table. "Are you having the usual, Jared?"

"You know it," his friend replied. "Grunt's Paradise," he nodded at Joe, "You should try it. Rib eye steak and red beans and rice.

"Next time," Joe told him. "I haven't had good catfish in a long time."

Dora nodded. "You're in for a treat then. However, I must warn you that you will be addicted. Once you eat here, you can't help but come back." She winked at him before saying, "Would you gentlemen like cornbread or hush puppies?"

"You cool with an order of each?" Jared asked him.

"Sounds good." Joe still was looking at Dora. Her smile widened. The beast he'd managed to tame between his legs roared back up.

"Okay, I'll be back with that in a jiffy."

"Jiffy?" Joe said, not wanting her to go just yet. "No one says jiffy anymore."

"I'm someone, and I just said it." A hand on her hip accompanied the words.

Joe smiled wryly. "You definitely are someone. I guess I'll just have to incorporate, jiffy, back into my vocabulary."

The look on her face screamed *is this man flirting with me*. Joe was sure it happened all the time at the restaurant. Military men didn't ignore beautiful women.

"I guess you will," she replied before spinning away to check on another table. Joe couldn't help admiring her backside. When she looked over her shoulder and caught him in the act, he smiled sheepishly and sipped his beer.

☆☆☆

Dora took the orders to the kitchen, and then went to the tap. Long ago, she'd learned to recognize the type of beer by the feel of the handle, so she didn't need to look at what she was doing. Instinctively, she knew when a glass was full, just like she knew when an order was ready, or where a certain liquor sat on the shelf.

Lowering her chin, she peeked at the table where the Captain sat with Jared, debating on whether or not she should apologize now or wait. The minute she noticed him in her restaurant her nerve endings went on high alert. She'd almost had herself convinced that it was only because of the confrontation earlier, but after interacting with him, she had to admit the man was a testament to raw masculinity. It was apparent that the two men had just come from working out. Jared wore gray sweats that still had a wet spot in the middle of his back and the word Army was stamped across the front. Captain Bolin wore a similar sweatshirt, but a good portion of his calves were bare under enormous shorts. What she could see was sculpted to perfection. Dora's overactive imagination started to picture acres of dark muscles underneath the rest of his clothes.

"Dora." She looked up to see Mr. Cook standing in front of her. She was shocked because he rarely left his chair once the dinner rush started. He would sit there and hold court as most of the customers would stop by and pay their respects.

"Dora," he said again a little louder, "you're wasting."

She immediately let go of the tap. "Oh, sorry," she whispered, wondering how much beer had gone down the drain. She wiped the glass with a rag and filled the other two drink orders. Mr. Cook looked at her oddly, yet he didn't say anything. Turning away, he shuffled back to his chair.

Dora delivered the drinks, and returned to the kitchen counter to pick up orders. As she moved through the restaurant, she noticed she wasn't the only woman keeping tabs on Jared and Bolin's table. Many seemed to be casting longing looks in their direction. Dora wasn't surprised when the two women sitting at the table next to them struck up a conversation. She couldn't hear the words, but their laughter and movements were animated.

When their food was ready, Dora let another waitress deliver. She'd decided she'd had enough of Captain Bolin for one day. However, she couldn't deny the satisfaction she felt when she innocently scanned the room later and discovered that Bolin was staring at her with such concentration that she wondered what the heck he was thinking about. She smiled, and although he smiled back, he looked a little embarrassed, which delighted Dora. She hummed as she delivered meatloaf to table thirteen.

She felt like she was thirteen again when twenty minutes later the Captain strode up to the bar where she was standing and her heart raced in her chest. Smiling her best fake smile, she said, "Do you need something else? I can send someone right over."

"No, I just wanted to compliment you on how delicious the meal was and pay the bill."

"Oh, thanks, I'll let the cooks know. Linda would have taken care of your bill at the table. You didn't have to get up." She took the bill and the money from him and quickly made change.

He shrugged. "I know. I wanted to talk to you."

Jared interrupted by slapping his friend's back. "Joe, it's my treat next time. Catch you later. Dora, it was great as always." He waved as he left.

Dora turned from Jared and looked at Bolin questioningly. "What did you want to talk about, Captain?"

"Please, call me Joe."

Dora nodded.

"I didn't get a chance to say much when we spoke earlier."

"I know. I have to apologize about that. The way my son told me...I was venting and said some unfair things to you. I know DS can be headstrong." She laughed softly. "I suppose he's a bit like his mother."

"I'm sure that's a good thing." He smiled. "Apology accepted, but I would really like to talk to you and Deshawn together, to make sure this is the right decision for him. I've already called and left a message on his phone. Here's my card. Give me a ring and we can set up a time."

The card slipped to the floor on Dora's side of the counter, and when she bent to get it, her hair escaped its knot and thick locks fell into her face. She looked at him through a curtain of black waves. It surprised her when Joe reached out with his good hand and tucked some behind her ear, his callused fingertips brushing her cheek. Heat shot from his fingers straight to the top of her thighs, making her gasp.

Joe's hand quickly left her face. "I'm sorry."

Apparently, he thought he had offended her. "No, it's okay," she assured him. "You just caught me off guard." Oh, how he'd laugh if he knew the truth. Maybe he did suspect something because his eyes were lingering on her lips. She raised his card. "I'll speak with DS, and we'll be calling."

"I'll be waiting." He turned to leave, and Dora shameless watched his tight butt and calves as he made his way out the door.

Maggie Clark, who had worked at Soul Kitchen even longer than Dora, had witnessed the whole exchange. "Um, that is one sexy man," she said in a croaky voice. "I wish he'd caress my face. Oh, I think I need a cigarette just thinking about it."

"Maggie, it's not like…"

"Shush." Maggie waved her protest away. "It's high time you looked at someone with a little gleam in your eyes. I swear when the man touched your cheek, you went cross-eyed. It's a wonder you can see now."

Geez, am I that easy to read, Dora thought. If so, she hoped Joe was illiterate!

Maggie was still talking, non-stop, "Running and biking aren't the only types of exercises that are good for the body and the soul." Her co-worker broke into a raspy cackle that quickly advanced to a hacking cough before she walked away.

☆☆☆

Later that evening, Dora thought about the events of the day as she watched *Nightline*. She couldn't sleep. Her son had come home from football practice hours ago, and despite the massive argument they'd had, he was sleeping like a baby.

DS had come into the house with an attitude, having already listened to the message from Joe. Good Lord, that's how she thought of the man now, not Captain Bolin, but by his first name. Groaning against the couch, she switched to *CNN*, hoping it would be dry enough to knock her out. However, her body still tinged with sexual awareness. It had been her long standing policy to have no boyfriends around DS until he was grown and out of the house. So her very few liaisons had been when he was spending the night at a friend's or with his grandfather. This arrangement worked great for her, but her partners either wanted to get serious, or moved on to more available women.

When was the last she'd had sex? Heck she couldn't even remember. She knew it had been with Daniel, a commercial airline pilot, she'd had a relationship with until he moved to Texas, yet she couldn't recall when. Obviously, it must not have been that eventful or she'd recollect every detail. She knew it would be more than memorable with Joe Bolin. He probably knew every way there was to thrill a woman's body. She recalled how he'd looked at her lips before he left. Had he been thinking of kissing her? Just the thought of his mouth anywhere on her body made her thighs clench.

A sleepy, "Mom, are you still up?" had her looking over her shoulder at her son standing at the entrance to the living room, rubbing his eyes.

"Yes, honey." Her son walked over and plopped down beside her on the couch, making the whole thing bounce. "Aren't you cold?" she asked, wrapping her robe more firmly around her waist.

Deshawn looked down at his boxers and plucked his tank-top. "No, I feel good. I had to use the bathroom and saw the light. Why are you up so late?"

Dora shrugged, "I couldn't sleep, so I thought I'd catch up on the news."

Her son yawned, then looked in her eyes. "Mom…," he paused and she could tell that whatever he wanted to say, it was difficult for him.

"What is it, baby?"

"I'm really sorry about yelling earlier. I'm still going to join the Army and that's not going to change even if we meet with the Captain, but I shouldn't have shouted like that. I love you." He leaned over and hugged her, making her heart melt.

She rubbed his shoulder length braids and uttered, "You're still my little boy." As soon as the words left her mouth she knew it was the wrong thing to say.

He immediately sat up, gently removing himself from her embrace. "Mom, don't get carried away."

Dora reached over and tugged a braid. "You know this will be the first thing to go when you report in." She knew her son loved his hair. He'd been growing it out for the last five years.

"I'm hip to that, mom. I don't go until after graduation in June, so I can savor it for a few months. I bet it's longer than yours."

"No, it isn't." This was a standard argument between them that they both enjoyed. "You'd have to grow it another ten years to catch me."

"Naw, you just don't want to face the facts. Maybe, I'll perm it before I let it go to prove it to you. You know Cat Williams' style," he joked, referring to the successful comedian who wore his long hair in waves as he often imitated pimps.

They both laughed. When they'd quieted down, DS said, "So when are we going to meet with the recruiter?"

"I don't know yet. I'll call him Monday. I'll probably suggest next Sunday since that's a light day for me."

DS yawned. "I'm going back to bed. See ya in the morning."

"Goodnight," she told her son. Wishing she could sleep so easily.

4

MONDAY AFTERNOON, Joe had just come back from a meeting with a high school principle when his clerk told him, "Ms. Dora Lamont called you, sir." Joe's eyes widen and his step quicken as he moved to accept the message slip from the man. "She said she'd be available at that number between two and three." Joe looked at his watch. It was 1:55. He told the private, "Thanks. Hold all my calls until you hear otherwise."

Joe dialed the number and waited as the phone rang several times. He was preparing to leave a message when someone finally answered, "Soul Kitchen," a male voice shouted. Joe was taken aback, realizing she'd called from the restaurant.

"May I speak to Dora Lamont, please?" He loosened his tie as he spoke.

He heard a clunk and assumed the phone had been put down. Someone yelled in the distance, "Dora, phone."

Although he fiddled with a pencil, he refused to call what he was feeling nerves, anticipation maybe, but never nervousness. Why would he be anxious? Maybe because the woman invaded your dreams last night. In his slumber, he'd gone to Soul Kitchen in full dress uniform with an enormous appetite only to be served by Dora. Miraculously, they were the only ones in the place, and she wore a pink waitress uniform instead of jeans. When she bent over to do something, he realized she wasn't wearing panties. Suddenly, he was behind her and his clothes had disappeared. With no further ado, he was deep inside her, groaning while she squealed in absolute joy. The dream had been so vivid. He could smell the citrus in her hair, feel the warmth of her skin as he gripped her hips. He thickened against his boxers just thinking about it. When her shouts of pleasure became piercing, Joe awoke to realize he'd fallen asleep with the television on, and the station was conducting an Emergency Broadcast test.

Joe's musings stopped, and he accidently snapped the pencil in half when he heard someone pick up the phone, and then there was a breathless, "Hello."

All business, he said, "This is Captain Joe Bolin returning your call."

"Oh, hi, thanks for calling me back. I don't have much time because the suppliers that were supposed to be here at eight this morning just showed up, and if I don't watch them, they'll just put boxes anywhere, and I'll never find the packing slips."

She suddenly stopped talking as if she realized she was rambling. Was she nervous, too? Joe smiled, liking the idea.

"I wanted to set up a time for the three of us to meet," she said in a rush.

"What's best for you?" he responded.

"Sunday evening around six. Would you mind coming to the house? I don't live far from the restaurant."

"Certainly not, just let me know where." She gave him her address.

Joe smiled as he hung up the phone.

☆☆☆

Jesus, Dora, stop being a nitwit and pick something! She stood in her small closet, surveying her options Sunday night around five. She didn't want to be too formal or too casual, but she had to wear something when Joe Bolin showed up besides the t-shirt and panties she had on now. She'd given up asking herself why it mattered. It just did. She was attracted to the man with his quiet strength and strong demeanor. Whether or not she'd act on that attraction remained to be seen, but she was determined to look good tonight.

As she picked through clothes, she tried to think back and remember if she'd ever been this hyped about seeing a man. Plummeting into love with Deshawn Sr., had been a slow process where he'd wooed her young heart over several months. Once she fell, it had been deep, however she'd never experienced this lightening spark that flashed bright with just the thought of Mr. Bolin. "You are really being stupid." She told herself. "The man is coming to discuss your son's future, not get it on with you." With that in mind, she chose to wear tan Capri pants, a pink fitted tee with a v-neck, and pink slippers.

Ten miles away, Joe sat in his underclothes on a large leather armchair, sipping a Heineken with his sock-clad feet on the coffee table while the Oakland Raiders and the Seattle Seahawks battled it out on the gridiron. His body was still, but his mind raced. Inexplicably, he was looking forward to this evening as if he had a romantic date, instead of business meeting.

Joe knew he was an appealing man, still in his prime, and women were attracted to him. He believed that if two adults were willing, then there was nothing wrong with sharing a night together. He wondered if this would interest Dora, if they didn't have the complication of her son. If they had met in a café, or club, or just on the street, could they spend some commitment free time together? Just the idea was enough to send blood speeding to his groin.

In the past, casual affairs satisfied his needs and suited his transient lifestyle. Now, he was coming up on his twentieth year, and he had to decide if he wanted to re-enlist. He was leaning towards retirement. After being stationed at Fort Lewis for three years, he kind of liked coming home to the same place at night. Besides, he wanted to try something different. Talking to recruits about options available in the military made him look at changing his career. He had two years of college, and the idea of going back and getting a business degree was appealing. Being the most successful recruiter in the region convinced him that he'd excel in sales or marketing. His thoughts returned to Dora, and he wondered could he excel in a relationship if he wanted to? Would a woman want him long term with all his baggage, missing parts, and occasional nightmares?

Looking at his wristwatch, he pushed to his feet, put the half full beer on the coffee table, and headed to the bathroom to get ready to visit the Lamonts. A picture of Dora appeared in his mind, and he couldn't deny the electricity that coursed through his veins at the thought of seeing her again.

An hour later, Joe pulled up to the light blue house. She lived in what appeared to be a quiet neighborhood, filled with single story homes. Joe parked, walked through the gate, and rang the doorbell when he got to the porch. Deshawn answered within seconds. "Come in, man, we've been waiting." The kid opened the door wide. Joe stepped over the threshold and shook his hand while the kid pulled him into a quick hug. Glancing beyond, he saw Dora standing about five feet away wearing pants that stopped just below the knees, a pink shirt that showed just a hint of cleavage, and ridiculously furry slippers. She looked good, and he liked her style. Heaven help him because seeing her was enough to bring his dream to the forefront. When she noticed him looking, her face lit up in a smile, and she joined her son in welcoming him.

"Come into the living room where we can have a seat." Dora led him through a short hallway, filled with photos tacked to the wall. He saw Deshawn in all phases of his life. The same was true of the living room, although Dora and an older gentleman where now in some of the pictures. He and Deshawn sat on the cushy, floral couch while Dora settled into the matching armchair across from them.

"Can I get you anything?" she asked. Joe's imagination had fun with that one before she continued, "water, tea, soda?"

"No thank-you, I'm fine."

"Well, I hope you're hungry because mom hooked us up with some food." Deshawn bounced in his seat.

Joe grinned. "I would love to eat after we finish talking. It's not often I get a home cooked meal." Dora and Deshawn burst out laughing.

He must have looked confused because Dora said, "Forgive us. I seldom cook because I hate it. It's a longstanding joke between me and my son. I have to confess that I nabbed our dinner from work. I hope you like fried chicken."

Joe rubbed his hands together. "I'm sure it'll be better than the frozen dinner I was going to eat."

After they quieted, Deshawn turned to him. "Can I ask you a personal question?"

Joe nodded.

"What happened to your hand?"

In the past, the question would have made Joe flinch, but he'd been asked so many times that now he was used to it. He crossed his legs before saying, "I was in Iraq in a covered truck with about twenty-five other guys, travelling through what was supposed to be a safe area. All of a sudden, someone throws a grenade in the truck. Without thinking, I picked it up, stumbled to the back, and threw it out. Unfortunately, I didn't move fast enough and lost a couple of fingers." Joe held up his disfigured hand and looked at it. "However, we didn't lose a life that day, and for that, I'm grateful."

"You're a hero." The kid shouted.

Joe shrugged. "That's a matter of perspective. The army brass appreciated what I did, and I received the Distinguished Service Cross."

"Is it like the Medal of Honor?"

"Not quite. The Congressional Medal of Honor is the highest award. The one I won is the second highest."

"Oh, yeah, I think I saw that on T.V. You have to just about die to get the Congressional one, so maybe it's good you got the Cross instead."

That drew a laugh even from his mother.

"Can I see it?" The boy's excitement was infectious. Dora smiled and nodded her head as if she agreed with her son that he was pretty unique. *Hey, if the medal makes her like me more, I can handle that*, he thought wryly.

"No, I don't travel with it, but enough about me, let's talk about you. I am really happy that you want to join the service, and I fully believe that you will make a fine soldier, however, I'm curious, why do you want to join the Army?"

The kid held up a finger. "First, it seems like fun, man."

Deshawn was focused on him, so he didn't see his mother roll her eyes. "It is fun, but there are lots of challenges as well. People serving today are facing some of the biggest tests of their lives."

"I know were at war, Captain Bolin. I also know I could go. That doesn't scare me."

He was full of so much bravado it was hard for Joe not to smile. Instead, very seriously, he said, "It scares me, Deshawn. War should frighten everyone, but sometimes we have to do it. That's why I joined, to be a part of protecting our way of life."

"I hear you, man, but that's not the only reason I want to join." The kid paused and appeared to be gathering his thoughts. "My grandfather is really like a dad to me, and he's a real cool cat. Anyway, we spend lots of time together and ever since I was a little guy, he'd tell me about what it takes to be a man. He told me to be responsible, stay out of trouble, and pay my own way. With the Army, I can take care of my tuition."

"Deshawn!" Dora stood. "I've been saving since before you were born for college. You don't need to join for that." Her hands settled on her hips as if she were preparing for battle.

"Yes, I do, mom! Use the money to get the restaurant. You know Mr. Cook is just hanging around, waiting for you to buy it. All the banks have turned you down, so use the dough you've saved. Also, the Army is giving me $20,000 just for signing up. I'm going to save it and use that to help me go to college, too. I don't want your money!"

It was obvious to Joe this was the first time Dora was hearing this, and she was taken-aback. She looked at him, and he could tell she was hurt. Very stiffly, she sat down and crossed her legs. "We will discuss this later."

Deshawn continued as if she hadn't spoken, "Mom, listen to me, please, really listen. I know you've had this plan for my life, and you've sacrificed a ton so that things would be the way you want them to be. I appreciate the love and effort that went into that, but it's not what I want. I want to be a soldier. I want to see the world before I settle down to go to college. I'm not trying to be a criminal or a hustler, mom. What I want is legal. Honorable. Can't you just support me in that?"

Joe began to feel as if he shouldn't be there. This was getting too personal.

Dora uncrossed her legs and leaned forward. "Of course I want to support you. Haven't I done that all your life?"

"Yes," her son answered quickly. "You've been the best mother in the world." Tilting forward, Deshawn clasped her hands in his. "You couldn't have raised me better, mom. Now it's time to let me fly on my own. I'm nineteen, not nine."

Dora shook her head without saying anything. Her eyes were bright, and Joe had the sense she was fighting tears. He remembered how his mother had wept when he left to join the military. Even his father had tears in his eyes as he hugged him goodbye. Joe wouldn't have admitted it to anyone, but he cried at the bus station bathroom. Growing up and leaving the nest was difficult for the kids and the parents.

Dora pulled her son into a brief hug before sitting back. "I'm tired of fighting you. If this is what you really want, go with my blessing."

You would have thought the boy had won a lottery the way he jumped up and hollered. He pulled his mother to her feet and swung her around, causing her pants to hitch up, giving Joe a prime view of her gorgeous legs. They were tone and tapered just right.

"Whoa." She clutched her son's shoulders. "Be careful or you'll hurt me. You're stronger than you think, Baby Hughie."

Deshawn put her down, saying, "Now that that's settled, can we eat?"

His mother reached up to pat his cheek. "You're always thinking of your stomach." She glanced at Joe, and he couldn't read the look in her eyes. "Come on." She led the way into the kitchen and through a doorway to a small area where there was a dinette table and a matching China cabinet.

Joe considered himself no slouch in the eating department; however, it was truly amazing to watch how much food Deshawn could put away. Joe had never seen fried chicken, mash potatoes, and green beans disappear so fast. And the boy drank grape soda by the gallon. As he watched in fascination, his mother just shook her head. In between bites, Deshawn asked him questions about the military. The boy was on his second helping, when he said, "Do you have any regrets? Would you join all over again if you had the choice?"

"Sure would," Joe answered. "I won't lie and say I enjoy being a soldier every day because, like with any career, sometime it really sucks. However, the overall satisfaction I get from knowing I'm an integral part of our nation's security system, is immeasurable.

Dora looked at Captain Joe Bolin and thought, *this is a real man's man, someone other men probably look up to, and I'm sure mano y mano is his mantra.* Over the years, Dora had become very independent, and she apologized to women everywhere as she daydreamed about what it would be like to be under this man's protection. Perhaps it would be similar to a big, soft blanket fresh from the dryer.

Rubbing his belly, DS looked at his watch. "Hey, it's time for me to go to work. Mom, are you giving me a ride or can I just take the car?"

"Go ahead." She waved her hand. "I don't plan on going anywhere tonight." Her son stood up, kissed her cheek, then grabbed the empty plates before leaving.

Joe was shifting in his seat, looking as if he was about to leave as well. "Would you like some dessert? I have some peach cobbler." Lord what was she doing?

With a smile on his lips and in his eyes, Joe said, "I would love some."

By the time she returned from the kitchen, her son had already banged out the front door. They were truly alone, and Dora's heart began to beat just a little faster. She placed the warmed up cobbler in front of the Captain.

"Umm, this looks good." An appropriate thing to say about the peaches floating in oozing, syrupy sauce under a golden crust; however, he was looking at her face, not the food.

"Yes it does look appetizing," she managed to say as her heart beat elevated to a pounding staccato.

She watched as he lifted his head and closed his eyes, moaning around the first bite. "I could eat this every day." His eyes opened, and he smiled wide at her. "Aren't you having some?"

"No, I overindulged yesterday. That's why I'm trying to get you to eat the rest of it. DS hates cobbler."

"What's wrong with the boy? How could he not love this?" He took another bite.

"I know. If I hadn't been there, I'd wonder if he's mine because I love the stuff."

Joe chuckled, taking the time to wipe his mouth. "Where does your son work?"

"At Burger King. He's been there a couple of years now."

"That's great." Joe was scooping up the last bite.

"Yes. One thing you can say about Deshawn is that he likes to have money in his pocket. He learned pretty early that the only way that was going to happen was if he worked. He started cutting lawns at thirteen, and he's had some sort of job since then." Dora glanced at his plate. "Would like some more? I have enough for another serving."

With a hopefully expression that made him look boyish, he said, "Are you sure?"

"Yes." She laughed. "You'd be doing my hips a favor." *Oh Lord, why did I say that*? It sounded as if she were fishing for compliments.

Joe jumped to the bait. "You look just fine to me, and I'm sure a little peach cobbler would only enhance the affect."

Dora slipped in the kitchen without responding. After she gave him the second plate, she said, "I'm sorry that things got a little emotional with DS earlier. I didn't necessarily want you to witness that."

Joe looked her in the eyes. "This is a big decision, feelings that are close to the surface get raw at times."

Dora leaned her elbows on the table and put her chin in her hands. "I imagine you must see this type of thing a lot."

"Every now and then, but it's better than parents who don't really care about their kids. I hate situations like that. It's not really good for anybody."

Dora nodded.

"What are you doing for the rest of evening?"

Shocked, she sat up straight. Was he going to suggest something? "Nothing. I plan to relax and get ready for tomorrow. How about you?"

"I'll probably do the same after I do my ironing."

A man who ironed? Dora laughed. "You do your own laundry?"

"Some of it. I shine my shoes, too. Does that surprise you?"

"Yes," she admitted.

He glanced her way with a mischievous gleam in his eye. "When you get to know me better, you'll see I'm full of surprises."

She did her best to stifle her gasp, but a little escaped as a heavy breath. He was flirting with her. She swallowed her panic.

If he noticed, he did a good job of pretending he hadn't. He leaned back and rubbed his stomach. "That was delicious."

Dora sat back, too, not saying anything. With the food gone, there really wasn't a reason for the man to stay. He appeared quite satisfied with his feet stretched out, slouching in his seat.

He looked sideways at her. "I suppose I should be saying good-bye now."

"Yes, I believe that time has come." She looked in his eyes and read that they were on the same level, neither of them wanted him to go. "That was a very brave thing you did with the grenade. Why did you say it was a matter of perspective when DS said you were a hero?"

Joe smiled rather sadly. "You know, no one besides one doctor has bothered to ask me that question."

"I'm a waitress, remember. Like bartenders, we're lay psychiatrists."

Joe chuckled, before saying, "Don't sell yourself short, lady. I sense there are many dimensions hidden behind that beautiful face."

Dora felt the heat rising to her cheeks. "So many compliments, you really don't want to answer my question, do you?" Sitting beside him, she crossed her arms and legs, proud that she was able to speak calmly.

☆☆☆

Joe looked at her posture, remembering some crazy course the army made him take about interpreting body language. According to the instructor, the way Dora was sitting meant she was closing off to him. *Bullshit*, he thought. Looking in her eyes, he saw only curiosity. For some reason, he decided to tell her more of the truth than he'd told anyone, including the doctors.

He began talking before he changed his mind. "All right, I tell you how I really feel. I was angry about losing my fingers. I couldn't shoot a gun and use my skills to defend our country in combat. Also, I felt like I wasn't whole anymore. The fact that I saved lives didn't help at all when I felt the pain or looked at my hand. Slowly, I adjusted, and now I love being a recruiter because I'm still contributing. But, when the event happened, I was acting purely on instinct, self-preservation. I was trying to save my own hide, not thinking about others. So I don't feel like I did anything special. In fact, I feel guilty every time the award comes up."

Dora looked at him, expression neutral. "There were a lot of other men in that truck, right?"

He nodded.

"I'm sure many of them saw the grenade, didn't they?"

"Yes, it rolled some before I grabbed it," he answered.

"And how many of them went towards the grenade?"

"None." Joe wondered where she was going with this.

"Don't you see it, Joe?" His back stiffened, the opposite of how he was feeling because he loved the sound of his name on her lips. "No, I'm not trying to offend you." Her hand went to his arm and he felt the warmth through his shirt. Automatically, his hand lifted to hold her fingers on his bicep. With her touching him, it was hard to focus on what she was saying. "You did what others were too terrified to do. You acted when others were paralyzed and that's what makes it heroic regardless of your inner motives. You are an ordinary man who did an extraordinary feat and lived to tell about it."

"Okay, okay. Keep it up and you'll have me blushing, and I'm much too manly for that."

That made her laugh. Then she squeezed his three fingers before gently pulling away. "Thanks for telling me the truth. I realize you don't know me well, and it would have been very easy to give me some pat answer just to shut me up." Suddenly, Dora stopped talking. Joe didn't fill the silence, wondering what she would say next. His wait was short. "Well, anyway, I appreciate your candor." She got up and grabbed his plate. It was a definite signal for him to leave.

He stood as well. "Thank-you so much for allowing me to invade your Sunday evening, and, as I've told you before, the food was a true treat."

"You're welcome." She put the plate down. "I'll see you to the door."

She led the way and her hand was on the door knob, when he said, "Do you enjoy the arts?" She quickly turned to him, and he plunged all the way in. The most she could do was say no, and although it would be bruised, his ego wouldn't break. "The Alvin Ailey dancers are coming to the Pantages Theater in Tacoma, and I can get a couple of tickets. Would you like to go with me this Saturday?"

"They're wonderful, aren't they? I saw them a few years ago in Seattle. I dragged DS and a couple of his friends. Although I believe they really enjoyed it, they insisted they would have been bored stiff if the women weren't so beautiful."

Joe smiled and waited for an answer to his question. He watched several expression flit across her face before she bit her lower lip and said quickly, "Yes, I'll go," like she was trying to rush the words out before her lips managed to say something else.

Joe felt stiffness leave his shoulders. He didn't realize how tense he was until she said yes. "Good, I'll pick you up at six."

"Actually, it'd be better for me if we met there. It's always been my policy to keep this side of my life away from DS."

"I can respect that. How about we meet at the Pantages at 6:30?"

"Okay." She smiled as she opened the door to let him out.

Grinning from ear to ear, he jumped and clicked his heels on the way to his car. She'd agreed and maybe he could get her to consent to a few more things in the near future.

5

ON THE NIGHT of the event, Joe stood in the foyer of The Pantages wishing he could ignore social mores and physically dispose of the stranger standing next to him. He'd moved twice and the man had followed.

"The only thing good thing about being here is that I get to see lots of skin, in the audience and on the stage," the parasite said.

Joe didn't respond as he waited for Dora to appear, standing upright in his tuxedo. After introducing himself earlier as Melvin Patterson, the man told Joe he was waiting for his wife who was in the ladies' room. Joe wished she'd hurry the hell up and come get her husband. He barely responded as the man spewed a steady stream of conversation while sipping beer.

"My, my, my look at the one that just walked in." The man had uttered this same phrase several times.

Glancing in the general direction of Melvin's finger, Joe saw who he was referring to, and told him, "Eat your heart out. This one is mine."

He left the sputtering man and approached Dora who looked stunning. She wore a black dress that fell in soft folds just above her knees. Her shoulders were bare except for the spaghetti thin straps that held the dress in place. The neckline was modest and exposed just enough cleavage to get Joe's blood racing. Her hair was pulled away from her face and anchored at the nape of her neck in an elegant bun, exposing the diamonds that sparkled in her ears. A matching solitary diamond twinkled from a necklace she wore. Over one arm hung a floor length black coat.

"Let me get that for you." Joe said after kissing her cheek. He took the coat from her and led the way to the coat check, whispering, "You look absolutely stunning."

Dora absorbed the comment. She'd never felt more beautiful than she did at this moment. The expression on Joe's face when he'd approached had been worth the money she'd splurged to buy the dress, matching stilettos, and costume jewelry. The almost burning look of what she decided to interpret as appreciation made her heart churn and her stomach drop to somewhere between her legs.

Maybe that's why she found herself studying him just as thoroughly while he checked her coat. Her eyes journeyed from impeccably polished, black shoes to the razor sharp crease in his black slacks. Both of which were complimented by the red tie that shined from his starched, cream colored shirt that rested beneath his black suit jacket. When he turned to her, she slowly allowed her gaze to reach his eyes. "Thank-you for the compliment, Joe. You look quite fabulous yourself."

The look in his eyes smoldered, and Dora turned away, finding it to be more than she could stand. She'd never wanted to pull a man to the nearest private place and get buck wild. The evening was just starting and her thoughts were already out of hand. Never a shy woman, she decided she wouldn't be able to survive this evening if some ground rules weren't put in place. Joe had a hand at her back to help guide her through the crowd. As they walked, she felt his hot gaze on her often. When they stopped near the bar and before he could ask if she wanted anything, she lifted to her tiptoes, and he took the hint and leaned down. "Joe, you've got to stop looking at me like that."

"What?" He smiled, letting her know he knew exactly what she was talking about. Still he said, "How am I looking at you?"

"Like I was on the menu at Soul Kitchen, and you wish we were alone with a few less clothes on." On bated breath, she waited for his reply.

He leaned in close until his lips were a hairsbreadth away from her ear. He had her full attention. "You're wrong, lady." Warm breath brushed her lobe. "I want us to have no clothes on."

A shiver passed through her, and she didn't know if the cause was hot breath in her ear or the vision of them writhing naked. She was so aroused she feared she wouldn't be able to walk straight. Stiffening her spine while telling herself to get a grip, she put a hand in the center of his chest and pushed gently, hoping to create distance. He didn't budge. She imagined to the uninformed her gesture looked like a lover's caress. "This is our first date, and if you don't behave, I just might have to leave." *Hah, more like jump you.*

The house lights dimmed, letting them know it was time to find their seats. "Okay, Dora. I promise to be good," Joe whispered, moving back.

Her hand was still on his chest. Sliding her palm slowly down, she removed it when she reached his stomach. With a wink, she whispered, "Not too good, I hope." So much for ground rules. The man was too sexy for her well being.

Oh, so the woman does like to play with fire. A crooked smile planted itself on Joe's face. "Maybe we should find our seats before I can do something bad."

"Yes, I certainly need to sit down."

The sexy way she said it had an immediate effect on Joe. He was hard enough to pound nails, and he wanted to take her right there. Instead, he placed a hand on the small of her back to escort her to their seats, happy that the darkness and his position behind her hid his condition.

The performance began with the signature piece, "Revelations," and the audience cheered, whooped, and hollered when the curtain rose to reveal the famous pyramid of dancers. Although they were only fifty feet away from the stage, that's the last thing Joe remembered seeing clearly. His eyes were drawn to the brown skin revealed when Dora crossed her legs. He tried his best to pay attention to the attractive, well-conditioned dancers as they performed their spectacular routines, but they were no match for the woman sitting next to him. Giving up, as unobtrusively as possible, he relished the view. His left hand hung from the end of the armrest, and it was just inches from her smooth looking calf, encased in stockings. Even in the dim light, he could detect well-defined muscles that left him wanting to see more. Part of her thigh was also visible, and he couldn't help imagining what was hidden behind the smooth fabric of her dress. He was so aroused it was becoming painful sitting as he was, so he decided it might be prudent to look down her leg as opposed to up. His eyes grazed the flesh over her knee, down the shin, to her high heel shoes. Damn, why did he look at those shoes? His mind was filled with images of her coming to him, wearing nothing but stilettos. He had to lower his lids until he had himself under control.

Thirty minutes into the show, Dora shifted to cross her right knee over her left. Although this angle didn't provide a full view, it was just as appealing. He continued to lavish his attention on the superbly shaped limb, all but disregarding the performance. A loud drum beat drew his attention to the stage. A female was dancing alone under a spotlight. She was short and wore a form fitting, shift dress that flowed as she moved gracefully and sensuously around the stage. Over the years, he'd seen quite a few females' bodies, and he took an educated guess that Dora's was similar to the dancer on stage. He watched lost in fantasy that Dora was dancing for him alone.

Joe was surprised when he felt something against his leg. Assuming it was an unintentional bump from Dora, he shifted to allow her more room. There was a distinct tightening in his chest when the movement continued. Looking down, he realized Dora had shifted positions again and her stocking clad foot was rubbing his leg. He watched, his eyes caressing her skin as she moved languidly against his calf. The pace of the music picked up, gathering energy, taking his heart beat with it. As the music climbed to a climax, Joe's eyes traveled up Dora body. She sat calmly, hands holding the program in her lap, the only movement being her leg. However, when he reached her eyes, they burned with the fire of awareness.

He leaned over until his lips were real close to her ear. "You'd better stop, or I won't be responsible for what I do."

"Deal." She removed her leg. "As long as you quit torturing me and keep your eyes on the show."

There was thunderous applause and the house lights came on

announcing intermission. He felt like a bad boy who'd been caught with his hand in the cookie jar. It didn't stop him from smiling, though. "I'll try, but I find you much more fascinating than the program, Dora."

"Uh, huh." She didn't sound like she believed him. "Well, you can work on it while I visit the ladies' room."

Dora didn't really have to use the facilities, but she had to get away from Joe before she did something else stupid and completely out of character. "You caressed the man's leg," she whispered as she made her way through the throng of people. She'd never been so forward in her life, preferring to sit back and let the man flirt. Yet this man had her so hot by staring like he wanted to devour her. It didn't help that the dancers were engaging in several sensuous numbers. She felt as if she was smoldering in eroticism, and it was making her crazy. The proof was in the action because she'd have to have been out of her mind to actually move her foot against him as she had done.

In the bathroom, she fought to get to a mirror where she checked her make-up, washed her hands, and finished composing herself. "Okay, girl, you can do this," she whispered to her reflection and made her way back to her seat. Joe behaved enough during the second half of the show that she was able to keep her attention focused on the dancers, but every once in a while, she still caught him ogling her legs. Dora breathed a sigh of relieve when the final bows were taken. She'd survived without doing anything else overtly sexual.

Although they drove in separate cars, Joe insisted on following her home to make sure she was safe. None of Dora's other dates had offered to do this when she'd driven herself. She appreciated the gesture even though she didn't think it was necessary. At her house, she parked in the garage and left the door up as she walked to Joe's car to thank him for a wonderful evening. It was only 10pm, and she knew DS was seeing a late movie with friends. He wouldn't be in for some time yet, so she wasn't concerned about him seeing her with Joe.

"It's not too late for a nightcap." He had stepped out of his car.

"How about I take a rain check?" Dora didn't want the evening to end either, but her strong reaction to this man scared her. She needed to get away and think.

"All right. Enjoy the rest of your evening, Dora." He kissed her cheek, causing desire to rage in her. She stepped back quickly and waved bye before rushing to the garage.

6

TWO DAYS LATER, on Monday, Joe was back at Soul Kitchen. He'd wanted to come sooner, but contained himself. It was about five p.m. and not that crowded yet. Mr. Cook was sitting at a table near the bar with another older gentleman. Two wooden canes were perched on the wall within reaching distance.

Seeing so many pay their respects to the owner the previous time, Joe decided to do so also. He walked up to the man. "Hello, I'm Joe Bolin, sir, and I enjoy your place."

The two shook hands. "Thank-you, but it ain't me. His daughter's been running the place for the last ten years now. Isn't that right, Jasper Pete?"

The man nodded. "Dora does do a fine job."

So this is Dora's father. Joe shook his hand as well. "It's a pleasure Mr. Pete."

Jasper laughed. "Pete's my middle name, last name's Williams."

Before Joe could respond, Mr. Cook asked, "Are you a soldier, son?"

"Yes, sir." He was wearing fatigues, so his occupation was obvious.

"Well, heck, sit for a spell and have a beer. We need some fresh conversation."

Joe sat down. Suddenly, his neck prickled, and he didn't have to turn around to know Dora was nearby. He looked over his shoulder and there she was balancing a tray of food, making the Soul Kitchen t-shirt that was tucked into jeans strain against her breasts. He knew he was going to need the Lord's help when she saw him, and her face lit up in a wide smile. "Hi Joe. I didn't see you come in. I'll take care of you in a jiffy?"

If only that were true. Looking at her father, he tried to rid his mind of all lust.

"So you know my daughter." Mr. Williams nodded in Dora's direction.

"Yes, sir." He decided to be completely honest with the man. "Actually, I met her through your grandson. I'm an army recruiter."

"Ah." The man laughed. "According to DS, Dora gave you quite an earful."

Joe chuckled. "She did indeed, sir."

"Hum, she doesn't seem to be mad at you now. For what it's worth, I think the boy's doing the right thing. DS is a daredevil. The military's a place where he can do exciting things to fulfill that side of his nature. Besides, my daughter needs to live her own life, and that'll be easier with DS out of the house."

"No, what she needs to do is buy this place, so I can retire." Mr. Cook slapped the table for emphasis.

"Daddy, Mr. Cook!" Dora had reappeared. "Please stop telling my business."

"All right, all right. I was just talking to him since he was part of the business of your son being recruited," her father retorted.

Shaking her head, she looked at Joe. "What can I get for you, Captain?"

Now there's a question, he wanted to say, but flirting was definitely not appropriate. "I'll take a Heineken and the hot wings with fries."

"Coming right up."

He tried not to stare at her bottom. He'd feel like a pervert if his normal reaction popped up in his pants while sitting with her father. If the military had taught him anything, it was control, although he seemed to have anything but around Dora.

"Hey, my grandson tells me you're a war hero. Is that so?"

Joe nodded and began talking when both men insisted on details. Engrossed in the story, they scooted closer, sandwiching him in. When Dora returned with the beer, her pelvis brushed his back as she maneuvered to place the glass down. Through the material of their clothes he could feel the heat. When she brought the food, her breast grazed his shoulder, and he smelled her citrus scent, both of which drove him crazy.

By the time he'd answered all of the men's questions, the place was very busy. Dora still came to check on them regularly while Joe enjoyed talking to the men. Mr. Cook had served fifteen years in the navy before opening the restaurant. Mr. Williams was a retired Boeing employee and full of stories. Before Joe knew it, hours had passed.

The restaurant was less crowded, and when Dora came by, Mr. Cook said, "Rest a minute, chile and come sit with us." Joe jumped up and grabbed another chair, helping her scoot in once she was seated. Soon the three of them where engaged in a heated debate about the fate of the Seattle Super Sonics. Mr. Cook believed the city of Seattle was at fault and the new owner should take the team to Oklahoma, while Dora and her father seemed ready to commit violence to keep the team from leaving. Joe liked being an observer. Dora was smart, articulate, and witty as she got her points across. The topic shifted to football, and he was drawn in since he was a rabid Denver Bronco fan.

Dora managed to maintain the dialogue even though she got up several more times to take orders or close out a bill. Also, many customers interrupted them to say hello to the older gentlemen. It was after ten, the staff was cleaning up, and Joe knew it was time to leave. Deshawn arrived with a burst of energy, dishing out hugs and high fives to just about everyone. "Captain Bolin," Joe heard the surprise in the kid's voice as the boy pulled him into a hug, too.

"How you doing, Deshawn?"

"Pretty good. I see you've met my pappy and Mr. Cook."

"Yes. I came to eat and ended up having great conversation."

The kid nodded. "It's all good." Looking at his grandfather, Deshawn said, "You ready to go home Pappy? I have your car out front."

"Yep, I suppose I am," he said around a yawn. Deshawn helped him to his feet. "Mom." Dora's head lifted from the till. "We're outta here."

"Okay, thanks for taking daddy home, baby."

Joe pulled out his wallet. Mr. Cook's voice stopped him. "Naw son. Thanks for keeping a couple of old men company." Mr. Cook rose shakily to his feet.

"Thanks, sir." Joe rushed to help him and the old man waved him off.

"I can still get 'round by myself. I'm just stiff. Hey, everybody, I'm gone. See ya'll tomorrow." Leaning heavily on his cane, Mr. Cook moved to the door.

"I'll follow him just in case," Joe whispered to Dora.

"No need. We're done here and everyone is leaving."

Joe left and made his way to his Jeep Cherokee. He sat and watched, making sure everyone made it to their cars safely.

"Damn!" the loud curse echoed across the parking lot, followed by a slamming door. Joe's hand stopped turning the ignition. He got out of his car and walked over to Dora. Everyone else had left. "It won't start."

"I have a flashlight in my jeep. Pop the hood, and I'll see if I can get it going."

"Don't bother." She leaned against the driver's door arms crossed, head down, like she was avoiding his eyes. "I ran out of gas."

Joe held back his laughter. "All right, I've got a gas can. Let's get you some?"

She cursed a blue streak, surprising Joe. This time he threw back his head and laughed before saying, "I didn't know you could cuss like a trucker. It's very endearing."

"I'll call a cab." She began marching to the restaurant.

"No." He touched her shoulder. "Let me help you." With a hand at her elbow, he led the way to his car.

"Are you sure?" Relief inched into her face.

Joe told himself he was squeezing her arm reassuringly, yet some might have interpreted the movement as a caress. "Absolutely."

It was a short ride to the gas station and back, but it was long enough for the mood to change as soon as they were enclosed together. Joe thought it was because they were two people who were intensely attracted to each other, and he wondered if they were going to do something about it. Silence ruled as they smoldered in the atmosphere.

Back at her car, Joe put the gas in, then insisted on following her to the station where he filled up her tank. Annoyed that he wouldn't let her pay, Dora said, "I'm not destitute you know. I can afford my own gas."

"I'm sure you can," Joe said, replacing the pump handle. "I just want to make sure it's full, so I don't have to worry about you running low for a while."

She made an exasperated noise and got in her car. He yanked open the passenger door and leaned in. "Being the gentleman that I am, I'm following you home."

Her only response was to start the engine. Joe hopped in his jeep and caught up before she left the lot.

Driving home, Dora wasn't nearly as irritated as she pretended to be. The man was such a gentleman mixed with just a touch of bad boy, and he was melting her heart. A funky attitude was her only defense against it. But why are you fighting? A little voice asked. She doubted that Captain Joe Bolin was serious about her, so why not follow her motto of companionship with no strings attached? Companionship, goodness, she just bet he was good at that! "Get your mind out the gutta," she whispered as she pulled into her garage. Her inner voice teased, *why not let it stay in the gutta, get a taste, enjoy it while it lasts, and get him out of your system.*

He waited in his car as she walked up to his open window. "Is my rain check still good? I'd like to offer you a drink for helping me out tonight?"

His eyes widened before he said, "You don't have to ask me twice." He followed her through the garage into the kitchen. She placed her keys on the counter and led the way into the small living room.

"I have beer, whiskey, soda, and water. What would you like?" It was the first time she'd really looked at him since inviting him in. Joe's dark brown eyes glowed as he looked down at her. His gaze appeared to devour her face, especially her mouth.

Anticipation flooded her. That he wanted her was more than apparent. Suddenly, the look was gone to be replaced with polite friendliness. "I'll take a beer."

She went in the kitchen to get it. When she returned, he was sitting on the couch. She handed it to him and sat in the armchair.

He took a sip. "You didn't have to put it in a glass."

Her eyes widened. "I don't mind."

"You're not drinking with me?"

She crossed her jean clad legs, remembering how he'd stared at them a few nights ago. "No, I'm fine."

"Yes, you certainly are."

She laughed. "That was pretty corny."

"Hey, I was attempting some serious flirtation. You're not supposed to find it funny." The twinkle in his eyes let her know he wasn't really upset.

"If that's the best you can come up with, we're in trouble."

"Oh, I can come up with better." He raised his eyebrows salaciously.

"Can you now?" Suddenly, she felt self-conscious. "Too bad I've been working all day and probably smell like fried chicken."

"I love fried chicken."

She smiled. "You're being lame again." Despite her words, that wasn't how she felt. The heat had returned to his eyes, making her moist in unmentionable places.

"Is your son here?" He took another sip, pinning her with his gaze.

Meeting his stare, she said, "No, he's staying with his grandfather tonight. He does that from time to time."

"Oh, so I can get comfortable?"

"Don't be too presumptuous. I haven't made up my mind about that, Captain. Remember, I only invited you in for a drink."

"And here I am finished with my beer. Should I leave?"

Dora felt as if she were at a cross road. She didn't answer his question. In fact, she said nothing at all, just sat there with her arms crossed.

"Enough said." Joe stood and put the glass on the coffee table. Apparently, he was absolutely clueless that still waters ran deep, and there was a tsunami building inside of her. Dora lifted from the armchair, and they were standing quite close together.

"Thank-you for your hospitality." He bowed slightly. "I'll see myself..."

Before he could say another word, she reached up, cupped his cheeks and drew his mouth down to hers. For less than half second, he was unresponsive. Her heart crashed to her feet as she cursed herself for being a fool.

But then, Joe started kissing her back, his tongue slipping between her lips as if it belonged there, or at least had been there several times before. He tasted of beer mixed with mints, a combination she found that she liked. She also enjoyed when his hand possessively covered her back as he pulled her against him. If the kiss wasn't enough to erase doubt, then the enormous bulge pressing against her stomach sure did the trick. She stood on her tiptoes, moaning and wiggling as she was enclosed in his big, brawny arms. Wetness rushed from her and all they'd done was kiss. Lord, she'd probably drown them both when they got to the actual act. As it was now, she quivered while hot lips and hot hands maneuvered over her, making her body crave more direct contact.

His hands settled on her bottom, and he straightened as he lifted her off the ground, keeping their mouths connected as her legs wrapped around him. "Here or the bedroom." He arched between her spread legs, making her squeal and rub against him.

"Does that mean here, baby?"

She nodded frantically, not wanting to delay. Soon, she was on the couch with Joe on the floor, kneeling between her legs. While he continued to kiss her senseless, a warm hand slid under her shirt, up her ribcage, to cup an achy breast. A thumb passed over her bra covered nipple, and Dora gasped into his mouth.

Seconds later, she broke the connection with his lips to lean back and lift her arms. He obeyed the silent command and removed her clothing. Her hair clip came off with the shirt, causing him to groan when her plump breasts and hair sprang free from their confines. Dark locks cascaded down her shoulders, and Joe muttered unintelligible as he buried his face in hair and breasts.

He trailed kisses up her neck and whispered, "God, you just don't know how good you look, sexy jeans, bare-chested, and waiting for me." His lips captured hers again. One hand fondled her breast while the other travelled down her stomach, to unclasp her jeans, and venture inside. He made a low sound and whispered, "Yes," when he encountered wetness. Where his vocalization ended, hers took off when his fingers pressed into the drenched folds, gently exploring. When he brushed the bud of her clitoris and sucked her tongue into his mouth at the same time, she almost lost it.

No God, please no, she silently begged because she'd never in her life come more than once, and she wasn't ready to give into that pleasure yet. Unknowingly, granting her a reprieve, he lifted his fingers from between her legs to grasp her breasts with both hands. "I'm really going to enjoy these when I'm inside of you. Maybe one day you'll let me put more than my face here." Her chest heaved. His words were making her hotter. "You'd like that wouldn't you? I'd make sure you do."

Too aroused to speak, Dora lifted her hips. Immediately, he understood and peeled the pants off her body. After he was done, he yanked off his fatigues to her delight. She lay there feeling completely wanton as the muscled flesh she'd imagined became reality. "My goodness," she said when his erection bounced free. Realizing she spoke aloud, her gaze leapt to his face to see what could only be described as pure male pride. Feeling emboldened, she reached and ran a hand down the center of his chest where sparse hair grew. His eyes darkened. Leaning up further, she intended to do some of the taking, but apparently he had other plans because his hands and mouth were on her again. "I'm going to lick, kiss, and suck these in every way I've imagined since I first saw you." As he thrilled her breasts, her hips arched and she ground herself against him.

"Um, I get it. This part wants attention, too." He moved down her torso. Lord, how could he not know, Dora wondered. The scent of her arousal was so strong, it was awkward. But somehow she was way past feeling uncomfortable. Heck, she was too damn comfortable and ready for what he was about to do. Yet, knowing her one time rule, she intended to delay him. She even put hands to his shoulders, but by that time, he'd already reached his goal. All thoughts of stopping flew out of her head at the first flick of his tongue across her over-sensitized nub. She moaned as the spicy, hot pressure of his mouth sent jolts of pleasure radiating outwards.

Dora would have never thought she'd want someone to talk while doing this, but when he said, "Delicious," and some other choice words right against her clitoris; she found the deep timbre and vibrations to be just as magical as what he was saying. He wrapped her legs over his shoulders, and her hands clenched the couch. Next thing she knew, one maybe two fingers entered and zeroed in on a bundle of nerves that she'd heard about, but didn't really believe existed.

"Oh, God, it's real," she hissed near delirium. Never had she imagined something could feel as good as his fingers combined with the wet, hot, sucking of his lips. Her belly knotted, her bottom left the cushion as she came screaming like it was her first time.

Dora lost all sense of time. Minutes or days could have passed for all she knew. Her hands ached when she unclenched them to cover her eyes. "That was so good it must be against some law. If the cops aren't here, I guess I'm just going to hell."

"If so, I'll be right there with you, babe."

Her hands moved to her cheeks, and she saw Joe kissing the inside of her thighs. When he grazed her nub, she jumped. "Joe, you're going to kill me."

Joe chuckled against her fragrant flesh. Killing her was the last thing on his mind. He looked, loving what he saw, flushed face, glassy eyes, and mussed hair spread in a sexy halo; not to mention her pointy nipples and the red, moist flesh glistening from between her legs.

"No, babe. You might faint from coming too much, but that's about it." He began kissing his way up her torso and she quivered. He was tickled she was so responsive after coming like a freight train.

"Humph." She smiled when he reached her face. "I've never had more than one. It's all good though, as the kids say, because that was a hell of an orgasm."

He hovered near her lips. "You're legs we're pressed against my ears, but if I heard correctly, you didn't know you had a G-spot either. Remember, you're in Joe's world now, where anything is possible." Not giving her a chance to answer, he nibbled and kissed her deeply as he tested the entrance to her body, not wanting to hurt her.

"Wow, that's thick." She slanted just enough to look down their torsos. "And wonderful." With a wicked smile, she pulled him in for another kiss. Tilting her hips, she drew him in to the hilt. "When did you put on a condom?"

"When you were in La La land, I took care of business."

"Umm, I love efficient men."

"Do you?" He began moving out and in, and she didn't answer. "Getting excited?" His tongue played with her earlobe.

"Yes," she admitted, "but that doesn't mean a thing. Usually, it's just enough to frustrate me, not get there again."

"Oh, yeah." His arms hooked beneath her knees, and he made sure the base of his penis brushed her clitoris with each stroke. She squeezed, pulling him deeper. Thighs bracing, feet on the floor, he leaned in and captured a nipple with his lips.

"Oh, that's so good," Dora crooned. She held her breasts as he lavished them with attention. She began grinding against his pelvic bone, and Joe knew her flesh wasn't overly sensitive any more. Unhooking one of his arms, he licked a thumb and moved it between their bodies. He vibrated it gently in a fast rhythm over her nub.

"Damn, I feel that in my toes." She pushed her breasts in his face, and he bit her nipples.

"You're going to come, with me inside of you," he growled, swirling his thumb even faster as he pumped long and hard.

She grabbed his face and drew him up for a heat searing kiss. Then against his mouth, she said, "I think you're right," before throwing her head back and arching her torso. When the spasms stopped, she slumped against him, looking dazed.

"Stay with me, babe. We're not done yet."

Her smile came real slow. "I know." She kissed him gently, almost preciously, then her body went real still. Placing her hands on his hips, her lower stomach started rolling in a steady rhythm. Pleasure washed over Joe. The sensation surprised him. It was like her body was a large, slick hand working him to perfection. He had planned to come pounding as hard as she could take and here she had him paralyzed, scared to move because it felt so good. When she cupped his sac and squeezed gently, he exploded while she milked him dry with the endless motion of her body.

He slumped, angling to the side so he wouldn't crush her, his good intentions were for not when she pulled him to her. He lay there, leaning into her body, his nose buried in her neck. She smelled of citrus and him. He quivered from the intensity of his orgasm and from the eroticism of smelling himself on her.

"Damn, what'd you do to me?" He asked when he could breathe again.

She tightened her muscles around him, and his penis jumped, trying to respond. "Pilates and yoga. You're not the only one with surprises."

"Do you know you almost killed me?"

She smiled slyly. "Join the club."

"Hell, I want to become a charter member."

Her throaty chuckle was incredibly sexy. "That can be arranged."

Dora was so content and spent that she frowned in protest when Joe shifted, so he was lying flat and she was on top of him. "Mmm," she murmured, snuggling into his neck. His heartbeat beneath her cheek was soothing, and when he began rubbing her back, she fell into a tranquil haze. That is until her foot cramped.

"Ouch," she yelled, vaguely aware that her elbow dug into his flesh as she twisted and almost fell to the floor.

"What?" Joe moved until her back was to the couch and he was on the ground.

She managed to squeeze out, "Cramp, foot."

He grabbed the one that was twisted inward. "Ahh," she screamed when he began pressing the ball of her foot with both thumbs.

"Trust me. This will help, try to relax."

Closing her eyes, she attempted to do as he said while he moved from her instep to the arch, massaging firmly. The pain began to ease. "How often do you get these?"

She shrugged. "I'm on my feet a lot."

"Where's your bathroom?"

She pointed, assuming he asked because he had to use the facility. When he returned with vanilla scented lotion, she wondered what he was up to. "You're couch is wonderful, Dora, but what I have in mind works much better in a bed."

With raised eyebrow, she asked, "What are you going to do?"

"Something you'll enjoy. I promise."

"Whoa," she yelped when he scooped her up, although she quite liked the end result, being pressed against his chest. Automatically, her arms wrapped around his neck.

"Where's the bedroom?"

She nibbled at his ear as she told him. Her room was simply furnished. A bed, nightstand, dresser, and stand alone mirror where the only furnishings. A bouquet of wild flowers rested on the dresser with several candles. Dora was in the habit of pulling the sheets back when she made the bed, so she could just slip in when she was ready. Joe placed her on the soft cotton sheets.

Dora eyed Joe's bottom shameless as he picked up matches from her dresser and lit the candles. The scent of vanilla filled the room as he turned off the overhead light.

"You know you're doing this backwards if you're trying to seduce me."

He chuckled. "Turn over." He ran a hand down her stomach.

She did as he asked, looking over her shoulder to keep an eye on him. He was semi-erect, making Dora think she knew where this was headed. He started with the same foot, his hand moving much easier now that he used lotion. It felt so good all she could do was moan. He moved to her other foot and gave it the same treatment. The press of his palms over her calves and thighs was absolutely magnificent, and by the time he reached her buttocks, she'd been reduced to a wet noodle. Climbing on the bed and settling over her bottom, he began working on her torso. Dora was in heaven, yet couldn't help but notice that his fully erect penis now rested on her lower back. His hands were magical and as he worked her arms, Dora feel into a light sleep. She woke when he settled in next to her, his raging erection at her side.

"Let me take care of that." She shifted and reached downward.

He grabbed her hand and kissed it. "Shush, keep relaxing, this is about you."

Dora leaned over and kissed his shoulder. "Thank-you." Then she pulled his hand to her lips and kissed each of his three fingers before holding it to her breast. He squeezed her to him in reply and his lips met her forehead with extreme tenderness. With his other hand, he stroked her back until she drifted off again.

7

A FADED PINK was just beginning to light the sky when Joe inched his way out of bed. Logical ruled over emotions because all he wanted to do was kiss her awake and love her until they both fell out, exhausted. He bet they could repeat the process for a week or two if they really put their minds to it.

Dora's breathing was even and slow as he paused at the edge of the bed. She was sprawled out on her belly, and the sheet had twisted in such a way that only her bottom was covered. His eyes roved over her lean back and smooth legs. One was bent while the other was straight, creating an interesting visual that disappeared under the sheet. He wanted to put his lips there, bury his tongue in between those gorgeous legs, and have her wake screaming as she quaked against his mouth. He refrained because he had to meet with his superiors in less than an hour, and he didn't know when her son was coming home. However, he couldn't resist her completely, as he lightly touched her hair, gently stroked her cheek, and leaned down to press the briefest of kisses to the side of her face.

His clothes were in the living room. He quickly retrieved them and got dressed. He returned one more time to peer down at her. She hadn't moved, sleeping deeply with a light snore now. He knew he had to leave pronto, or he wouldn't be able to drag himself away from her golden brown skinned body at all. Still, it wouldn't be right to go without leaving some word. He pulled a card from his wallet and found a pen on her nightstand. He scribbled a note and placed it on the empty pillow beside her head. As he slipped through the door, he gazed at her once more. She turned slowly, trapping an arm under her body, and exposing lovely breasts. Joe caught himself drifting back in the room. He shut the door softly, creating a barrier between the two of them.

Dora woke up alone the next morning with sunlight streaming through the window. She squinted and turned her head, yelping when something scratched her face. Feeling under her cheek, she lifted a business card. "Why would he leave me this?" she said as she flipped it over. "Oh," she read Joe's blocky, slanted print. *Last night was wonderful! You're wonderful. I'll call you. Joe.*

Dora smiled and stretched, feeling like she was on top of the world. She hadn't slept so soundly in years. Glancing at the clock, she realized she had a few hours before she had to be at the restaurant. She burrowed into the pillow Joe had used, reveling in his scent. She remembered how she'd kissed his big, beautiful shoulders, wide enough to ease a girl's burdens. When was the last time someone had gone out their way to take care of her? Oh, DS did little nice things, but that didn't count. Not even Deshawn Sr. had put his needs on the back burner to deal with her stress. Being pampered was rare in her life, and she wasn't ashamed to shout to the rooftops that she liked it. The evening had been truly fantastic and the lovemaking, incredible, yet Dora knew that his tenderness and his caring would be what she remembered most about him.

☆☆☆

"Dora! Hey, Dora!"

Dora's head jerked up, and she realized she'd been wiping the same counter for quite a while.

"What, Maggie? Why are you screaming?"

The older woman put a hand on her hip. "Honey, I have been calling you for at least an hour. The food service company is on the phone. Did you work up the order?"

"Yes, it's in the office. I'll take the call in there."

Dora rushed to the back. Goodness, she was tired and it was just Tuesday. The past three weeks had passed in a blur. Working, mothering, and spending time with Joe was beginning to catch up with her. There was only one day last week when she hadn't seen him and the ache that burned in her scared her, especially when she realized the longing had nothing to do with lust. She missed his companionship, his sense of humor, his unique view of the world.

In fact, that's what they spent most of their time together doing, talking. Joe would come by Soul Kitchen to eat lunch or dinner at least once a day, and at some point, they'd end up talking about their lives, or politics, or local sports usually at a table or over the bar. He'd asked her about Deshawn Sr., and she'd been truthful up to a point. He'd looked in her eyes and said he'd never abandon a woman with his child, and he'd always be there for the lady he loved. Deep in her heart, she believed him, and when she'd asked if he'd ever been in love. His head had shook, but then he said, "I believe that's changing." A wave of joy had rushed through her that left her grinning like a fool for the rest of the evening.

They had only been together physically one time since that night. A drunk driver had hit a pole, taking out the power to the restaurant, so Soul Kitchen had to close early. Dora had called DS and told him she was going shopping, but she really went to Joe's house for a few hours. His home was beautiful, making hers look like a small shack in comparison. It was a lovely tri-level house with large porches and vaulted ceilings. The kitchen had new appliances and granite counters that Dora became intimately familiar with as Joe lifted her on top and proceeded to rock her world more than once. Her eyes squeezed shut at the lusty memory and her legs got all achy. Lord, she felt addicted and that wasn't her style.

Forcing herself to concentrate, Dora placed the order, then hung up the phone and her thoughts returned to Joe. Although he didn't say so, Dora got the distinct impression that he didn't take many women to his home. First off, the place didn't have a woman's touch. Except for new appliances, electronic stuff, and flat screen televisions, the place was sparsely furnished. There was a couch, loveseat, and beds in the rooms, but there were few pictures and no knickknacks. Second, the almost shy way he showed her around and watched for her reaction let her know that her opinion was important to him. That meant that either not many women came there, or she was special. The latter was scary and delightful territory. So, she told herself that this was like all her other interactions with romantic interests. It was a casual fling and nothing more. Yeah, right, her consciousness teased. *Then why does he always invade your thoughts? Why do you get absolutely giddy when he compliments you? Why do your knees turn to mush when he walks through the door? Why are you thinking about contacting a lawyer to do something you should have done years ago?*

"Dora?"

She looked up to see Maggie.

"Honey, you've been in another world for more than a few days. It wouldn't have anything to do with our newest regular would it?"

Dora stood up from the desk. "I don't know what you're talking about?"

"Yes, you do." Maggie's smile was a mile wide. "I've never seen you like this. It's nice to know you're normal."

Dora was organizing loose papers into piles. Her head snapped to Maggie. "Of course I'm normal!"

"Oh, don't get offended. I'm truly proud of the way you've raised that boy and didn't put your personal interest ahead of him. But he's old now and it's okay to let the woman in you come forward." Maggie chuckled. "I'd imagine it must be impossible to hold that femininity back when a man that fine is interested."

Dora stared at Maggie in horror. They had never talked about her love life, and she wasn't sure if she liked a woman who had gone through three husbands commenting on something so private.

"Anyway, I just thought I'd let you know that you're number one soldier just came in. I was going take his order, but I thought I'd leave that pleasure to you."

"No go ahead. I have to call the beer company and make an order before I go back to the floor. I'll be there in a minute."

"Okay." With a wink, Maggie was gone.

As soon as the door closed, Dora sat back down, put her head on the desk and groaned.

When she finally returned to the dining room, she was surprised to see that Joe wasn't alone. He was with Jared and two other men she recognized as customers, but she didn't know them well. She didn't go up to their table, just smiled and wiggled her fingers as she passed by. Jared and Joe waved back. Maybe, just a little distance would help to sort out her feelings. As she checked on the kitchen staff, carried orders, and spoke to customers, she couldn't help hearing little bits of Joe's table's conversation. Once she got the gist of it, an odd tighten happened in her chest.

"Joe, did you see the one that gave me a lap dance? She could wiggle each breast independently." Jared said excitedly.

"Precious. That was her name," one of the other men said. "I wonder if she could do that while it was in my mouth?"

Dora noticed that Joe looked uneasy when their eyes caught as she walked passed.

Good, she thought.

"Didn't you have fun, Joe?" Jared asked. "That one girl…" Dora had heard enough. Apparently, the Saturday that they hadn't seen each other, he'd gone to a strip club. Fury made breathing difficult as she went to the office to cool off. She didn't want him seeing other women.

She jumped when someone entered the office without knocking. "Joe, how did you get here?"

"Maggie showed me the way." He closed the door and moved towards her.

"What are you doing?"

"Clearing up a misunderstanding. Dora, nothing happened Saturday night." He put his hands on her shoulders.

"Oh, you didn't get lucky," she spat, then instantly regretted it. She had no claims to Joe. "Sorry about that." Her voice was still too hard. "It's really not my business."

She twisted away from his hands, still facing him. Her little inside voice told her not to say anything else, but she blabbed on. "Just because you're enjoying me doesn't mean you can't screw someone else." She hoped her face was as neutral as her tone. "Lord knows I believe in a warm bed whether you're there or not." *Lying is a sin*, the little voice reminded her.

Joe looked furious, standing there with his arms crossed and his legs spread wide in Army fatigues and boots. His jaw was tight, making his cheek bones even more prominent.

There was a knock on the door, then Mr. Cook's head popped in. "Ya'll all right in here?"

"Yes, Mr. Cook. We are just talking. I'll be there in a moment."

"Are you sure, gurl?" He looked at Joe's face and raised his cane.

Going around Joe, Dora got in between the two and gave Mr. Cook a hug. "Nothing's wrong. I'm fine." She gently shooed him out and shut the door.

"It's time for you to leave," she told him.

Joe snatched her up in his arms and his mouth closed over hers in a punishing kiss. Emotion overruled logic and her arms twined around his neck before she could even think about it. When she realized she was kissing him back, she tried to pull away, and Joe let go just as quickly as he'd grabbed her. His face was ablaze with anger, and he had her pinned against the door with his body and arms on both sides above her head.

"I guess I should have told you upfront. I don't share!" With that, he stepped back, and she quickly moved away from the door. The next instant, he was gone.

8

IT WAS AN HOUR past closing time, and Joe felt like a stalker hanging out in his car at the Soul Kitchen parking lot. He was in his Ford Taurus, a car he rarely drove, so he knew no one from the restaurant would recognize it. Three people were left inside: Mr. Cook, Maggie, and Dora. He didn't know what he'd do if they all left together.

He'd left the restaurant in a rage to drive around for hours, trying to calm down. When he eventually did, he felt like an animal for mauling her the way he had. He'd never put his hands on a woman in anger, yet the image of another in her bed had overwhelmed him. Not even when he'd caught a lover with a soldier from his unit did he feel so bloodthirsty, and here, all Dora had to do was suggest it, and he wanted to kill. Putting his head back, he had to admit that this was more than a fling. He wanted Dora with him, and the right to know where she was when they were apart. He wanted to tell her where he was and have her on his arm as he strolled through base. He'd never felt this possessive, and now he understood why animals marked their territory.

That's why he was here tonight. He had a gut-wrenching need to see her, to explain how he felt, and to hear her say sorry after she found out she was wrong about the strip club. Sure, he'd gone, but only because he'd committed himself weeks ago. The guys wouldn't take no for an answer when he tried to back out. Joe had left early. He kept comparing all the women to Dora, and he wasn't interested in seeing if any measured up.

The fates were on his side, he decided, when Mr. Cook and Maggie left together. Dora waved from the door, then went back inside. He waited until both were in their cars and driving down the road before he hopped out of his car and trotted to the entrance.

He tried the door and, for security reasons, he was happy it was locked; but, for his purposes, it sucked. He could see her through the window next to the door because the drapes hadn't been drawn. It looked like she was doing a final check, walking around, straightening napkin holders and bending over to wipe a table. Her jeans tightened on her bottom, causing a similar reaction in his boxers as he studied her. She turned, facing his way and saw him standing at the window. She dropped the rag and her eyes widen. He knocked. She grinned, picked up her towel, and whirled it in the air like a helicopter before walking to the door. When she reached him, her smile disappeared, and she yanked the curtain closed.

"Dora, open the damn door! I'm not going away!" He was tempted to break the window when surprisingly, he heard a click and the door was open.

"I don't want to talk to you," she said holding the towel like she was going to snap him with it.

"Good, don't talk. How about closing your pretty little lips and listening." He locked the door, and she retreated to the bar, leaning against it. He walked up to her. "I went out with the guys, I didn't enjoy it, I came home early."

"Why are you telling me this?"

"Because you want to know, that's why." He stopped within inches of her. She had to crane her neck to look him in the face. "Let's get something straight, right here, right now. I'm not sleeping with anyone but you. I don't want anyone but you. If you feel differently, we need to end this thing now because after tonight I'll tear apart anyone who comes near you."

Joe couldn't read the expression on her face. He stared, wanting to kiss her senseless and stake his claim right there. She must have been thinking something similar because suddenly she reached up and pulled his head down into a hard kiss. As if unleashed, Joe was all over her. One hand was in her hair, his tongue was in her mouth, and his fingers went straight to her breast.

Dora moaned while she greedily sucked Joe's tongue. She'd been jealous, then so angry, and now that he'd explained, she was relieved and happier than she wanted to admit. Rather than analyze her feelings, she decided to focus on the lust, so when he lifted her, she wrapped her legs around his torso. They continued to kiss and she could hear him doing something behind her. She wasn't surprised when she was lowered to an empty table. His lips moved down her neck, and he tongued her breast through her t-shirt as he removed her shoes and all the clothing below her waist. Cool air and the cold table were in direct contrast to his hot mouth. "Mine," he said right before he spread her wide and latched on to her nub. Teasing, sliding, and flicking, in no time at all she was clutching his head with her hands screaming, "Yes!"

She'd barely finished climaxing when he had her on her feet and flipped around. Shirt still on, pants at his ankles, he slid himself up and down once before sinking all the way into her body. Bracing her hands on the table, Dora's head lifted, and she saw them in the mirror behind the bar. She gasped. It was so earthy, so basic, so real, and the fact that he wore fatigues only added to the effect. Her eyes looked crazed, her face was flush, and her lips were kiss swollen.

Joe's face looked feral as he moved in a circle inside her. Dora knew he was making a statement, staking a claim. *You are mine, exclusively.*

She squeezed and watched as Joe grimaced and thought, *Yeah, buddy, I've got you, too.* Widening her stance, she crooned as Joe gripped her hips and pumped harder. She met each thrust eagerly causing her breasts to bounce vigorously despite the bra and shirt she still wore. The sound of flesh slapping was terribly erotic to Dora especially when it was combined with their harsh breathing. She clenched tightly when Joe's hand left her bottom to reach around and rub her clitoris. In response, he moaned and pressed his finger harder. She whimpered and ground against him, undulating, until she came hard enough to make her legs weak. Joe's hand returned to her hip, and he began stroking rapidly again. Dora watched in the mirror, fascinated as his face contorted and he thrust hard enough to lift her. He fell forward, landing on her, but balancing on his hands so he didn't crush her. She could feel his stomach trembling and his heart pounding against her back, and each breath was like a bellow. When his breathing slowed, he buried his face in the back of her neck.

His head lifted and their eyes met in the looking glass. Joe looked happy and relaxed with his lids half-closed and a smile hovering on his lips. With her mussed hair and dilated eyes, Dora decided she looked kind of freaked out. "Good Lord, where is this going, Joe?"

He kissed her back and shoulder through her shirt as he drew them into a standing position. With his hands under her shirt, he fondled her breasts. Although he was softening, he was still in her body. Maintaining eye contact in the mirror, Joe said, "I thought this was casual, Dora. It's not for me. Each time I'm with you, it means more. I want to stick around and find out if it means serious like, love, or maybe something more permanent, like living together or marriage?"

He had slipped from her body, and Dora was turning in his arms when she said without thinking, "Well, I'd have to get divorced first."

The look on his face caused her to lower her arms.

"What did you just say?" The words come out very slowly.

"I'm married, but…"

"Married!" Joe shouted the word reverberating in his skull while stepping away from her, almost tripping because his pants were still around his ankles. He yanked them up. "What the hell are you doing with me? Killing time?" An ache started in the center of his chest, his breathing became heavy. He should have known this was too good to be moral.

"Joe, will you listen."

Naked from the waist down, muscled legs flex, she was sexy as the sin they'd just engaged in. Damn, he did not do married women much less fall in love with them. No he wasn't in love. He refused to be serious about someone who could be that conniving. "And you had a conniption fit because I went to a strip club. Talk about the pot calling the kettle black."

She had the nerve to look irritated. His hands clenched as he watched the anger building in her narrowed eyes and in her jerky motions as she snatched her clothes up and hopped into them. For some reason, fury just about blurred his vision when she grabbed a napkin and snatched their condom off the floor.

"Hiding the evidence," he spat.

"No," she hissed back, "Just cleaning up a mess."

The laugh he intended was more of a snort. "You're right about that, baby." Ugly words flew out of his mouth before his internal editor could filter them. "They have names for women like you. Low life who scream about honor, integrity, and protecting babies one day and live by the ends justify the means the next. Had me believing you wanted to be on the down low to protect your son when it was your own dirt you were trying to hide."

"That's not true, Joe. You don't understand…" she stepped towards him.

"If you're somebody's wife, that's all I need to know!" They stared at each other as he waited for her to say something else. When she didn't, he slammed out the door.

☆☆☆

Dora's arms wrapped around her waist as she tried to process what the hell had just happened. She felt as if she'd drifted into another dimension where her body still tingled from their lovemaking, but her mind reeled from their argument. Why wouldn't he let her explain? Then, she thought, *even if he had, would he have been satisfied*? She had no love for Deshawn Sr. and hadn't seen him in almost twenty years, but technically she was still a wife.

Numb, she just stood there for several moments before going into automatic as she locked up and drove home. In her bathroom, right after she brushed her teeth, the cocoon encasing her broke away, and she fell crying on the floor. Reaching up, she managed to turn the sink on full blast to try and cover the sound of her sobs, hoping DS wouldn't be able to hear in his room. She lay there a long time, grieving on the cold tile.

The next day she rose very early after a sleepless night. She had a few hours before she had to be at the restaurant, so she dressed, went to wake DS to find that he was already up and in the kitchen, eating toast. She told him she had some errands to run and was about to leave when he said, "Mom, I've noticed the Captain is at the restaurant a lot."

That stopped her cold. "Yes, he probably likes the food."

DS laughed. "I'm not stupid, mom. I think he likes you." Her son's smile was mischievous, and Dora didn't quite know what to do. They'd never discussed anything remotely close to this before.

"I'm cool with it. I think the Captain's an okay guy. I just wanted to let you know that I know so if it gets serious, you don't have to sneak around…"

"Deshawn! That's enough!"

Her son threw back his head and laughed while Dora stared at him. When he calmed down, he said, "Sorry I shocked you. I just think with me grown, you need other interests in life, and maybe it's time to divorce my dad." He walked over and hugged her. Patting his back, she couldn't help thinking how ironic it was that her son would tell her this when whatever she had with Joe was already crumbling.

Dora got in the car and drove on autopilot as she relived the event from the night before, going over every word, berating herself for not handling it differently. Maybe she should have grabbed Joe and held on until he listened to what she had to say, but her vow had been in the way, the promise she'd made after Deshawn Sr. left to never beg or run after a man. It was probably wishful thinking he'd care anyway. He was so upset that he most likely wouldn't have cared she hadn't seen her so called husband in almost two decades.

When she reached her spot, she threw the car into park. She sat inside the Maxima on the edge of Spanaway Lake and let memories of her mother who had died of heart failure when she was twelve wash over her. At the worst of times or the best, Dora came to lake because it had been her mother's favorite place, and she had so many memories of them fishing, swimming, or boating together. Like she always did, she felt her mother's presence and let it soothe her.

"What should I do, mama?" she asked staring out at the green water barely visible through the gray morning drizzle. No lightening struck and no answers flew into her head. "You're not going to help me with this one are you?" She threw her head back and closed her eyes. Images of Joe teased her until her lids flew back open. "Okay," she rubbed her face. "I'll try once and if he doesn't want to hear it, so be it." She grabbed her cell phone and dialed Joe's mobile number and then his house. No one answered, so she left a message on his home phone. "Joe, I know you're angry, and frankly I don't blame you. I didn't mean to tell you that way. It just sorta popped out, but what I want you to know is that I haven't seen Deshawn's father since I was pregnant. That was a long, long time ago. I didn't expect to have…strong feelings for someone again and now I do. It's my deepest regret that I didn't take care of things years ago. I should have divorced the man who means nothing to me." She paused, gathering her thoughts before continuing, "I won't beg you. I won't stalk you. If you want me, you know exactly where I am." She pressed the end button and rested her head on the steering wheel whispering, "I've rolled the ball to your court, Mr. Bolin. Hopefully, you'll pick it up and bring it back to me."

9

JARED STARED at Joe wide eyed and slack jawed. Then he walked to the front of the Racquetball Court and picked up the broken racquet. "Man, what is up with you?"

Joe gave his friend an irritated look before jogging up and taking the racquet. "It just flew from my hand with the swing. I didn't mean to throw it."

"Uh huh. That's why your poor assistant was trembling at his desk when I came to your office. You had the private so riled about misfiling the papers I thought he was going to wet his pants."

"I have another racquet in my bag. Let me get it."

"Hell no. I'm not playing you anymore. It might be me instead of the wall you hit next time. I will treat you to a beer if you promise to tell me what the problem is. Maybe I can pull the thorn out of your paw at Soul Kitchen."

Just the mention of the restaurant caused his gut to clinch. "No, I don't want to go there."

Jared looked at him oddly. Than an ear to ear grin split his face, and he shot his pointer fingers at Joe like they were guns. "Would your crappy mood have anything to do with a sexy waitress?"

Joe glared at him, and then began gathering his stuff to leave the court. Jared followed him into the weight room at the gym on Fort Lewis. Joe dropped his bag, grabbed the eighty-pound dumb bells, and started doing curls. "I thought you two were hitting it off a couple of weeks ago when we were at the restaurant. Come on buddy, do you two have a thing going?"

"Jared, go away." Joe began doing squats.

"Naw, it's too much fun hassling you. I was in there the other day and guess what, Dora bought the place. It's finally official."

"Really." Joe's mouth dropped open. He was proud of her, but he tried to hide it when he said, "I'm sure she's happy about that."

"Yeah, she was all smiles, unlike you."

That hurt, and Joe wasn't sure why. Maybe because he wanted to be there to share in her happiness. He alternated back to curls, and he wanted to slam the weight against his chest, hoping it would help dull the ache there. The ache of betrayal, he reminded himself, but despite his wishes he felt more frustration than anger. Thirteen days ago, he'd first listened to her message, and he'd replayed it at least a dozen times since then. Each time he heard it, he came away with chinks in his armor. He vowed not to listen to it again because he needed his shields at full strength to deal with seeing her like he did the other day. Deshawn's football team made it to the playoffs, and the kid called asking him to come. Telling himself he was only supporting a recruit, he went. Dora displayed absolutely no emotion when she saw him in the concession's line. After greeting him like he was an acquaintance, she ignored him and talked with the other parents the rest of the game. The woman was cool as the Pacific Ocean, and he truly knew if he wanted their relationship to be over, it was over. Putting the dumb bells down, he breathed heavily while taking a brief break.

"You're depressing, man, lifting weights like a robot, and do you know you look like crap."

Joe didn't respond, thinking about how beautiful Dora had looked at the game. Skin glowing, eyes round full of excitement as she watched her son, although it did look as if she'd lost weight.

"If you don't want a beer, I'm gonna let you stew in your own bad mood."

Joe picked up the weights. "Good."

"I'm still going to Soul Kitchen, though. Maybe I'll try my luck with Dora."

"Not if you want to live," Joe growled.

"Ouch." Jared stepped back. "It's like that then. Well, why didn't you say so? You two had a lover's spat?" Joe looked at him, letting all his irritation show. His friend didn't get the point. "So, let me get this straight. You don't want to see her, but no one else can inquire?"

"That's right."

"Well, it doesn't work that way, bro, especially with a woman that hot. Why don't you tell me what's really up."

Joe started lifting the weights above his head. "She's married."

"What!" Jared stepped back.

"That was my response, too." Joe put the bells down again and his hands settled on his hips.

"Where the hell is he?"

Joe shrugged. "He's been AWOL for about twenty."

"Wait. She hasn't seen him in that long?"

Joe nodded.

"Then what the hell is the problem? The marriage thing is just a technicality."

"That's not how I see it." His hands tightened at his waist because he was so full of justified angst he hadn't thought of it quite that way.

Jared's head tilted to the side. "That's because you're blind. Is she willing to get a divorce?"

"Probably. We didn't actually get that far once I found out?" He scowled, knowing how stupid it sounded.

"Man, you're not blind, you're a damn fool!"

Joe just stared at him before picking the weights up.

"Okay. I'll leave you alone, but you're a nut if you let that go." Shaking his head, his friend left as Joe continued to take out his aggravation on the weights.

An hour later, a freshly showered Joe was leaving the gym, physically exhausted, and hoping he could sleep. His phone rang and he answered after recognizing Jared's number. "I'm here, the place is packed, and your lady is absolutely radiant. You better come get her."

"Go to hell, Jared."

"Naw, I'd rather stay here in heaven where the food and view is lovely. I'll leave hell to you. Goodnight." His friend hung up.

Joe cussed all the way to his car. At home, he slammed doors, kicked cabinets, and broke a glass setting it down too hard. "Shit," he yelled, then sucked the cut on his pinky. He grabbed a beer and plopped down on the couch in front of Northwest Cable News. He almost dropped the cold can when Dora's lovely face filled the screen. A white hot sword of pain cut through him. Damn, he couldn't get away from her. Turning the television up, Joe heard the newscaster congratulating Dora about being the new owner of a local landmark, then he was asking questions about the billboard where she kept count of the local and national soldiers killed in Iraq.

As he watched her face the microphone with pose and grace while she talked about her friendships, commitment, and gratitude towards the soldiers, something deep inside of him snapped. *Why couldn't it be as simple as Jared put it? In her message, she practically made it clear she'd get a divorce?* It was him, not her marriage that was the barrier to them being together. Tired of all the longing and the wanting, Joe made a decision. It had been thirteen days and absence was doing more than making his heart grow fonder, it was making it ache as it never had before. It was time to see what she really meant when she said she had strong feelings. Soaring hope had him lifting from the couch and heading to the door.

It was almost closing time when he made it to Soul Kitchen. Not even contemplating waiting until the open sign was off, Joe walked through the front door of the restaurant. Surveying the room, he didn't see Dora, but Mr. Cook and Mr. Williams were posted by the cash register. They both looked Joe up and down, suspicion in their eyes. Joe knew Mr. Cook must have told his friend about the episode in the office. Wishing he was wearing something more presentable than sweats, he walked over and shook both men's hands before turning to Dora's father. "My intentions are honorable towards your daughter, and if she'll have me, I'll do everything in my power to make her happy."

Surprisingly, Mr. Williams smiled and shook his hand again. "Good, maybe now she'll divorce that fool. But let me tell you, son. If you don't do as you say, both of us are coming after you."

He left the men and headed to the back where he ran into Maggie who threw her arms around him and squeezed. "Hey, I haven't seen you around here, stranger!" He hoped Dora would be as happy to see him. "If you're looking for the boss lady, she's in the kitchen. Want me to get…Oh, here she is." Dora walked through a swinging door down the hall.

"Joe," she practically shouted, obviously surprised to see him.

"Dora," he said in the same tone, walking up and gathering her in his arms. He swung her around as he buried his nose in her hair. Her scent fogged his brain, making him forget everything but how good it felt to have her next to him. He pulled her into a kiss, slipping his tongue between her lips to enjoy the salty sweet taste. She returned his kiss, leaning into him like she wanted to crawl inside. He ignored the polite cough, but Dora lifted her head.

Her eyes were watery when she said, "Good Lord, I'm happy to see you, too, Joe, but you have to put me down." His arms stayed around her as he followed the order. He barely registered that Maggie had been joined by several people dressed in white.

"Show's over, guys. Get back to the kitchen." She pulled Joe into the office. Wiping her eyes and then straightening her clothes, she moved to a far wall. Once there, she looked at him shyly before saying, "To what do I own this honor?"

Closing the distance between them, he said, "I'm doing as you suggested, coming to get you. Are you ready to be taken?"

A smile twitched her lips. "It sure took you long enough. A sister could just about dry up waiting for you to make the right decision. Are you positive my marital state no longer bothers you?"

"Not as long as it's temporary." He was standing right in front of her now.

"I've already hired a lawyer and private investigator. They've found him, and it doesn't look like he's going to contest the divorce."

Placing his hands above her head, he whispered, "Music to my ears. By the way, congratulations on buying the place."

She managed to utter, "Thanks," right before his lips closed over hers.

As Dora melted between him and the wall, she wondered if she shouldn't play a little harder to get. The darn man had made her wait almost two weeks! Yet, he was here, pressing against her, and she didn't want to waste any more time. "I love you," she whispered when they came up for air. The joy, then heat in his eyes made her want to say the words again.

"Is that so?" His smile was wolfish. "The time I spent apart from you was sheer hell. I've never missed a woman, nor wanted to be around her all the time." His eyes were bright and his Adam's apple moved up and down. "I love you, Dora Lamont, more than I thought was possible, and if you weren't already entangled, I'd be tempted to do something totally out of character and ask you to marry…"

"Yes!" Dora threw herself into his arms. Both of them ignored the knock on the door. In fact, they didn't separate until Maggie tapped on Joe's shoulder.

"I think you two better come out before the old gentlemen and all the employees come in here. I can only hold them back so long."

Looking in her eyes, Joe said, "We will continue this later."

"Is that a promise?" Dora's hand caressed his cheek.

"Yep. The kind only I can keep."

Walking from the office holding hands, the crowd greeted them with cheers, making Dora feel silly and giddy. She squeezed Joe's hand, rubbed against his solidness, and was completely confident she was the luckiest woman in the world.

☆☆☆

Going Commando

By
J.M. Jeffries

Books by J.M. Jeffries
Road Tested
A Bride to Treasure
Cupid: The Amorous Arrow
Cupid: The Bewildering Bequest
Cupid: The Captivating Chauffeur
Cupid: The Dazzling Debutante
A Dangerous Love
A Dangerous Deception
Southern Comfort
A Dangerous Obsession
Code Name: Diva
Blood Lust - paranormal
Sin and Surrender
A Dangerous Woman
Vegas Bites
Virgin Seductress
Creepin'
Blood Seduction
Suite Seduction
Vegas Bites Back
Soldier Boys

Dedication

In Memoriam
James Parker Pace
1947-2007

To Parker for thirty-seven totally wonderful years.
I am going to miss you every day for the rest of my life.
Thank you for believing in me, for supporting me and for encouraging
me to be the best.
I wish you could be here to share all this with me.
All my love, Miriam

Dedication

To the men and women of the United States Armed Forces:
Thank you for keeping our country safe
And thank you for allowing me to have a voice.
— Jackie

Acknowledgement

For Dee, Edwina and Angela
What a pleasure
Thank you Ladies
Miriam and Jackie

Going Commando

by
J.M. Jeffries

1

Georgina Landry still couldn't believe it. Mark Jones had left her. Alone. In the desert. At night. In a foreign country. In the middle of a war zone. In Manolo Blahniks.

She was screwed. How the hell was she going to find her way back to base camp?

The desert shone with pleasant silvery moonlight from the quarter moon. Stars twinkled overhead. If she hadn't been so annoyed, she would have enjoyed the clear night. Looking up she tried to spot the North Star, but couldn't find it.

The silky material of her cocktail dress ruffled around her legs. Sand began filling her crystal encrusted black satin sling backs. Clive, her personal assistant was right, she should have worn the pumps.

Georgina reached into her evening bag for her Zippo lighter, and lit it. The flickering flame showed her faint tracks from the jeep in the sand.

Although she had no idea how far she was from the base camp, where she'd done a USO show earlier, she figured she could follow the tire tracks and she would get back. Assuming camp wasn't too far. She tried to gauge how long Mark had driven, but couldn't really remember. It seemed a long time, but she hadn't been wearing a watch.

If she could survive the Hollywood jungle, four younger brothers and the set of her show BFFs, she could manage the Iraqi desert. She started walking. Though the night was brisk and cool, she was still angry enough with herself that she wasn't cold.

A bird hooted, the eerie sound echoing across the desert. Damn! Wildlife! The enemy she could avoid, but birds, bugs and snakes were not on her wish list. Maybe if she prayed hard enough she'd run into a Ritz Carlton. Hell, she'd settle for a Motel Six.

Go to your happy place and just keep walking.

☆☆☆

Lieutenant Dante Mayweather was twenty miles from his next check-in point when he spotted movement and a tiny flicker of light a quarter mile in front of him. He'd always had good night vision so he wasn't surprised. But he was confused. Whoever was strolling across the sand wore a dress and was doing a great impersonation of a woman. A tall curvy woman. He rubbed his eyes certain the desert was playing tricks on him. A damn good trick, too.

Maybe he'd been in the desert too long. He should have gone to the USO show instead of letting Vegas have the next couple nights off.

Silently he moved toward the figure, closing in on *her*. He took out his K-bar knife knowing he couldn't risk a shot. On a night like this sound traveled bringing who knows who investigating. And covert meant covert no matter what came up.

Ten feet away from the target, he heard mumbling. The voice was a woman's, she spoke English and she didn't sound happy. He considered the possibility of this being a trap. If so, it was best one he'd ever seen.

As he crept toward her, she stopped, lifted her foot and shook it. "Manolo fucking Blahniks," she muttered, the lighter flame casting a glow on medium brown skin and one lustrous brown eye.

Dante paused. He understood shoes, he had sisters.

He had to stop from laughing as he re-sheathed his knife and grabbed her. One hand went for the mouth and the other curled under the rib cage. For a second the soft skin and the fact she wasn't wearing a bra nearly stopped him. And the scent of orange blossoms and musk. God, her smell was intoxicating.

The lighter fell to the ground, sputtered and went out. She began struggling. He lifted her up and she elbowed him in his solar plexis and flung herself back, pushing his rifle into his chest. The ton of body armor he wore absorbed the impact, but he knew she'd bruise. Then one of the heels of those Manolo fucking Blahniks scraped down his instep, but was deflected by his boot. A fist sailed back, barely missing his nose, hitting him upside the head. Then she kicked back and her heel landed square in his nuts.

He half groaned, knowing the future of the Mayweather line might be in serious jeopardy. Pain radiated over his entire body and he almost let go of her. She squirmed and wriggled and kicked, and if he hadn't been in such pain he would have been impressed.

He whispered, "I'm American."

She froze and after a long moment he let her go. He wanted to fall on the ground in agony because his boy hurt, but didn't because he still had some dignity.

She whirled and threw her arms around his neck. "Thank you. Thank you," she cried.

Dante stilled. She was soft, so soft and for the first time since he stepped on to Iraqi soil, he cursed the need for body armor.

He put his hands on her waist and reluctantly tried to pull her off. She felt good, smelled good and was grateful. What a combination. "What the hell are you doing out here in the middle of the desert?"

She pointed back over her shoulder with her thumb. "That bastard left me." Her voice was a low vicious growl.

"What bastard?"

"Mark Jones. That low life cheating pond scum bastard."

She didn't need to say more. Mr Bad News Walking, as the soldiers who'd met him called him. The rumor around camp was that he did the USO tours just to score with women entertainers hoping one of them would help him get his big break in show business.

Not good. Shit was gonna hit the fan when the big brass discovered he'd endangered one of the entertainers. "What were you doing off the FOB?"

She peered at him, the moon reflected in her large, shimmering eyes. "What's an FOB?"

"Forward Operating Base."

Her voluptuous body shook. "I thought I was consoling a broken-hearted man."

He swallowed a chuckle, "In the *middle* of a war zone?"

Pushing a curl from her eyes, she growled. "He was crying because his wife is cheating on him and he was feeling—" her voice rose in indignation.

"Stop!" he commanded. "Take a breath and stop talking so loud." He glanced around. Even though the area was held by American troops and was relatively safe, he couldn't take chances. Snipers could be anywhere and he didn't want to draw their attention by loud noise.

The moonlight bathed everything in a shimmering silver, just enough so that he could see her face and realize she was just plain beautiful. No wonder Mark Jones had gone after her. The bastard had good taste, but lousy judgment.

She took a deep breath muttering softly, "Inhale a cleansing breath, exhale toxic waste." She paused for a second, repeated her mantra and said in a hushed tone, "I'm all better now."

She turned her full face to him and he recognized her. Georgina Landry from the TV show, BFFs. She was the rich mean one always holding a drink and looking to score with every man on the show. She was the funniest character on the show. He always thought she was hot. Great rack, an ass a man could hold on to, and juicy lips promising all kinds of fun. This was a page for his diary. "Ms. Landry?"

Her eyes widened in surprise. "You know who I am?"

"Yes Ma'am." *You are my living breathing fantasy.* Just the thought made his knees go weak.

Relief flashed across her face. She glanced around the desert. "What happens now?"

Funny, the pampered TV star sounded game to go. "Getting you back to the FOB is my priority."

Georgina turned around a couple of times. "Any idea how far away we are?" She kept her tone hushed.

He pointed east. "About fifteen miles that way."

Her eyes narrowed and she growled softly. "If I didn't want to beat the crap out of Mark Jones so bad, I'll tell you to shoot me now."

He liked a woman with a sense of humor. Humor was a must in the field.

"Now what fun would that be?"

She smiled. "Normally, I'm a role with the punches kind of girl, but today I feel like I went twelve rounds with Tyson in his heyday."

She didn't seem like the type to do anything other than shop, sip cocktails at stylish clubs and choose polish for her fingernails. "You know about boxing?"

She shrugged. "Brothers."

That explained a lot. Especially the way she'd fought with him. He still felt a burning ache in his groin. "We'd best get going. We have a long a walk ahead. Give me your shoes."

She stared at him for a second as if she processing his words. "But I'll be bare foot, I didn't wear panty hose."

He bit off a groan. Knowing she was pretty much naked under that dress sent hormones flooding through his blood.

This was the kind of stuff men read about in Penthouse magazine. Not that he read the magazine. His buddies did and discussed every page in minute detail.

He felt a tightening of muscles down below, which if he wasn't in the middle of the desert with a walking wet dream, wouldn't be a bad thing. But since she nailed him in the dick pretty hard he was glad to know everything was still in working order. "I'm going to make it easier for you to walk."

She handed him her right shoe. "How are you going to do that?"

He took the front of the shoe in one hand and the heel in another and broke the heel off.

She moaned. "But...but...they're Manolos."

"Ma'am, you can't walk round the desert in high heels."

She straightened, one hand on her hip. "Do I look like I'm a 'ma'am' kind of woman?"

No way, no how, but he'd been taught to be polite. "Not really."

One finger went up into the air. "Don't call me ma'am again."

He'd been told. He handed her the shoe. "Okay. May I have your other shoe?"

She took her shoe from him and slid her foot into it. "Thank you."

For a second he was puzzled. "For what?"

She gave him a heart-stopping smile. "For asking, instead of demanding."

"No problem."

She handed him the left shoe and covered her eyes. "Make it quick."

He snapped the heel off.

She whimpered and peered at him through the space between her fingers. "This is about survival right?"

"Yeah."

She bit her bottom lip. "I will endure."

He was glad to hear that, because he wasn't sure he would.

Her hands fell away from her face. She took the shoe and slipped it on her foot. "So what's the plan?"

The fifteen miles between here and the FOB was heavily patrolled and they had a good chance of running into one. If he could keep her at a brisk enough pace, the journey wouldn't take all night, depending on what kind of shape she was in. Though he had to admit, the shape she had already was pretty hot.

And if things didn't work out the way he planned, he had enough water and rations for both of them for probably two days. She didn't look like an anorexic actress who didn't eat. She had some tasty meat on her bones. Make that a day and a half.

He shrugged out of his pack off, opened it and took out two spare pairs of socks. He handed them to her. "Put these over your shoes."

"Okay. Why?"

He caught his breath as she bent over to pull a sock over one raised foot, the dress split and he witnessed the eighth wonder of the world—Georgina Landry's cleavage. For a second he couldn't catch his breath enough to answer her. God bless America. Now that was what he was fighting for. He took a deep breath and said, "To make walking a little easier on your feet."

She glanced up. "Are you okay? You're hyperventilating?"

"I'm fine."

"If you need time to catch your breath…" She finished her make-shift boots. She stood, her breasts thrust out like beacons as she stamped her feet more securely into the socks. "Or if you need to rest, I understand."

Her delicate scent meandered over him and his libido kicked up another notch. "We need to get moving ASAP." He started urging her forward. His night patrol hadn't shown any enemy activity, he was not a man who took chances. He urged her forward.

She took a few steps and then stopped to look back at him. "But I don't want you fainting on me."

As if she was going to save his ass. "Thanks for your concern. I'm fine."

He handed her his combat jacket. "Put this on."

"But you'll be cold." Concern echoed through her voice.

That number she wore looked great on the red carpet, but it wasn't going to survive the desert. "I'll be fine." Besides the heat she generated was enough to keep him toasty in the Arctic Circle in January wearing nothing but his skivvies.

She slipped on his jacket. It hung down to her thighs.

He urged her forward again when she suddenly stopped. "Can I have a gun?"

"No."

She balanced her hands on her hips. "Why not?"

"Have you ever fired a weapon?"

"I played a gun toting gangster on an episode of *Cop Time*. Point and shoot. What's so hard about that?"

He had visions of her shooting herself or him. "Really?"

"It was the first acting job I landed after I moved to Hollywood."

"And that's going to help you how?"

She trained her big, velvety eyes on him. "I need a gun."

Damn, she did a great Bambi impression. His head started to throb and he was thinking about shooting himself. "Why?"

She said, "Because, I'm one with the vagina."

2

HE RUBBED HIS temple. Did she just say what he thought she said? She used the V word.

"If I had known I was going to be stuck in the Iraqi desert, I would have left it home in my safe. But silly me," she said as she hit her forehead with the palm of her hand. "I packed it right up along with my passport, hiking boots, and digital camera. If we run into the enemy they are just going to kill you. But they're going to want to party with me, if you know what I mean. If I wasn't going to let Mark 'I'll-help-your-career-if-you-gave-me-a-taste,' Jones, I'm not going to let anyone else inside either." She took a deep breath and eyed him soulfully. "Except maybe you, because you're saving my life and a muffin basket with assorted goodies just doesn't say thank you the right kind of way."

His mouth fell open and couldn't quite get the hope out of his voice. "Are you serious?"

Shock spread over her face. Damn, now she was going to back pedal. The TV star giveth and taketh away.

Georgina rubbed her temples. "I can't believe I just said that. When I'm nervous I tend to be a bit of a potty mouth. I'm sorry."

Dante touched her shoulder. "I'm really flattered." Yeah that sounded good, like he really knew she wasn't serious. He urged her to start walking again. They had too far to go to be constantly stopped to chat.

Without missing a beat, she said, "So can I have a gun?" She batted her eyelashes at him.

Her voice was so persuasive he reached for his side arm, but stopped himself just before he grabbed the butt. He counted to five remembering who she was. "Let's just think positively that we're going to make it back to the FOB without incident." Because God knows that's what he was praying for.

"Is that all you're going to do?" she demanded, "Send good vibes out to the cosmos, because it sounds like a lame-ass plan to me. I was hoping for a little more action."

He liked her fighting spirit, but he still wasn't handing over a weapon. "No gun."

She stopped, turned around and faced him. Her shoulders went back and her hand went to her hip and that delectable finger went up. "Fine, but if some serious shit goes down, I'm going be really mad at you if anyone gets near my cha cha."

Dante forced himself not to laugh, because that would have been wrong. "I'll protect your cha cha with my last breath," he said as sincerely as possible. No one was getting near that cha cha except him, because he didn't want a muffin basket for saving her ass. A man had to have a dream.

"You said cha cha with a straight face." She laughed.

"I use those words all the time."

"You're funny."

Stopping himself from rolling his eyes, he shook his head. Two weeks. He had only had two weeks left before he was outta here and back to the States. "No, the situation is funny."

"No, it's not!" She glanced around the empty desert.

"It could have been worse."

Georgina sighed. "I'm still hoping Ashton Kustsher is going to jump from behind a rock any second now and tell me I'm being *Punk'd*. Or maybe I'm having a bad dream because I ate one too many Dove bars. Or I'm at one of those parties and someone slipped something in my drink."

"I'm sorry to say that show's off the air. There's not a Dove Bar to be had, and no one's had a cocktail party in this neck of the woods for years."

"You watched that show?" She sounded impressed.

"Yes, Ms. Landry?"

She waved her hand. "Just call me Georgina. We're going to be stuck together for a while we don't have to be so formal."

That was nice of her except for that part about being stuck together. "If you insist."

She stopped walking. "All this time we've been chatting and I don't know your name."

But he knew she'd brought her vagina with her. That made them even in his mind. "Mayweather."

"Is that your first name?"

"Dante."

"How do you do?" She stuck out her hand. "Dante Mayweather."

"I'm doin' alright, Georgina Landry." He reached out and took her hand. Dear God, her skin was soft. He wanted to keep holding her hand until the peace treaty was signed. His stomach was all in knots and he could barely grasp his next thought.

"An officer right?"

"Lieutenant." Now that surprised him. "How did you know?"

She gave a low, hushed chuckle and started walking again.

He really liked her laugh. She did it like she meant it and wasn't being polite.

"My brother Jeff is stationed in Afghanistan and my brother Vince is stationed in Kuwait. He's a doctor. You just have that 'tude about you, but not in a bad way."

He released her hand. "So coming here was more than just getting some good P.R." Trailing next to her, he thought about all the Hollywood people who came to entertain the troops. Privately, he thought they were just getting some good press.

"I think the men and women in the Armed Forces do a hell of tough job. Letting them take photos and signing autographs is the least I could do. That's why I got my glam on, I wanted to do my Marilyn Monroe impersonation. And until tonight, I was having a really good time. And I did get to see both of my brothers. So that was great."

Boy was she a talker, but at least she was honest. He liked that about her. "The troops appreciate it." Too bad there wasn't more light so he could get the full effect of her 'glam'. Because as wonderful as his laptop might be, that tiny screen wasn't enough to contain all this woman.

Her mega-watt smile could have been picked up on satellite. "You're welcome, Lieutenant. Glad to do my part."

They walked in silence for a while.

She stuck her hands in the pocket. "Are you going to get in trouble for helping me?"

"I'm gonna go with 'no' on that one." Not that anyone was going to slap a medal on him. Most likely Mark Jones would be kicked out of the country with a no return ticket for endangering someone he was supposed to keep safe.

She snorted, which sounded odd coming from such a beautiful woman.

"Well I'm in big trouble. God, I could kick myself for being so gullible. Normally I can tell the bad news guys the second I see them."

Dante had wanted ask about the details of how she got out, but figured it was a sore subject. "He does have a reputation." And a shitload of connections that until now had given some immunity. Dante figured that was over, though he doubted Mark would suffer too much. Mark was the kind of weasel who always landed on his feet.

"I'm wondering," she mused, "If I castrate him, could I claim extreme duress and just get off with community service. It's not like I was driving under the influence."

He winced. "Not a good thing to get on your bad side."

She slipped and when he tried to help her right herself, she brushed him off. "I'm considered one of the nicest actresses in Hollywood, according to *People* magazine. I just play a bitch, but for Jones I'd be happy to let people see who I really am. Monica Wentworth Bryce, that's the name of my character on *BFFs*, would have him castrated and then make his balls into a pâté."

Ouch! "And you're good at it. Playing a bitch I mean." What else could he say after that remark? Pretty and lethal. His kind of woman.

Georgina held up two fingers. "Two Emmy nominations and a Golden Globe win. I love the role."

"I think you should win." And he meant that. She was funny and while she was on the screen, she stole everyone's thunder. Yeah he liked watching her and not because she was drop dead beautiful.

She laughed. "So you watch the show?"

"A lot of guys think Destiny Knight is hot." Plus half the camp had her sex video on their laptops. He'd seen it, but had to admit watching rain fall was more interesting.

"Thin is in." She turned to him. "Did you and your buddies download the sex video?"

Oh so busted. He couldn't admit to seeing it. He didn't want to seem kind of disrespectful to Georgina in a weird sort of way. And the last thing he wanted to do was disrespect her, not because she was a lady, but he figured she'd give him a run for his money in a fight. "You're thin and she's boney."

Her head shook. "Thank you, but in Hollywood, I'm a fattie."

She had to be about five feet ten and looked to weigh around a hundred and forty pounds give or take. He didn't have a problem with her body at all. In fact she hit him in all the right places. "In my neck of the woods you're a woman, she's a boy with an incredibly big head."

She snorted again. "You noticed that?"

How could someone not notice her big head, it just wasn't natural. "It's so big. Is it all her ego? Or has her brain swelled up, or something?"

"One could only hope," Georgina said. "I'm waiting for her head to fall off and roll across the sound stage."

There were some issues there. Couldn't be envy. In his opinion Georgina had nothing to be jealous of. With her pin-up body and cover model face, she was damn near the perfect woman. And that snide sense of humor didn't hurt either. He'd bet his last dollar she was smart too. "Not a lot of love for the skinny girl?"

"Did I sound mean?" Georgina snorted again. "I didn't mean to." She paused. "Really." Then another pause. "Did I sound convincing?"

He held his two fingers close together. "No, but I'm not going to hold it against you." He understood. He had men in his unit that if he ever met them on street, he'd run them over and back up a time or seven. When they worked together they were a unit but once in the real world again, he wouldn't give them the time of day.

"I like Destiny just fine."

Now she was trying to bullshit him with some lame ass lie. "You're lying."

"If I didn't have to work with her five days a week and sometimes on Saturdays. That affects my opinion too."

Okay, he wasn't much into gossip, but keeping Georgina talking not only ate up the time, but kept her moving more quickly. They'd covered nearly half a mile in fifteen minutes. Keeping her calm would go a long way toward keeping her moving. "Tell me all your dirty Hollywood secrets."

A strand of hair fell over her eyes and she pushed it back. "I can't."

"Who am I going to tell out here in the middle of nowhere?"

"You never know."

"Of course," he continued, "if I get caught by the enemy I might let it slip, only because they're pulling on my right pinkie toe with hot pair of pliers. Anyone else, I'm not going to tell anything, because you are thinking about castrating Jones and frankly, I think you could do it and not even chip a fingernail or break a sweat." Now he was beginning to sound long winded like her.

"Look there is a fifty thousand bounty on anyone who tells dirt about what happens on the set."

A faint grinding sound reached his ears. He grabbed her upper arm pulling her to a stop, his fingers over her lips to keep her quiet.

"Stay here," he whispered. He removed his hand from her mouth. With her full lips pressed up against his hand, his boy had jumped to attention. A thought of what she could do with that mouth just wandered through his head like a rushing river.

He pulled on his night goggles and proceeded to shimmy up a little hill to take a look around. He scanned every little hill, every shadow. The desert looked flat, but he knew it was filled with gullies and washes that could hide an army. He waited for the sound to repeat, but after five long, agonizing minutes it didn't.

He turned over and slid down the hill on his back. Georgina sat on a boulder, her arms wrapped around herself. He took a second to admire her. This woman was playing havoc with his sense like no one's business. He was in serious lust with a TV star, as dumb as that sounded.

"Are we okay?" she whispered as he approached.

"Yeah, I think so. Nothing moving, but a few night birds."

Grabbing his hand, she started walking, pulling him along. "I think we should move a little faster."

She took off at a fast pace and he jumped to keep up. When she moved, she moved.

He eased his rifle into a more comfortable position. Despite the distraction of this heavenly woman, he couldn't afford not to be vigilant. Her safety was in his hands.

"I swore to protect your cha cha," he said. "I think you can trust me to keep your secrets." She made him nervous and he couldn't remember the last time a woman made him this nervous. One would think he was trying to get some play from her. As if a woman like her would ever be in his league.

She was a beautiful, successful woman and didn't need a man for anything but decoration. If she did need one, she'd pick some super-star stud with gym perfect muscles and white teeth and a bank roll to buy her those damn shoes. Not a regular guy who was happy with a lukewarm shower and MRE's to eat.

She was the kind of woman a man put on a pedestal and not just to look up her dress. She was a star made to shine in the night sky and the best he could hope for was to be a rock he hoped she didn't trip over.

Being around her made him feel thirteen years old again and asking Tanya Benson to the Spring Fling. He'd screwed that up to. Jesus this was embarrassing.

3

GEORGINA MULLED over in her mind what she could say to Dante Mayweather. Dare she spill those deep dark secrets of life on the *BFFs* set? She figured he kept her talking so she wouldn't freak out, which was okay with her, because she was about five seconds from having a meltdown. If she did have said meltdown, she worried he'd leave her. If someone she wanted to help went into bitch mode she'd leave them—no problem. And wouldn't even be ashamed.

And he was so nice. And strong! She could feel it in the grip of his hand and the solid feel of his body when he exuded a sense of safety. Even in the moonlight, she could see his dark brown skin and beautiful mouth with dreamy chocolate brown eyes. Lord have mercy, he was tall, too. At least six foot three. In other words he was a casting agent's wet dream of soldier. This was like being in a movie. She was the damsel in distress and he was her knight in sandy brown camouflage.

She was getting carried away with the fantasy. She needed something to distract her so she didn't have to think about the big nasty pickle she'd gotten herself into. Or the repercussions arising from said pickle. She was going to have to give her publicist a raise for this. And let's face it, if this guy wanted to do anything to her and her cha cha, he'd have done so by now and *hidden* the body. No one would ever know he'd run into her and Georgina Landry would disappear forever.

Speaking of which, what would Mark Jones say when she didn't return to base camp. How would he weasel out of an explanation. Just claim ignorance. He wasn't going to tell anyone he'd kicked her out of the jeep and left her to fend for herself and if she didn't come back he'd be free and clear.

Her mind whirled back to the show. What would they do without her? All the secrets and gossip about Georgina would be leaked to the world and Destiny would revel in her exposure. Secrets upon secrets. She glanced at Dante. After a half hour she was pretty sure Dante Mayweather would take them to the grave. She just knew he was the kind of guy a person could trust with their life. "Swear on your honor as an officer and a gentleman." She'd seen *An Officer and a Gentleman* a few too many times.

He lifted his big strong hand. "I swear."

And it's not like she wasn't still fuming over contract negotiations. "First of all Destiny is bulimic. How anyone could stand to kiss her with that breath is beyond me. There are not enough mints on the planet to take care of her rank stank. I always put some scented cream under my nose when we have to do a scene together."

"Nothing secret about that. Anyone can tell just by looking at her she's unhealthy. I want the nasty dirt."

As did everyone else. "In my business we call that a teaser. I'm just warming you up for the fun stuff."

He inhaled. "Warm up faster."

If they could stand still for a moment, she'd put her hand on her hip, put her finger in the air and roll her eyes, but they had to keep moving. She clutched his jacket close to her. The night had gotten even more chilly and despite the two pairs of socks on, her feet were cold. "We just signed new contracts and do you know what she had put into all of our contracts?" With each step, her feet sank into the sand and grit had started to collect between her toes.

"No, but I'm all ears."

Where is a tabloid reporter when you need one. If she thought she could get away with it, she blab to everyone. "First of all, no on the show can make the same amount of money as her."

"Did they hose you?"

She chuckled. "Nope, just a gentle sprinkle."

"How much is a sprinkle?"

"We all make five cents less. Can you believe that shit?" She held up her hand and wriggled her fingers. "Five freakin' cents." She had dropped a little behind and found herself staring at his back. He thought she had a rockin' body. But he was pretty good in the shape department himself. "As if the show would fold without her."

"She does get top billing." He glanced back at her and she hurried to keep up.

You're losing points with me, Dante Mayweather, she thought. "Destiny can't act her way out of a wet paper bag with three sides down."

"Are you jealous?"

His low sexy voice swirled all around her. Damn right, she was. She busted her butt and that little bag of bones was treated like a queen. "I might have an envy issue or two, but that doesn't mean it's not the truth."

"As long as we're being honest. There's more isn't there."

Well since they were being honest and she could deny everything, and she lied well when she needed to. "Did they give you a therapist patch at boot camp, too?"

"Nope, I—"

"Are you going to torture me next?"

"Ms. Landry—"

"I told you to call me Georgina. Tonight you are my BFF." But she'd left the best part for last. "The kicker, done especially for me, is that I can't lose more than five pounds unless it is a due to a health problem, but I can gain as much weight as I want to."

"Sounds like she's jealous of you."

Not really. Destiny thought her size negative two self was the hottest thing on the planet. If she was jealous it would be over her Emmy nominations. The Golden Globe win put Destiny on a bender for weeks. It was fabulous. Good ole Destiny could wilt her waist to nothing, but until she practiced her craft she was going to be nothing more than a pretty face parroting lines. "Threatened is a better word. Plus, she's mad at me."

"Who could be mad at you?"

Let me get you a list, she thought. She'd been navigating the Hollywood jungle for years which made her wonder why she'd been so easily tricked by Mark Jones. Ordinarily, Georgina Landry wasn't a gullible person. "I have small production company. We've done a few things that garnered critical and commercial success. Destiny wants to be in one of my films, but I refuse to ask her. Though she does a lot of hinting." Call me a bitch. She had to work with Destiny on the show and that was enough.

"Why would she care."

"I've gotten most of my co-stars and a lot of the crew to do the projects."

"Why not her?"

She smells bad, can't act and is generally a bitch. "She's a one-trick pony. When this show is over she's going to be a has-been."

"And you're not?"

She deserved that question. And since he was the only thing standing between her and certain death, she'd answer it. "It's a crap shoot, but I'm building myself a nice future with my film company and I've been asked to do some stage work."

"You're a busy woman."

She liked that he sounded impressed. She'd worked hard to get where she is. "Keeps me out of trouble."

"Are you going to do Broadway?"

"Don't you think I'd be a great Katherine in *The Taming of the Shrew*?"

His eyebrows rose. "But you're…"

Georgina lifted her eyebrow although she figured he couldn't see it. "What? Too tall for the role?"

He laughed. "That's not what I was going to say."

She knew exactly what he meant. What a lot of people meant. "Denzel Washington played Don Pedro of Aragon in *Much Ado About Nothing*." He proved them wrong and so would she. After she left Iraq, she was going to New York for an audition. Assuming she made it back alive and in one piece. "I can play Katherine?"

"I think you'd be a great shrew."

Was that a subtle jab at her? He was brave. The man had character. Few people had the stones to get mouthy with her. "Thanks, I think."

"You're welcome."

The conversation lulled after that. She wanted to stop and take a break. She was having a potty emergency and damn she was starving. At this rate, she'd drop five pounds and more before she got stateside, then she'd be out of a job. She just wanted to sit down and cry, but didn't want to slow him down or worse.

☆☆☆

Dante figured they'd been walking about four hours. Georgina had lapsed into silence after her huge exposé. Though she kept the pace up, he could tell she was tiring. "You doing okay?"

"I'm fine."

She didn't sound as if she was lying. "We can take a break if you need to."

"How far do you think we've gone?"

"About seven, maybe eight miles. Do you want to rest? We're doing good on time."

She picked up the pace a bit. "I'll get plenty of rest on the plane."

He grabbed her arm and stopped her. "I don't want you to collapse on me."

She shook her head. "No, I'm fine I power walk about five miles every day. I have to."

"To look good for the camera." Now why did he ask her that question? He'd just about accused her of being vain.

"I walk for my babies."

"You have kids?"

"Dogs."

Now that surprised him. He'd pegged her for a cat person, but then again maybe like a lot of actresses, she had one of those little dogs she could put in a designer purse and walk down the red carpet with it slung over her arm. "You don't seem like a dog type."

"I'm normally not, but a couple of years ago I was doing this charity thing for the Hollywood animal shelter and there they were. Sitting in a cage staring at me with those big take-me-home-and-love-me or I'll-be-put-down brown eyes and I couldn't say no." She sighed. "Don't tell anyone, but I'm a sucker that way."

"What kind of dogs are they?"

She shrugged her shoulders. "I had them tested. They're all over the place. A Pit Bull, Akita, Rottweiler mix. They are big as mountains and pretty much eat me out of house and home."

The picture in his head of her being lead down the street with dogs the size of Shetland ponies must make a good photo op. "I'll get you home to them."

"I know you will."

God, please don't let me be talking shit here. He heard the tremble in her voice. She was frightened no matter how she tried to play it off. "Keep thinking good thoughts."

☆☆☆

Who knew the desert could be so bumpy. Georgina had already stubbed her toe a dozen times and half the sand in the whole desert was stuck in her socks. She stumbled and Dante caught her and set her back on her feet. He was strong and every time he touched her a hot thrilling pulse of pure electricity radiated through her.

She pretended she was on a date and having fun with Dante Mayweather. He radiated hotness. Why weren't the guys in Hollywood like him? He was real and respectful. He wouldn't ask her to dress up like a nun and do the nasty with him ten minutes into the first date.

Just because a guy was the latest action hero, he thought he could get freaking on a girl, before he knew her. Sliding a glance over at Dante, she figured him for the Catholic School thing. She would definitely consider the plaid skirt and patent leather Mary Janes for him. Or she'd play POW interrogation with him. Hmmm, these are not the thoughts she should be having alone in the desert with Commando Man. Because there was nothing they could do about it. But mostly even though he didn't act like it, he probably thought she was the world's biggest pain in the butt.

Georgina made a promise to herself; she was never going to be ungrateful for anything ever again in her life. She was a pampered over-paid actress and this guy put his life on the line every minute of every day and here she was whining like a cry baby. She wasn't dead and she wasn't starving. She could work with that.

"You're quiet."

"I'm just thinking I really did get lucky tonight." She patted him on the back. "I got you. I could have ended up with Gomer Pyle or worse yet in the hands of the enemy. Trust me I'm going with lucky. Of course, I'm thinking lucky is not the word I'd be using to describe your situation. I know you think you're not going to get in trouble, but they are going to be mad that you didn't follow the Army game plan. I'm sure rescuing me wasn't one of your training scenarios. Don't you have to go and do a commando raid or go blow something up?"

"You have a very active imagination."

"Duh, actress." And tonight her imagination was working overtime. Between being stuck in the desert and waiting for trouble to find her again, she was kinda crushin' on Dante.

"I'm doing the world a favor rescuing you. I'll be fine."

He sounded so confident; she wanted to be lulled into believing him. "Okay if you say so."

His soft laugh swept over her. "You know what, you're okay, Georgina Landry."

She was thrilled he liked her. She couldn't remember the last time someone had liked her just for herself? "Thanks, you're not so bad yourself."

"Good to hear."

"How much longer are you going to be in Iraq?"

In a wry tone, he said, "Two weeks, three days, eleven hours and about ten minutes, but I'm not counting."

She smiled. "So you like Iraq."

"With all my heart."

What she really wanted to do was to invite him to stay with her for a few weeks and play house. Which kind of surprised her. Normally she took a long time to warm up to a guy, but Dante Mayweather really put her at ease while at the same time he sparked her interest. Deep down, she was really attracted to him. He was calm, cool, collected and seemed to have enough ego to make him interesting, but not enough to make her want to hit him over the head with a hammer. "What are you going to do when you get back to where ever you came from?"

"I'm from Detroit. I don't know yet what I'm going to do when I get out. My cousin is on the Detroit PD and said he'd put in a good word for me. I also have a friend who does high end security. Though I do think I'm going to be a bum for awhile."

A movie trailer started playing in her head starring the beautiful actress and the sexy bodyguard. Move over Whitney and Kevin, I'm re-writing your movie. "If you're interested in bodyguard work, I'll be your walking, talking résumé." Very smooth, Georgina, are you going to pack his underwear, too. He'd stay at your house and be your love slave.

"A job and a muffin basket," he said with a soft chuckle. "I have hit the jackpot."

Georgina couldn't help insisting, "You should think about getting into standup comedy. You'd be a hit."

They had come to a ravine that slowly descended between two sandy hills. He stopped and looked down the shadowed path. Then started walking again going around rather than between the two hills. "I'll leave the performing to you. I don't like being the center of attention."

"You're a good looking man, all you'd have to do is stand still and be all alpha male. Women will go crazy over you and men will want to be you." Not that she wanted to share him.

"I don't think that's for me. Why did you choose acting?"

As if she didn't get this question a billion times. "I'm lousy at pretty much anything else."

"Come on you're a smart woman. You could have done anything you wanted to."

Dust balls had better SAT scores than she'd managed. "I love being the center of attention." That was the press junket answer the real one was too personal. Too telling about who she was.

"Is that all?"

Damn he was digging deep as if he wanted to know the real her. "Wasn't the egotistical answer enough for you?"

"You are deeper than that."

"Okay, Mr. Look-Below-The-Surface, I'm going to tell you. I'm shallow, vain and egotistical."

"You are a good actress, I almost believe you."

Most men weren't as interested in who she was as they were in what she was. She could handle that. It was complicated, but letting someone know who you were was like giving them the combination to the family safe. In her business that wasn't done, especially if a person wanted to keep a part of herself private. "Once during an acting class, I convinced Robert De Niro I was an Icelandic cucumber."

"That makes you a great actress, but you're not shallow."

He was good at not letting her dodge the question. He could be a journalist on *Sixty Minutes*. "Are you always this nice?"

"I try to be."

"Makes it easier to get laid?" Good answer, Georgina. Talking about sex wasn't personal and it always distracted people from anything important.

"Your mind is in the gutter."

He held out a hand and helped her over a particularly rocky area. His skin was hot and she could hear the sharp intake of his breath as she bumped against him.

And she was so ashamed. "I used to tell my mom if she wanted me to be a lady, she shouldn't have had so many sons."

"You're avoiding my question with chit chat."

She would have loved to see his face when he said that. How he seemed to maintain his manliness was a miracle to her. "I never heard a big strong guy like you say chit chat before."

"Did I tell you I was trained in interrogation tactics?"

And was that supposed to scare her? "Are you going slap me around?"

"I'll torture your shoes some more."

She shuddered, he'd found her weak spot. She would tell him anything he needed to know. "That's low. My shoes are innocent."

"Then answer the question."

"I forgot what it was." She kept her voice light and friendly, because he was probing beyond her comfort zone.

4

THIS WOMAN could talk circles around anyone. He kind of liked that about her. She made him work for every little answer. "Why acting when there are about five billions jobs that are much easier?"

She didn't answer right away. They walked a few yards more before she finally said, "When I'm acting it's like being five years old again running around my mom's living room with the towel tucked in the back of my pajamas. Now, I do that every day and get paid."

He imagined her as a little girl running around after her brothers, trying to be as bad they were. "What you're saying is that you never grew up."

"Part of me never will, but for an actress, I'm pretty stable."

"Compared to whom?" he asked curiously. Considering how unstable the whole Hollywood scene appeared to be, hearing her say she was stable was interesting. Maybe he'd get that bit of insight into what she guarded so carefully.

"A whole boat load of people I can name."

"But you won't." No big secrets about what was going on in the entertainment field, the paparazzi made sure of that.

"Well, not until after you save my cha cha."

He started to get excited again. What he wouldn't do to get a taste of her cha cha. If the guys knew he'd used her term, he'd be laughed out of his unit. "We do a lot of talking about your cha cha."

"Keeps coming up in the conversation."

She sounded so innocent, but below that smart-assed remark, he sensed her fear. The danger and the uncertainty was beginning to wear on her. Did he stop, or push her harder? "Is your cha cha really that special?"

She drew herself straight and proud. "I never used my cha cha to get a job, but I like to think she is special."

Everything about Georgina was special. She was the type of woman he'd introduce to his mom. "I'm not touching that one."

"So back at you. Tell me your life story."

"I'm not interesting." Especially, when everything about her was.

"We still have time to kill. And if you don't talk I will, and then you will think I'm your typical self absorbed actress."

Hell, he admired her. Hardly a complaint out of her despite the grueling trek, the cold and her broken shoes. "I would never think that about you."

"Sure you would."

"I was born in Detroit."

Georgina grinned at him. "A page turning beginning."

"Are you saying I'm boring?"

She snorted again. "That would be rude."

Dante stole a glance at her. The moon caressed her face and she was smiling. The silvery light added shiny highlights to her dark brown hair. He'd seen that smile on TV and it was just as dazzling in person as on the screen. "I grew up in Detroit well actually Grosse Point."

"Any brothers and sisters?"

"Three sisters. No brothers."

"No wonder you joined the military."

She was right, but he didn't want to admit it. He loved his sisters, but being the youngest child and only boy had been a challenge. "I'm a patriot."

"What do you parents do?"

"My father was a design engineer for Ford. Mom stayed home to keep her knuckle-headed children in line."

"She did a good job. You turned out okay."

He'd tell his mom that he had the Georgina Landry Seal of Approval for child-rearing. His mother had her doubts. "I did all right."

"Where did you go to school?"

"Annapolis."

"You're a navy man, what are you doing here?" She spread her arms to indicate the desert.

"I'm Delta Force."

"That's it?"

He didn't want her to get under his skin anymore than she wanted him to get under hers because he didn't like what was there and she wouldn't either. He was a killer, not the kind of nice man a woman could take home to her family. "I hit the high points."

"How old are you?"

The end of their journey was almost in sight. He figured another two hours and she'd be back where she belonged and he could get on with his patrol. "Twenty-seven. You?"

"I'm thirty but in Hollywood years that's about forty-five."

On TV, she looked much younger. "You make that sound like you're older than dirt."

"It's like dog years."

He couldn't help himself, he chuckled. "You don't look it."

"Black don't crack. Plus I'm not all skin and bones."

"Your skin and bones are great." And given a chance he would love to get up close and personal with them. He couldn't remember the last time he'd been this turned on by a woman. She interested his brain as much as his body. Sex with her would be more than a workout it would move the globe.

"I'm gonna hire you to be my body guard."

Dante would guard her body for free. "Can I kick the crap out of Mark Jones for you?"

"I'm going to do that myself. I just have to think about how I'm going to get away with it. He's married to the youngest daughter of Merritt Studios' head honcho and they have several of my projects under consideration."

"Delta Force, trained to be covert. I can kill him with a paper clip and some dental floss."

"Will it be slow and painful?"

"He'll scream like a little girl."

She sighed. "Sick and twisted. You are my hero."

Damn that was sexy. His gut tightened. "I aim to please."

"So why are you out here all by yourself? I'm assuming it's not because you got lost."

"I know exactly where I am."

"So do I. Iraq."

"We do solo patrols. Tracking enemy movements."

"Aren't you afraid of being out here all by your lonesome surrounded by the bad guys?"

As if he'd cop to being afraid. That's all she needed to know. "To admit anything less would be unmanly."

Sand crunched beneath their feet and the moon had gone down in the sky. A flicker of movement caught the corner of his eyes and he stiffened as a lizard darted out of the shadows and raced across the sand. He stopped and held up his hand. What had startled the lizard?

"Stay here," he ordered. She sat down on a small rock and he eased forward, rifled ready, toward the spot where the lizard had bolted from. He found nothing. Slowly he widened his search, but the area was clear.

When he returned, Georgina sat stiffly on the rock, her knees bent to her chest and her arms wrapped around them. The last bit of moonlight showed the fear lurking in her eyes.

"Let's get going," he said and held out his hand. She unbent and let him pull her to her feet.

"Is everything all right?" she asked in a hushed tone.

"Nothing out there."

She breathed a sigh of relief as she fell into step with him. "About that gun," she said.

"No guns."

"Damn," she said. "I'm not afraid."

He grinned. She never gave up. "You should be. We're not on a picnic here. Even I'm afraid." Afraid of the unexpected, afraid of the child bomber who looked so innocent he couldn't even pretend to think about killing a child. "Every minute of every day." Afraid of doing the wrong thing and sometimes the right thing.

Georgina didn't say anything for a long second. He hoped he didn't scare her finding out the man she'd placed her life in was just as anxious as she was.

"How do you live with that?"

No one had ever asked him before and he didn't have a ready answer. "There's a job that needs to be done and I just do it."

"How long have you been over here?"

"A year and a half." Being Delta Force meant longer times in the field. Sometimes he wished he'd turned down the offer and stayed with his ship. He much preferred water to land.

"How do you watch people you work with get shot at and die?"

Now that was one subject he wasn't going to touch. "Let's not talk about dying."

"Is it like bad luck or something?"

"We live with that thought every day we go out into the field. We just don't talk about it."

"Why not? Talking is therapeutic."

Who the hell was this woman? "You ask a lot of questions."

"I'm an actress. I have to get under people's skin to know how to be them. When am I ever going to get a chance this good again?"

"You said your brothers are in the military. Do you talk to them about what's going on here?"

"One's a doctor. He has some interesting stories, but he could never do what you do. And the other one is in military intelligence and he can't tell me anything. We call him Agent Orange. But you are the real deal. You get in the dirt and you do the real soldier job."

She sounded like she admired him. "Thanks."

"You're welcome."

They walked a few more minutes. "Wanna stop?"

"No. I'm not tired."

She didn't sound as if she was lying, but he knew she was exhausted. "You need a break. You aren't trained for this."

"The only thing I want right now is some Chicken McNuggets."

"I'm fresh out."

"It was more of a rhetorical need."

He knew that, but he wanted to keep the banter going. "If I could I'd get you some."

"I bet you would."

"With a smile on my face. If only…"

"You know if they put a Starbucks, a Wal-Mart, and a McDonalds right in the middle Bagdad there would be no war."

"What?"

"Shopping and eating. God knows they are two of my favorite things. Maybe not the route to inner peace, but it makes a hell of a reason not to fight."

The logic was a little out there, but she might be on to something. "I'm gonna give you that one. Because the Big Mac does put me in my happy place."

"Caramel Frappacino with extra caramel and extra whip, and I'm a happy girl."

"Georgina Landry, you are a unique woman."

She stopped walking and looked to the sky. She raised her arms up. "And that is why I ended up in the desert at night in a foreign country in the middle of war zone. Next life time I'm opting for normal."

"Don't."

"Don't what?"

That would just kill him. He liked her just the way she was. "Be normal."

"You're kidding?"

"This the best night I've had since I got here."

"Your life must be pretty boring, outside of the keeping yourself alive."

"In between bullets, yeah it is." He chuckled. "But you made it all worth it."

"I bet you say that to every wayward actress you rescue."

"I never said that to any woman."

"Of course you—"

He heard something. "Shhh."

5

HE PUSHED her down on the ground behind a jumble of rocks. A prickly bush scratched her leg as she lay down. The sand was gritty under her hands and didn't like to think all the places sand could get.

Had she done something wrong? She started to ask, but he put his hand over her mouth.

Georgina's instinct was to pull his hand away, but didn't. He would hardly manhandle her if something weren't getting ready to happen. Her heart raced and she closed her eyes tight.

Dante pulled her close to him and whispered, "Not a sound."

Then why was he talking? She began trembling. At any moment something on her body was going to be knocking together and then they'd be found and taken captive and then she'd be…Oh God she was getting light headed. Dante slipped his hand in hers and in an instant she settled down. This man wasn't going to let anything happen to her. She would be okay. He was her hero.

And damn did he smell good. Like a man. All man. Not pretty like one of those Hollywood boys. Which really amazed her, because he should smell bad. After all, he'd been in the desert for God knows how long. Was she really thinking about how he smelled? Here she was about three seconds from being the love toy of some terrorists and she was smelling him. And liking it.

Voices carried on the night wind. Arabic or Farsi or whatever the hell they spoke here.

God if *People* magazine could see her now flat on the ground, hiding behind a rock, ready to pee her thong because she was so scared, she'd finally have her cover.

Dante squeezed her hand.

He felt so strong and in control, which made her feel more like a ninny. Where was her inner Lara Croft? It had to be there somewhere. Well maybe if she'd have played an action adventure heroine she would know how to feel like one. She was going to have to put that on her list. Yeah things to do *if* you make it back home alive. No, think positive *when* you make it back home alive.

If only her palms would stop sweating. How could the enemy not smell her fear, or hear her heart pounding. Maybe because Dante was so cool and his coolness canceled out her fear. He was still as a stone as if he did this kind of stuff every day. Oh wait a minute he did. She closed her eyes and sent a silent prayer up to God for dropping her in this amazing man's capable hands. If she was alone, she had no doubt, she'd be dead or captured by now.

One of the men laughed as they passed Georgina and Dante's hiding place. They just walked by as if they were taking a stroll in the desert. She never had that kind of cool.

What if Mark Jones got caught? She wanted him to be punished, but not by the enemy. If even half the things she heard about them were true, no one deserved that. Besides she wanted the sole pleasure of punishing Mark herself. That jackass had left her out here when she wouldn't give up the good stuff. And if Mark Jones was captured, he'd tell all those lonely men she was out here alone with a big target on her back.

Georgina, you are obsessed with getting violated. What the hell is wrong with you? After living thirty relatively safe years, she figured she was due. Oh, that was crazy. *Just relax. Be calm. You will get through this. You have big strong Dante to protect you. He's a really hero, he will never let anything happen to you.* And strangely enough that made her feel good. As good as could be expected, while stranded out in the Iraqi desert during a war.

Dante lowered his hand from her mouth. "Relax," he said in a whisper. "We're not moving for a bit. I want them as far away as possible before we start again."

Hell no, she wanted to yell, but didn't. She had so much adrenalin pumping through her she could probably fly back to the FOB in about twenty minutes. Just point her in the right direction and she was off like a bullet. "Why?"

"These guys are probably tracking us."

She shuddered. "Can't we just take another direction? If we double back, we'll fool them right?" Why was she questioning him? He was the expert.

"They aren't dummies."

Why couldn't she get the stupid ones? "That's what I was afraid of."

"I'm no dummy either," he reassured her.

She leaned back into him. His chest was solid, broad and reassuring. She took deep breaths and waited, the minutes ticking by, the moon going lower in the sky. She wondered how long until dawn. When she thought she could safely speak again, she said in a low whisper. "I know I'm getting on your last nerve."

He squeezed her hand. "I've done hostage rescue, before. You're fairly easy to deal with."

She wasn't the pain in the ass she thought she was. God, she needed a cigarette, a martini and a burger—in that order. "Thanks. I needed to hear that. If I get you killed, I'll never forgive myself."

"Won't happen."

"How do you know?"

"I promised my mom, I wouldn't die in this country."

"Okay I'm reassured." This close she could see the shape of his mouth. He had a beautiful set of lips. Not just for a man but for a human being in general. If those full luscious lips were on screen, there wouldn't be a dry pair of panties in the house. Georgina leaned forward just to get a closer look at his mouth. And before she realized what she was doing she planted her mouth smack dab on his and began kissing him. His lips were soft and warm and he opened his mouth under hers and his tongue slipped inside her mouth and she thought she was going to die right then and there. Oh. My. God. This guy knew how to work it. A bolt of heat went down her body and her toes finally warmed up.

He tasted like mint.

Georgina started shaking and she felt his arms go around her and he pulled her body to his. Her breasts became mashed up against his body armor. This was so hot. She slid her hands to his face and felt the day's stubble on his cheeks. She didn't ever want this to end. She could kiss Dante until the world blew to hell.

Georgina knew this was crazy but she didn't care, she wanted him. This might be the wrong time and wrong place, and maybe it was the extreme circumstances she was under, she didn't know. She just knew that with every fiber of her being she wanted to make love to Dante.

He suddenly pulled away.

Georgina rolled back. The heat of embarrassment crept up her cheeks. "Oh my God! I'm so sorry. I didn't—"

He took a deep breath. "Listen I was right there with you."

"My timing sucks."

He smiled. "Yeah."

"I could have gotten us killed." She bit her bottom lip, still warm from his kiss. "I'm so sorry."

"I'm not." He stood up.

"Where are you going?"

"I'm going to walk this off."

He's leaving her? Panic welled up in her chest. "What?" She tried to stand, but fell on her butt. Sand grated on her bare legs. This was so humiliating.

"There are no cold showers around here."

"Are you going to leave me?"

"I'm going to see if our friends have moved far off enough for us to start moving again."

Relief flooded her for about two seconds. "I thought we were going to stay here?"

"Change of plan. Don't move and don't make a sound."

☆☆☆

Dante moved off into the night. Jesus Christ what the hell was he thinking? Never in his entire life had he done anything so stupid. He needed to get his mind back on his job and get Georgina Landry as far away from him as possible.

Though the moonlight was fading, he could still see the tracks scoring the sand. He trailed behind them for the next ten minutes.

Something hit him in the head. He spun around.

"Hey, Weatherman," came a hoarse whisper.

He let out a breath. This was defiantly not the enemy. "Crush."

A man stood from behind a low hill. He raised a hand as he approached. "How's it hanging?"

Dante stared his team member. "You won't believe my night."

Crush took a step closer to him. "Let me guess. You found a hottie named Georgina Landry wandering around in the desert."

Surprised, Dante stared at Crush. Shit the word was out. "How did you know?"

"Cause you are always the luckiest bastard."

Another man stood carefully and Dante recognized Vegas. "Vegas. What up?"

Vegas hitched a thumb over his shoulder. "Just taking care of the tangos on your ass."

He opened his mouth to reply just as an ear piercing scream pierced the night.

Georgina! He took off running.

6

GEORGINA KICKED the man in his stomach and promptly fell on her ass, her dress skidding up. Sand crept into her nether places. *As God as my witness*, she thought, *I'll never wear a thong again.*

At least the guy went down, which surprised her. She didn't think she'd kicked him that hard. She pushed herself to her feet and started to run.

"Thanks, Ms Landry," came a man's voice. A man who spoke English.

"You're American?" She forced back the sob that had risen in her throat.

"Yeah." He stood up then bent over and picked up his rifle. "Sorry I scared you."

She held out her hand to him. Squinting at him she could tell he was a white guy with an accent she couldn't place. "It's okay. I'm sorry I hurt you." What else could she say?

"Next time I have to rescue you I'll sing *Yankee Doddle Dandy* first."

Before she could answer, she heard the sound of running behind her and a second or two later three men raced around the boulder. One of them was Dante.

He stopped. "What the hell happened?"

She shook finger at the man she kicked. "He touched my hair."

"I said I'm sorry. She didn't need to throw some kickboxing moves on me."

Dante slapped him on the shoulder. "Freeze, you're from Alaska so you haven't dealt with a lot of sisters. You don't mess with the hair."

Dante knew the deal. She fluffed her flat dirty curls. "Thank you. My weave is Korean. It just doesn't get better than that."

Freeze held up one hand. "My bad."

Dante turned to her. "You know kickboxing?"

"It's a great workout. Three times a week. I'm out in an hour and half." She shrugged. "Who knew it would come in handy."

One of the men looked at Dante. "You really didn't need us did you, Weatherman."

Dante grinned. "Had everything covered, but I'm not mad at you."

Georgina let out a long breath. "So does this mean I'm officially rescued?"

Freeze checked his watch. "Yes Ma'am. We just radioed the helicopter and it's on the way. ETA—ten minutes."

There they go with the ma'am again. "How did you know I was missing?"

A round of laughter sounded from the men. "An incoming patrol found Mark Jones driving around the desert."

Mark Jones mentioned her? "Really?"

Freeze shook his head. "Yeah. He was crying like a baby, promising cash to anyone who found you."

Georgina felt her hackles rise. "Is he back at the base?"

Freeze looked up to the sky. "Oh yeah."

"Sweet."

A whoosing sound filled the air. "There's our ride."

Georgina took a long look at Dante. Part her relished the challenge of being out here with him. They had some unfinished business to attend to. Strangely enough that made her sad. Her great big adventure was coming to an end. And it didn't have the happy ending she wanted.

☆☆☆

Dante looked up at the imposing façade of the former president's palace. Old Saddam knew how to live. He walked through the doors and hurried up the stairs. He knew Georgina's room was on the third floor.

He'd spent the last two days typing reports, talking to his superiors and generally trying to stay out of the way of the shit hitting the walls. No one on a USA tour had ever been put in harm's way before and for one man to upset the whole balance of the USO programs was grounds for expulsion. Mark Jones, no matter who his political contacts and entertainment ties were, he was never coming back to Iraq.

Dante walked into the palace. Though it was a shadow of its former glory, the entryway was still opulent enough to awe him with its gold encrusted columns, tiled walls and intricate inlay floor. If he were smart, he'd head back to the field and forget Georgina Landry, but Dante wasn't long on smarts at the moment. He had to see her. He wanted to see her. Just one more time. He told himself he just wanted to make sure she was okay and not feeling any after effects of her night in the desert. Like any compassionate human being would do. He wanted to see if she was surviving her round the clock exposure on *TMZ.com* after she beat the living crap out of Mark Jones and told the entire world he was a lying cheating scumbag coward. Her words, not his. Her adventures replaced Britney as the lead story of the week.

He stopped at the ornately carved door of her room and started to knocked, but stopped. Did she really want to be reminded of her desert time?

Oh what the hell. He wanted to say goodbye. He knocked. The door opened and a tall thin black man barely stopped from running into him.

"Hello?"

Who the hell was this guy? Dante swallowed the golf ball sized lump in his throat. "May I speak to Ms. Landry?"

The man put his arm up to block his entry. "She's not—"

"It's okay, Clive," Georgina said. "You can let him in. He's a good guy." Her voice washed over him.

Clive pointed a finger at him. "You're Commando Man?"

Dante smiled. "That would be me."

Clive threw his arms around him. "Thank you for saving her." He sniffled. "You're my hero."

"Ah thanks." Was all Dante could say.

Georgina stood in the center of the elegantly furnished room. Though Saddam Hussein's castle had taken a hit in the decorating department and wasn't quite as opulent as it had been before the war, it was still beautiful. The elaborate canopy bed against one wall was original, but the hangings were gone and the massive Oriental carpets that had graced the marble floor were now in some other person's home. The crystal lamps that had adorned the gold side tables had been replaced with less expensive replicas. Fortunately the elaborate tile work on the walls was still in good shape.

"Clive, honey," Georgina said, "let Lieutenant Mayweather breathe." The half smile on her face seemed to be only for Dante.

The man let him go, stepped back, and looked like he was going to cry.

Georgina rubbed her forehead. "Why don't you go down to the mess and have some lunch."

"But—"

"Honey, I'll be fine."

Clive huffed. "All right."

He pushed passed Dante and out into the hall.

"You have to forgive Clive," Georgina said. "He's my personal assistant and he bought me those shoes you killed. He's still a little emotional."

Dante stepped inside the room. "And what about you?"

She slanted a glance at him. "Okay, grateful."

He wondered how grateful should could be. Instead, he decided to just keep things neutral between them. "How are you doing?"

She shrugged elegant shoulders. "Well, at least when I show up in L.A. I won't look like a hot mess."

Who was she kidding? Now that he could really see her in broad daylight, she looked great. Her long hair flowed over her shoulders like silk. Her skin glowed like dark copper. She wore khaki colored pants and a dark green shirt molded tightly to her generous curves. An amber bracelet adorned one wrist and diamond earrings twinkled in her ears. Hell, she was gorgeous. Despite her night in the desert, she looked none the worse for wear. "You look great."

She flashed him a mega-watt smile. "I'm going to need to."

"You're not the bad guy in all of this."

Her brown eyes widened. "Are you the only person in the world who hasn't seen me on the internet?"

Her ass-whipping on Mark Jones was playing 24/7 on the Internet. Some enterprising soldier just happened to be in the right place at the right time. "I think there's some guy in Fiji who missed the action, too, but I could be wrong."

She put her hands on her hips and tilted her head at him. "Don't make me laugh.

But he wanted to make her laugh, to make the not quite sad look in her eyes go away. "What are you going to do?"

She shoulder drooped. "My publicist thinks I should go to Paris and hide until Lindsey Lohan goes into re-hab again."

He checked his watch. "That'll be twenty minutes."

"I wish." She folded a pair of jeans and laid them in her suitcase. "The only thing I can do is go home and face the music."

"You have nothing to be ashamed of."

Covering her face she snorted. "The beat down I put on Mark Jones can be forgiven, but the 'you're married to one of the most beautiful women in the world and still can't keep it in your pants. What kind of moron are you?' comment. Well that's a different story. I humiliated the daughter of one of Hollywood's mega-players. So that forgiveness thing, I'm not so much expecting."

If Jones had done that to his one of Dante's sisters, no place in the world would be able to hide him. "Nothing is that bad."

Georgina snapped the lid of her suitcase closed. "Hollywood is not a forgiving town unless you make a lot of money. I'm thinking my big money potential might have just dried up."

He refused to let her feel sorry for herself. She'd gone through a traumatic situation and come out in one piece. That earned his respect and the respect of every soldier in Iraq. "I was with you in the desert. You hung tough. You'll survive."

"Maybe." She put the suitcase on floor. "I know this is totally off the subject, now that I can really see you, you are gorgeous."

Heat flooded his face. "Thanks."

A sly smiled curved her mouth. "The cigarette lighter did not do you justice at all."

What does a man say to something like that? He liked that she thought he looked good. "I don't know what to say."

"No comment needed."

"Everyone treating you okay?"

She sat on the bed. "Well outside the whispered comments, everyone's been nice. The women have been extremely supportive and the guys are giving me a wide berth. I don't think I'll be invited back anytime soon though."

"You okay with that."

"I'm sorry I told the world Mark Jones is an adulterous pig."

"I'm surprised." He wondered what else she was sorry about.

She walked over to him and stopped about inch in front of him. "I'm not sorry about kissing you. I'd do it again in a heartbeat."

And he was going to let her.

Georgina planted her hands on his chest.

Dante lowered his head and took her mouth. She opened her lips and his tongue slid inside. She tasted sweet and hot. He loved the way her body molded next to his. He trailed his hands under her shirt to caress her bare skin. She was so velvety soft. Her sleek smooth skin warmed his hands. He could become addicted to this woman.

Georgina found his zipper and he heard the rasp as she pulled it down then reached inside his pants and palmed his cock.

A shudder wracked his body. This lady was all business.

She broke the kiss. "Very nice." Her fingers continued to stroke him. "I knew you would be."

"You can keep doing that."

A sultry laugh left her full lips. "I have a lot things I want to do to you."

"And I'm going to let you."

She rubbed her breasts against his chest. "Good."

Dante grabbed her around the waist and lifted her up. Her long brown legs circled his waist. God he loved her body. Bubble ass, lush tits, she was a walking talking sex bomb and she was all his today. He pushed her down until she lay on the bed staring up at him surprise in her eyes.

She raised a perfectly arched eyebrow and he got on his knees between her legs, pulling her pants down until green silk panties were revealed. His mouth watered as he stared at her silky cover mound. Slowly he pulled her down until her butt was on the edge and knelt between her legs, slipped a finger under the elastic and found her already hard clit. He brushed his finger across her engorged flesh and she moaned.

"You're wet," he whispered.

She closed her eyes and thrust her hips up.

Dante took his finger away. "Look at me."

Her eyes opened and she bit her bottom lip. "Please."

"You want me bad."

Georgina nodded.

He smiled. He stripped her quickly. For a moment he admired her as shaft of sunlight shining through the window illuminated her velvet skin.

"Beautiful." Her chocolate nipples were hard. He bent over and took one into his mouth. She gasped as he sucked her. Gently he sank his teeth on the hard point. She tasted sweet and salty at the same time.

Georgina gripped his waist with her long legs. He could feel her bare heels digging into his skin.

Under him, her body writhed and he thought he would shoot his load right there. He had to get inside her soon. With the tip of his tongue he licked his way over to the other breast.

"You are so bad," she moaned.

He answered by nipping the underside of her full breast. "In a good way?"

She nodded. "Oh yeah."

"Then I'm all yours." At least for today, he thought.

Dante worked his mouth down her flat stomach pausing only to swirl his tongue in her belly button. He worked his shirt off and she ran a hand up and down his chest, her fingers stopping to tug at his nipples, then make their way up to his face. He licked the base of her throat, the valley between her breasts and trailed kisses down her stomach to her mound.

Moving his tongue over her damp flesh, working his mojo on her, he grasped her butt and lifted her to his mouth, feasting on her, thrusting his tongue inside her, thinking he'd never get enough of her taste.

He was ready to burst, but he wanted her to come at least once before he got inside her. Carefully he eased a finger inside her tight channel. She clinched around him immediately and he swirled his tongue around her clit. He slipped another finger inside her slick heat. With his other hand he massaged her breast, her skin like fiery silk. Her stomach began to undulate and he could tell she was close to coming. He just had to work her a little more.

She started trembling. Her soft gasps spurred him on. Suddenly she arched her back and cried out while the muscles around his fingers tightened and spasmed. Her juices flowed over his tongue and he stayed with her until her body stopped quaking.

Georgina took a deep breath. "That was perfect."

Dante lifted his head from between her legs. He licked her juices off his lips savoring her musky flavor. He sat her up and pulled her head down until their lips touched, kissing her gently until she melted against him. He fumbled his way out of his uniform and into a condom. "We've only started."

A knock sounded at the door. "Georgina?"

"Clive's timing sucks." Her head fell back on the mattress. "Give me a minute."

"You have five," Clive said through the door. "They want you on a plane and gone."

Dante rolled on his back.

She jumped up and started pulling on her clothes. "You can come to L.A."

He knew he couldn't. "I can't." He stood and started pulling on his uniform. Instead of getting laid he was heading back to the trenches.

She put her shirt on. "Why not?"

"I don't who I am outside of this place. Not anymore."

"I like you now."

"I'm not the kind of man you need."

She stopped buttoning her shirt. "How do you know what kind of man I need?"

He just did. "I know it's not me." He finished dressing in silence. He opened the door and pushed Clive out of the way. Maybe he was being stupid, but he knew the best thing that ever happened in his life was slipping through his fingers and there was nothing he could do about it.

☆☆☆

Georgina sat in front of the vanity mirror in her cheerful yellow and blue bedroom, cell phone to her ear listening as her agent told her the one thing she most wanted in her life had just happened.

She hung up the phone, dazed, staring at herself in the mirror. The French doors were open to the covered patio and the sweet scent of her wisteria vine and the gentle sound of water from the fountain wafted into the room. She twisted around in the chair and stared at the people fussing over her, staring at her bedroom, so unlike the regal perfection of Saddam Hussein's palace in Baghdad.

"Well," Clive demanded. "Do tell."

"I'm going to play Katherine. I'm on Broadway." If she hadn't been groomed within an inch of her life she would have fallen on her knees and wept.

Jen, her hairstylist yelled, jumping up and down, her dark hair flying. Clive high-fived her. Then he came over and air-kissed Georgina, not wanting to ruin the makeup job. Blair, her make-up artist was doing some kind of crazy white girl dance along with Andrea, Georgina's stylist.

"This is just extra sweet," Clive said.

She knew what he meant. Since her return from Iraq her professional life had been off the charts. She'd expected to be a pariah for beating up Mark Jones, but the reverse had happened. Her new best friend was Mark Jones' soon to be ex-wife. Two of her film projects had been green-lighted. Oprah called, Diane Sawyer was her new email buddy, and Glen Beck sent her a muffin basket and an invite to do his news show.

Georgina was the new poster girl for the fight against sexual harassment. Tonight she wore Vera Wang, the designer having personally delivered the dress to her house and fitted it to her. For free.

Destiny Knight was in such a tizzy she gained two pounds and promptly went on a diet to lose five. And the cherry on the sundae was the guest list for the fundraiser she had sponsored for the war vets. It was totally A-list and she was going to be queen of the ball with studio head, Walter Merritt as her date. The only thing missing in her life was Dante.

"Don't you dare cry and ruin my make-up." Blair ran a contour brush over Georgina's cheek.

"I'm not. I'm just feeling…" she couldn't find the right word. Empty. She felt empty. Her body ached for a fulfillment. The memory of those few minutes with Dante's hands on her body sent her into a spiral of desire.

Gail patted her shoulder. "I know, Georgina. We aren't the person you wanted to share the news with."

Was she so transparent that they all knew how she felt about Dante? She wasn't going to ever forget him. "You have all been my best friends since the dawn of time. Who else would I want besides my family?"

"Commando Man?" Clive asked.

She wasn't going answer him. A change of subject was in order. "Clive, is your date picking you up or meeting you there?"

"He's picking me up." Clive pressed his clasped hands to his thin chest.

"Anybody I know?" Georgina asked curiously.

Clive looked sly. "You met him...once."

How very unClive-like to not be up front. "Who?"

Blair dabbed berry red lipstick on Georgina's generous mouth. "No more talking, I'm working. Hell, I'm creating a masterpiece." Then she blotted the lipstick. "Get out, Clive."

Dismissed, he headed for the door. "Tootles."

Georgina watched him leave. And let everyone finish getting dressed.

☆☆☆

As was her custom, Georgina liked a little time to herself to prepare for a live appearance. She needed to find her calm, inner place so she would be nothing but courteous and professional.

Georgina stared at her reflection in the mirror. She had about twenty minutes before Walter picked her up. The yellow satin halter dress caressed every curve, exposing a sublime view of her cleavage. Vera Wang was a goddess. Except for the vibrant red lips, the make-up was subtle. Her hair was pulled into a sleek ponytail. She never looked better. She never felt worse.

She forced herself to reflect on the positive in her life. How could Dante think what she felt wasn't real. A good shrink would tell her she had Stockholm syndrome. He saved her, treated her like a real person and made her face her fears. Of course she was in love with him. He was like her father. A quiet man who did a job because that's what he said her do.

A knock interrupted her thoughts.

Glancing at her antique clock on the wall, she figured Walter was early. How unHollywood. "Come in."

Clive stuck his head in. "Walter Meritt called, he had an emergency and will try to meet you at the benefit."

Georgina sighed. "Is everything okay?"

"Nothing that can't be fixed." Clive stepped into the room wearing the black Armani tux she bought him. He looked handsome, but he also looked a little nervous.

"Are you going to be my date?" Georgina asked. She didn't know if she was sorry that Walter wasn't going to be her date or not. He was nothing but charming even if he wasn't the one she wanted.

"No," Clive replied with a little role of his eyes, "but I was able to get you someone."

Her eyebrows rose. "So quickly?" Clive deserved a raise.

He spread his arms wide. "Clive is a miracle worker." He stuck his head out the door and yelled, "Hey, Commando Man."

Georgina's mouth fell open. It couldn't be. "Dante?" She stood as he entered, one hand pressed to the base of her throat.

Clive wriggled his fingers. "You may call me miracle worker." Then he walked out the room.

"Hi Georgina." Dante's broad shoulders filled the door. He wore full